THE HEART'S
DILEMMA

No sooner had lovely, talented Prudence Schuyler arrived at Prosperity Farm than she found herself the center of attention of the town's most eligible young bachelors. First there was her new neighbor—sporting, boyishly handsome Rodney Gerard, owner of the large seafront estate with its private airport. Then there was dark, almost too good-looking Len Calloway, a lumber baron and the town's first citizen.

But Prue had set her heart against such wealthy and attractive young men. How could she trust any man again? Could she allow herself to forget the tragedy that had broken her faith in love?

Bantam Books by Emilie Loring
Ask your bookseller for the books you have missed

EMILIE LORING
HILLTOPS CLEAR

A NATIONAL GENERAL COMPANY

HILLTOPS CLEAR

*A Bantam Book / published by arrangement with
Little, Brown and Company*

PRINTING HISTORY
William Penn edition published 1933
Grosset & Dunlap edition published July 1946
Bantam edition published July 1968

2nd printing ...... August 1968   4th printing ... December 1968
3rd printing ... November 1968   5th printing .... May 1969
6th printing ..... October 1969
New Bantam edition published February 1971

2nd printing
3rd printing
4th printing
5th printing

Published simultaneously in the United States and Canada

Bantam Books are published by Bantam Books, Inc., a National
General company. Its trade-mark, consisting of the words "Bantam
Books" and the portrayal of a bantam, is registered in the United
States Patent Office and in other countries. Marca Registrada.
Bantam Books, Inc., 666 Fifth Avenue, New York, N.Y. 10019.

To
The memory of my brother
ROBERT M. BAKER

HILLTOPS CLEAR

I

The automobile lurched over deeply rutted roads. When it didn't lurch, it skidded. A cold, bone-penetrating fog transformed trees into ghostly giants, houses into weird dwarfs and filled the world. Moisture dripped from twigs and branches. A huge shape, which suggested a pre-historic monster with burning red eyes, loomed and was left behind. The faint far moan of a buoy drifted through the grayness with melancholy monotony. The smell of the sea crept behind the slackly fastened side curtains of the car. The lean, angular driver stopped the engine and climbed out.

"What is the matter, Mr. Puffer?" Prudence Schuyler inquired from the cavernous gloom of the back seat.

"Tires leaky. Guess they'll hold out till we get there, though."

His passenger valiantly swallowed an exclamation of concern. She patted encouragement on the hand of the woman beside her. She really needed someone to pull her spirit out of the pit of depression, she told herself.

A motor purred alongside; the glow from powerful lamps illumined the fog ahead, turned dripping moisture to sparkling jewels, the rutted road to a highway of gold.

"That you. Si? What's the matter? Tire trouble? Flat?"

The voice was hollow, muffled, a man's voice. Shut within the curtained car, Prudence could see nothing but the uncanny mist.

" 'Tain't flat yet."

From the gruffness of his answer she judged that

1

Mr. Puffer did not care for the person who had hailed him.

"Has the girl come?"

There was eagerness in the question, a hint of anxiety, more than a hint of arrogance. If the wheel under her could talk, she would have said that its shake was warning her to keep quiet, Prudence decided.

"Gorry-me, you wouldn't expect city folks to come to the country in this storm, would you? Whatta mean is, guess she'll get to the red brick house 'bout tomorrow."

The red brick house! Her house! The voice in the fog was inquiring for her, Prudence Schuyler! Why had Mr. Puffer evaded the question? She watched him as he resumed his seat. His great ears, which stood out from his long, narrow head like the ears of an elephant, were black cut-outs against the glow.

"Phone me the minute she arrives, Si."

A grunt from the man at the wheel was the only response. A red tail light shot into the golden mist of its own powerful headlights and dwindled to a spark.

Prudence leaned forward. "Was that voice, which sounded like a demon of the fog, inquiring for me, Mr. Puffer?"

"Yep."

"Why did you sidetrack him? Why tell him that I was arriving tomorrow?"

"Gorry-me, you wait an' you'll see, Miss Schuyler. Whatta mean is, by tomorrow you'll have kinder got yer bearin's an'll know what to say. Len Calloway'll tie you up tight to him, if he can."

"Tie me up! You're not alluding to a matrimonial tie by any chance, are you?"

The driver looked back. His blatantly artificial teeth gleamed in the faint light.

"Glad to hear you laugh. When I met you at the station, I was afraid you was going to break out cryin'. It sure is a mean night for you to arrive. Not much further to go. We're passing the Gerard place now."

It was evident that he considered the voice in the fog a closed incident. Couldn't he feel that she was fairly tingling with curiosity? Prudence asked herself. She had better seem indifferent. She said lightly:

"I'm glad to know there is something tangible to pass. This fog looks like one of the creeping horrors Edgar Allen Poe saw in the Pit and the Pendulum."

" 'Tain't always like this; just wait till the sun shines. Gerard is your neighbor on the east, that is, if you can call it being a neighbor when the houses are two miles apart. His folks come down only for the summer, but I reckon you've come to stay, judgin' by the truck load of stuff I carted up to the red brick house the other day."

For no reason she could explain to herself, Prudence Schuyler evaded an answer. With the intention of turning the driver's attention from her affairs, she suggested:

"Tell me about the Gerard family."

Her ruse succeeded. Si Puffer looked back with a suddenness which sent the car to the side of the road and Prue's heart to her mouth in the same skid. With a stifled shriek the woman clutched her seat mate.

"It's all right, Jane Mack," Prudence encouraged. "Please drive more slowly, Mr. Puffer. We people from the city aren't accustomed to skidding. Perhaps you would rather not talk when you are driving," she suggested tactfully.

"Gorry-me, I've driven this machine over these roads when there wasn't no headlights. They're not all's bad as this one; it's like running over a wash-board, ain't it? Just been makin' it over. The men left it to finish their hayin' an' haven't got to work again—notice that big road machine we passed? Of course I can talk an' drive. I'll tell you about the Gerards; perhaps 'twill take your mind off the rough going. The estate, which includes plane landing field, golf links, mountain streams, an' 'bout two miles of pond shore besides the sea front, belongs to Rod Gerard. His name's Rodney, but the townspeople call him Rod. He's one of those rich fellers you read about who fly airplanes, own a string of polo ponies, an' have a vally to bring up their breakfast, crease their pants, an' lay out their pink silk pajamas—but he ain't a bit stuckup."

"Sounds like a first family of Hollywood."

Mr. Puffer ignored the crisp interruption and dissuaded the car from making a slight detour up a bank.

"Whatta mean is, folks here think a lot of Rod, but he has an older brother Walter an' that brother has a wife. Walt was the son by old man Gerard's first marriage; that wife didn't have any money, neither did he. After she died, Gerard, who was a handsome, gifted man, married an heiress and Rod's their child. This place came to her from her father, who, years ago, bought about three thousand acres of land and built a house of stone and oak on a high ledge; that's the name of the place—High Ledges."

"It has a sort of approach-if-you-dare-sound."

"As I was sayin', Rod's mother loved every inch of the land, turned the abandoned quarry holes into gardens—builders used to come here for granite from all over the country—we carted tons of loam into them. She and her husband are buried in one of them. Old man Gerard died, then she went several years ago, and Rod—well, Rod was just out of law school and crazy about flying when he came into a big fortune; perhaps you've met fellers like that."

"Just like that!" Prudence concurred bitterly, and hoped in the next second that the man had not noticed the sting in her voice.

"He didn't show up here for two years after he lost his mother. Then last June he opened the place, and who'd he bring with him but Walt Gerard and his wife and little girl. Walt lit out pretty quick, but the Mrs. seized the reins of management and how she did drive. She's one of them women who's so busy helpin' God run his world that she lets her own folks get along as best they can. I guess she's what the newspapers call a society leader, one of the kind who's always headin' some sort of Charitable Board or other. She's all atwitter, winks one of her cold blue eyes when she thinks she's bein' smart; before you've been talkin' to her five minutes, she'll lug in a remark about 'my cousin, the Ambassador.' She kept the house full of company all summer, young folks, but the girls were so homely they'd have stopped even one of them electric clocks which is supposed to run forever. She's a wise one."

Prudence temporarily forgot the fog, the reason for her coming.

"I hadn't supposed there were any 'homely girls' now, they know so well how to look like a million. Why is Mrs. Walter Gerard wise? Not because she doesn't care for beauty?"

"Whatta mean is, Walt, her husband, is handsome as a movie actor. She is tall, with horses' teeth and a kind of horse-shaped face. Guess she was handsome once—the women here say she's a nifty dresser—must have been or Walt never would have married her. He—well, he knows where the corn crib is. Their kid is thirteen years old. She's cute, but that curious that folks lock up everything when they see her coming. Rod's awful good to her and she worships him. The Walt Gerards haven't much money; he's got some sort of an insurance job now, I hear. Rod gives them an income. That's another reason his sister-in-law doesn't want pretty girls around. 'Twould upset her apple cart terrible if he should marry."

"Has Mr. Rodney Gerard no mind of his own?"

"Yes—yes, he has, but since his mother passed away, Rod's kinder lazy; besides, he's got the idea some girl will marry him for his money." Puffer's voice deepened with affectionate anxiety. "You see, he has all he can spend. That is, I'm guessing so. If he ain't got it, no one'll ever hear a yip from him; Rod Gerard don't bellyache about nothin'. Perhaps he thinks, why should I work now an' take a job from someone else?

"Here we are, Miss Schuyler, this is your uncle's place. I forgot; it's yours now. Sorry you had such a tough night to arrive."

He stopped the car in the road before brick gate-

posts and sounded a lugubrious horn. In response, the
house door opened and let out a stream of yellow
light; a soft, cushiony voice called:

"That you, Si?"

"That's Mother—my wife," Puffer explained, as he
unfastened the curtains on Prudence's side of the car.
He helped her out, then extended a bony hand to the
gaunt woman who seemed to unfold like an extension
ladder as she stepped cautiously to the ground.

Prudence Schuyler's throat tightened as she blinked
at the red brick house she had inherited. Its white
trim, its hooded doorway glowed faintly through the
fog with a sort of phosphorescence. The effect was
weird. As she passed between the posts she had a
flashing vision of the wooden gate she would design
for it; then depression seized her in its talons again.
She set her teeth hard in her lip to steady it. A black
and white English setter charged from the door. He
leaped upon Puffer, then dashed toward the girl. He
sniffed at her skirts and rapturously licked her gloved
hands. Prudence stooped and encircled the dog with
both arms.

"Oh, you dear!" she whispered brokenly. "You
dear!"

She administered another convulsive hug before
she followed the walk of herring-bone brick and entered the house.

A woman, designed on the feather-bed plan, with
an extra chin or two in the best Rembrandt manner,
greeted her in the hall. Her eyes were small and
kindly; her strained-back hair accentuated the arch of
her eyebrows and gave the effect of chronic surprise.
She looked quickly away from the girl's face, patted
her arm with motherly understanding.

"Come right in and wash and take off your hat.
Supper's all ready, dearie. When you get something
to eat, things'll look different. Life can seem awful
dark and dreary on an empty stomach."

Prudence achieved a smile. "Thank you, Mrs.
Puffer. This is Jane Mack who has come to help me
keep house. She has been a standby in our family

since the first day she came to make little girl frocks for me. Will you tell her where to find things, please?"

As the two women disappeared, Prudence lingered in the hall, slipped out of her rain coat, pulled off her close turban. A steep flight of stairs dared ascent to the second floor. She entered the room on her right, a large room invitingly lighted by a blazing fire on the hearth and a gree-shaded student lamp on a magazine laden table. Her brown eyes, already black from emotion, dilated as she saw herself reflected in the long old-fashioned pier glass between the windows. Her blue knit suit made a spot of rich color against the neutral wall paper; her face was too white, her hands too tense, she told herself, but thank heaven for the permanent with which the Good Fairy had endowed her at birth. The dampness through which she had driven had marcelled her ruddy hair into soft curls about her temples.

"Not too bad." She made a gamin face at the looking-glass girl, before she turned to inspect her surroundings. The room was cozy, homey. Her spirit stirred damp wings. Her back-to-the-farm venture might not prove the flop it had seemed a few moments ago. Surely a house with such a fireplace and such a dog offered infinite possibilities for homemaking.

The dining room was cheery with crackling logs in the Franklin fireplace when she entered a few moments later. A huge platter of savory beef stew, garnished with fluffy white dumplings flanked by piles of plummy brown bread, gave out an appetizing aroma. For the first time since she had left New York Prue's heart felt warm.

"Oh, how tempting! That array of pickles and condiments would make the original 57 Varieties hide their heads in shame. Come, Macky, aren't you starved? Mrs. Puffer, won't you sit with us and serve? It will seem more homey to have you here."

Stark, thin-lipped Jane Mack, her high cheek bones flaunting red flags of excitement, took her seat with an air of being about to commit a social blunder. The rosy-faced stout woman plumped into her chair with a contented sigh.

"Dearie, I'll do just that. When you smile and that deep dimple pricks through at the corner of your mouth, I feel's if I could die for you—though I guess I can be more use to you living," she added practically.

After an interval devoted to serving and eating, she sympathized: "Hope you didn't mind the trip from the railroad station. Seven miles isn't far, but it's a long way to drive over a strange road in a fog."

"Only seven! I thought it must at least have been a thousand." The satisfying food was ringing up the curtain of depression. "That is ungrateful when Mr. Puffer diverted our thoughts by most interesting descriptions of our neighbors."

"He said there was something in your voice that did things to his heart an' that he talked like a house afire to cheer you up."

"He succeeded. I'll never forget his kindness."

Jane Mack made her one contribution to the conversation.

"Do you have movies here, Mrs. Puffer?"

"Three times a week in the village. The manager tries to show the films people want to see."

"Does he?" Jane Mack's eyes snapped. "I love mystery and gangster pictures."

Prudence gazed at the thin face in speechless amazement. She had known the woman almost all her life, had confided school and boy troubles, sports ambitions to her, but had she been taking her to a picture, she would have selected one with de luxe settings and smart frocks. How little one could tell what was going on in a person's mind, even the mind of someone near and dear.

"Something tells me that that profound conclusion has been reached before." Amazement at her bromidic reflection lighted her eyes. She said aloud:

"Now we'll help clear away and do the dishes."

"Not you, dearie. You go into what your uncle called the living room, and set. If Miss Mack wants to lend a hand, perhaps she'll be more contented to be busy."

Curled in the depths of a wing chair before the purring fire, Prudence smoothed the dog's head snuggled against her knee as she looked about the room—indubitably a man's room—which almost over night had become hers. It had the musty smell of furniture drenched with stale tobacco smoke. There was an air of mystery about the closed secretary; it made her think of secret drawers, missing wills, and stealthy fingers searching for a document which might change the pattern of a life or two. When her uncle had last sat at that desk, had he felt the faint far breath of eternity blowing toward him?

Her interested eyes wandered on. The Windsor chairs were good, the linoleum rug left much to be desired, the walls were cracked and dingy. Above the mantel hung the one picture the room presented: a delicately colored engraving of Franklin at the Court of France. Benjamin, stage centre, bent his head to receive a wreath from the gorgeously appareled Countess Polinac; while from a divan, Louis the Sixteenth and Marie Antoinette looked on with royal indifference.

They all had been real once, the girl mused; they had held their heads high while their hearts broke, they had smiled through tragedy, while she, with youth, health, opportunity, and her brother, had fairly wallowed in self-pity these last few weeks.

She sprang to her feet with a suddenness which toppled the dozing dog to the rug. She dropped to her knees beside him and smiled into his aggrieved, if evasive, brown eyes.

"I'll make a vow to you, now, that from this moment I foreswear self-pity. I will regard this experience at—at—what shall I name the place which has a lift to it? I know! Prosperity Farm! Grand!—at Prosperity Farm as an adventure which will lead to health for David and great, good fortune."

She snuggled her face against one floppy black ear. "What do you think of that? When you licked my

hand, the fog seemed to thin, I felt almost happy.
Happy. A name for you. I'll call you Happy. Happy!
Like it, old dear?"

The setter whacked his tail rapturously. Crouched
on the floor, the girl put her arms over his rough
white back ticked with black as he sat on his
haunches blinking at the fire.

"I thought I was coming to a treadmill of endless
monotonies, and within the first hour a hollow voice—
which set little merry-pranks picking through my
veins—rumbles through the fog:

" 'Has the girl come?'

"Meaning me—me, your new mistress, Happy. Why
does the man want to know the moment I arrive?
Why will he try to 'tie me up tight to him'? That
meeting was like a dash of tabasco on top of chicken
bouillon—chicken bouillon served in a crystal soup
plate being the most colorless proposition I can think
of."

Thoughtfully, Prudence scratched the dog's head
between his ears. He snuggled closer.

"Like it, don't you? You and I will be grand pals.
You won't mind if I talk out my problems to you, will
you, Happy? David mustn't know that I have any.
Let's forget them now. That was an interesting bit of
biography Mr. Puffer volunteered about our neighbors. I'm willing to wager my first crop of chickens
that I shall detest the Gerard heir. Rich playboy. I
have no illusions about his type. If I meet him, I'll be
colder than an electric ice-box running on high. Also
something tells me that Mrs. Walt and I will be
antagonistic from the start. Maybe, though, I won't
meet her; maybe she won't see her farming neighbor
even as a dot on her social horizon."

"Miss Prue, I'm ready to go up now," lean, lank
Jane Mack announced from the threshold. "Mrs.
Puffer showed me where to find the supplies. I guess
she'll be a good neighbor. Wish I hadn't seen that
procession in my tea cup, though."

Prudence valiantly disregarded the woman's lachry-

mose sniff as she took the tall brass stick with its
lighted candle.

"Now, Macky, don't look for trouble in tea grounds;
haven't we had enough fairly sitting in our laps these
last weeks without hunting out more? Come on up,
let's see the rest of the house."

She shaded the flickering spear of flame as she
mounted the steep stairs with Jane Mack and the dog
following close on her heels. He decorously accompa-
nied the woman and girl on their tour of investigation.
Interest in Prue's eyes glowed into excited anticipa-
tion as they went from room to room. Back in the hall
she looked up into the bitter-lipped face of the
woman.

"Macky, think of having a whole house in which to
spread out after years in an apartment! We'll make it
a dream. We will warm it with color till it makes
hearts glow just to come into it."

A faint pink crept under the woman's skin. Her
washed-out eyes shone with a lovely light.

"You'll make hearts glow all right, Miss Prue. Your
brother said to me just before we left the apartment,
'I'm not afraid for Prue. She'll make a home wherever
she is. She's like her mother.'" She almost smiled.
"'Especially,' he said, 'if she can find rooms to re-
paper.' Guess he was right; that was what you meant
when you said, 'warm it with color,' wasn't it?"

"Did David say that, Macky? He must be feeling
better, he always teased me about my re-papering
complex."

She slipped her hand within the crook of the woman's thin arm and for an instant pressed her cheek
against her hard shoulder.

"I suppose there isn't a person in this village who
doesn't know that my brother's wife ran away with
my sister's husband," she said in a muffled voice.

Jane Mack awkwardly smoothed the girl's ruddy
hair.

"There, there, Miss Prue, suppose they do? 'Twasn't
your brother David's fault nor your sister Julie's. If
folks here know about it at all, they know that. If you

make too much of it, they may think there's something back of it all you're ashamed of. I know folks."

Indignation jerked Prue's head erect, dried her eyes.

"As if David or Julie could have done anything wrong! But I see what you mean. Good-night, Macky. Be sure and name your bedposts the first night in a strange house."

Prudence smiled and patted the woman's bony hand before she entered the room she had selected for herself. She surmised it faced the sea. It was a ponderous room, lavishly furnished in black walnut and marble—the marble ghostly in the candlelight like nice white tombstones, she reflected, with a gasping chuckle.

Long after she had extinguished the light, she lay with wide-open eyes staring at the fog which hung like a curtain of gray gauze before the wide-open window. What waited for her behind it? Would life pick her up and whirl her in a merry-go-round of perplexities until she lost her sense of direction? Senseless question. That sort of thing was out-dated. One kept straight on. One met situations now with resolution—unless one were a puppet. The make the best of it philosophy never had appealed to her. Disappointment and disillusion always had been a challenge to her to face the situation and fight.

She watched the steamy fringe of water dripping from the window as she lived over the last weeks. As if his heart had not been sufficiently uprooted by the desertion and tragic death of his wife, David, whose health had been undermined by service overseas, had been ordered to give up work and live in the country.

The country! The inexorable command had staggered her at first. How could they go with no money for living? When the crash had come in their fortunes six months before, she had opened a studio and had worked professionally at what had been a delightful avocation—the craft of designer and maker of jewelry and silver boxes. Her brother's law practice had dwindled in the bleak years; he had received a small salary for his time, which, before, he had given to a Rescue Mission—crowded now with unemployed—which was the core of his heart. Each month had seen an increase in the number and importance of her orders; then had come the command to go to the country, which had meant that she must give up her shop.

While she was struggling with her problems and doggedly assuring herself that she would find a way to relieve the situation, a way opened, but not from her effort. Her father's brother, Austin Schuyler, had invested part of his small fortune in an annuity, then had made the dream of years come true by buying and stocking a Maine farm with the remainder. For the first time in his life, he had said, he had what he wanted—and then one morning he didn't waken. He had willed the Maine property and five thousand dollars in cash to his niece Prudence.

The legacy had providentially answered the on to the country problem. After the usual amount of conservative caution and investigation, the executors of her uncle's will had consented to her immediate occupancy of the house. She and her brother must get their living from the place, she had told them; except for the cash she needed for clamoring necessities, she wanted the balance invested.

Now that the strain was eased, she had but a confused remembrance of the days during which she had cleared and sub-leased the apartment. At the last moment, Jane Mack had begged to go with her. Her eyes were giving out for sewing, she had said, but she knew almost everything there was to know about a house, she knew how to care for milk and could make butter—she had been trained by a New England mother. Prudence had hugged her in her relief. Jane Mack might be grim and a confirmed pessimist but she could cook, while she herself farmed and, if opportunity and time allowed, worked at her craft.

Could she afford to keep Si Puffer as helper on the place? her thoughts ran on. She couldn't afford not to at present. Already he had stood like a guardian angel between her and the voice in the fog; how he had growled the name, "Len Calloway!" What had the man wanted? Something in his demand had antagonized her. "Tomorrow" was almost here. Soon she would know.

The muslin hangings swung into the room like two frail, transparent wings. Had the wind changed?

She ran to the window. The fog had cleared as if by magic. A keen salty breeze flapped the delicate white crêpe of her nightgown. She leaned out. The moon had risen rotund and ruddy above the horizon where sky and sea met. Its light flooded a field with silver, patched it with sharp blue shadows; turned the rocks on the shore to copper, the pines and cedars to obsidian sentinels; it threw a restless path of gold across the sparkling sea. The symphony of evening was at its height. Above the croak of frogs, the fluting of toads, rose the monotonous shrill of crickets and the weird hoot of an owl.

With a surge of indefinable longing, the girl looked up at the star-punctured heavens. With a shaky laugh at her own absurdity, she flung out her hands toward the man in the moon.

"Your excellency, I thank you for this royal welcome! Prue of Prosperity Farm salutes you!"

She hadn't realized the range and carrying power of her clear voice till faint and far off quavered the echo:

"Salutes you! Salutes y-o-u!"

II

Prudence stopped settling her possessions the next day at noon long enough to inspect the outside of her inheritance. Poor Mr. Puffer. He had been kept hustling, he was entitled to his lunch hour. The early September air was crisp and bracing. The house,

which had been called the red brick house as far back
as eighteen hundred, was large, with white wooden
ells and sheds which trailed from the rear like the tail
of a kite. The blinds were white, yellowed, but un-
questionably white. Boxes at the windows were spill-
ing over with pink petunias, spikes of purple vis-
caria, fluffs of blue lobelia, and trailing vines. She
could see Mrs. Puffer's hand in that bit of loveliness;
she looked like a woman for whom flowers would
grow. About a hundred feet from the front of the
house the main highway divided the property which
sloped from the ledges and hills, which serrated the
skyline, to the rocky shore which girdled the bay.

Prue's tour of inspection ended at the long weather-
stained barn. Her yellow angora sweater was like a
sudden shaft of sunlight as she entered the shadowy
building. She sniffed. How deliciously barny! From far
down the stall and stanchion-bordered lane of rough
flooring came a whinny; from near at hand a horse
answered. Swallows, like black witches, flitted above
the mows which dripped hay; a tortoiseshell cat with
sphinxlike topaz eyes brushed against Prue's white
skirt. The girl picked her up, stroked her electricity-
charged fur, and called:

"Mr. Puffer! Mr. Puffer!"

"Yep! Be there in a minute." The man's voice came
from somewhere outside.

With a frenzied "cut-cut-cut-cadaakut!" a black hen
flew down from the topmost loft. Prudence watched
her switch and cackle and flap through the open
doorway, before her eyes returned to the spot from
which she had descended. Had she been stealing a
nest? Could she find it? What fun!

She dropped the cat, tugged a light ladder into
place, and with excited agility mounted. As she went
up and up, she visualized her brother's whimsical
eyes watching her, could hear his voice:

"She would do that!"

He knew her flair for adventure, though one could
hardly list hunting stolen nests under the head of
adventure.

Past the first mow. Up to the highest, almost
touching the roof. Something brown flew in her face
as she peered into the shadows. With a startled little
shriek she tumbled to the hay. She regained her
balance and crept forward on hands and knees. That
black hen hadn't been sitting up here to see the
soldiers go by, she must have left a nest. She touched
warm feathers and called:

"Mr. Puffer! Mr. Puffer! I've found some eggs! E-g-
g-s!"

"Gorry-me! Don't stop to spell 'em! Bring 'em
down!" His voice, which must have started as a yell,
came thinned by distance.

"All right! I'm looking for more!"

Prue's cheeks burned; her eyes felt like big protrud-
ing marbles; wisps of hay prickled against her scalp,
tickled her neck, as she continued her search. A sharp
peck from a yellow beak dampened her lashes but
steeled her determination. Were all the ladies of the
poultry harem leaving home for stolen nests? She shut
her eyes tight and grabbed. She flung the squawking
fowl to an adjacent mound of hay where it made the
rafters ring with its outraged cackle.

Prudence sat back on her heels and counted. Eight
eggs!

"Si! Oh, Si!"

The cheery call came from below. A man's voice.
Not the Voice in the Fog. That had appeared in
person early this morning. Who could it be? Prudence
cautiously placed the eggs in her white skirt,
gathered up the front of it, and crept to the edge of
the mow. Curiosity tempted. She leaned too far over.
The hay slid. Struggling to retard her progress, she
went with it, down, down into the arms of a man.

"Boy! That was a narrow squeak!"

Prudence had closed her lids tight when she felt
herself going. She opened them wide, looked up into
the deepest bluest eyes she ever had seen. They were
shadowed with concern, the lips under a small
moustache were colorless. Her glance traveled on to
light hair which had an engaging kink at the temple,

then back to the face. Its expression sent a ripple along her nerves. Who was he? The muscles of his jaws were set, his arms still gripped her.

"Seems idiotic to say just 'Thank you' when you really—" Her smile was tremulous, her voice shaken. She shivered.

"Don't think about it. I was the man for the moment, all right. What possessed you to lean over that haymow?"

Prudence freed herself and stepped back. She resented the dictatorial question.

"Don't lose your temper." She noted with a little glow of satisfaction his light frown, the color which crept to his hair—a man did so hate to be accused of irritation. "That's my usual one-two-three-go! method of descending from haymows. Rather original—if you get what I mean." She nibbled a straw as she gazed at him with what she intended to be exasperating indifference. Now that his color had returned, the curve of his sensitive mouth set her on the defensive. It was so darn boyish for a man his age; he must be about thirty.

"Okay with me. Every move a picture. But is this method of transporting eggs also original with you?" His slightly raised eyebrows pointed his words as he glanced at her white skirt which she still gripped with one hand. From the side a stream of egg yolks was dripping.

"My word!" She looked from her skirt to his perfectly tailored gray sports suit. It was liberally splotched with yellow which had not been part of the weaver's design. The sight wiped her eyes and voice clean of assumed indifference.

"I'm sorry! I'm terribly sorry. I—I've made you look like an omelette."

His eyes deepened as they met hers contritely appealing. His lips tightened. Was he furiously angry because she had spoiled his clothes, did he think she was a country moron who didn't know better than to go about smearing smartly attired young men with egg yolk?

"Truly, I'm sorry. I haven't even thanked you for saving me from a horrid fall—I'd loathe being mushed—forgive me for being flippant. I hate to be crabbed at, and you—well, your voice wasn't all sweetness and light, was it? I am on my knees in apology for the damage to your clothes. Come into the house and Jane Mack will take off the spots. She's a demon cleanser."

"No, thank you, my man will do it."

"If you scorn our help, you will let me say 'Thank you,' won't you?" She held out her hand. "I am Prudence Schuyler of Prosperity Farm."

"Don't apologize for the damage, which amounts to nothing, or the snub which I deserved. I am—"

"Well, Rod, here you are!" Si Puffer in work-stained blue overalls extended a knob-jointed hand, thereby necessitating the release of the girl's which the younger man still held. "What you doin' here? Thought you left High Ledges last week." His eyebrows, which resembled nothing so much as bristling gray moustaches gone up in the world, registered surprise. "Whatta mean is, didn't know you and Miss Prue was acquainted."

So this was the glamorous Rodney Gerard! The playboy whom she had planned to treat with superb disdain when or if they met! Life certainly had a nice sense of humor to fling her into his arms. Prudence jerked her thoughts back to the present and debonairly answered the question in Si Puffer's slate-color eyes.

"We aren't—that is, we weren't, but quite suddenly I took the quickest way down from the haymow, Mr. Man-of-the-Moment caught me—and look!" She held out her skirt.

"Well, I'll be darned—and eggs forty cents a dozen! You'd better chuck the mess an' go get that skirt cleaned."

"I'm going. Good morning, Mr.—Mr. Rod, and thank you again." Prudence smiled and nodded to the two men watching her. She whistled to the dog. He deserted the mouse hole at which he had been noisily snuffling and bounded after her as she left the barn.

"Pretty as a movie star and smart as a steel trap," Si Puffer commented, as he watched her out of sight.

Rodney Gerard overturned a bushel basket, kicked it to the wide doorway, and used it as a seat while he lighted a cigarette.

"Who is she? What is she doing here?"

Puffer perched on a keg and began to whittle.

"Haven't you heard? Austin Schuyler left all his holdings here to that slip of a girl. He'd just got the place stocked with poultry, bought a gun dog, a couple of A. R. Guernseys—Advanced Registered, in case you've forgotten what your Pa used to keep—an' two horses for farm work—he could buy them cheaper than tractors. Hadn't done nothin' to the house except put in plumbin'—when he up an' died, just after he'd paid a lot of money for an annuity too. Can you beat it! Miss Prue came last night with a hatchet-faced woman who's goin' to be the housekeeper. She's come to the farm to see if she can get her brother David's health back. They say he had an income enough to live on—he was a lawyer—besides his practice till the crash came. Two years ago his wife walked out on him with his sister Julie's husband."

"Schuyler! Is that the family! That rotten scandal staggered even the most hard-boiled people I know. This Miss Schuyler's sister Julie was charming but too domestic for the man she married. Her husband wanted a woman who would make other men stop, look, listen. His wife's sister-in-law was that type, so he stepped up and took her. He didn't have her long. Mrs. David Schuyler was smashed up in an automobile accident a week after she ran away."

"Gorry-me, when I hear of human beings—who have had every chance to know better—bein' so promiscuous, I say to myself, 'Rabbits!' Yes sir, that's what I say, 'Rabbits!' I'd heard the woman died, didn't know how though. Makes me think of them words in the bible, 'an' the wages of sin is death.'"

Folks say David Schuyler put in all his spare time helping the down-an'-out at a Rescue Mission. Miss Prue's got grit. Whatta mean is, last night when I brought them in, the road was so thick with fog you could cut it. Once when I looked round I could see tears glistening in her eyes, but she kept her voice like music. I'll bet she sings."

"So she intends to farm! Haven't they any money?"

"Lost it; investments wiped out as quick and as clean as you can wipe writing from a slate—perhaps you've heard we've just pulled through a slight depression."

"You're out of date, Si. We now speak of 'the state of financial tension.' "

"Well, whatever you call it. Whatta mean is, they lost their money, that's the talk in the village. Beats all how some folks always knows other folks' business, don't it? She can get their living all right from the place if—if—only she will stick it out. In spite of radios an' movies, I guess 'twon't seem much like the city. Thought you'd gone, Rod. What'd you stay over for? Don't you usually go flying or playing polo or visiting this time of year?"

Rodney Gerard looked quickly at Puffer's inscrutable face. "You're not crazy about me as a solid citizen, are you, Si? I was going, but Len Calloway held me up. He wants my decision on the timber now so that he can make his contracts for the increase in his cut. I don't know whether the price he offers is fair. If it were anything else I owned, I would let it go and not be bothered, but I know every tree and hollow in the woods he wants to log. The pines and spruces and cedars are like friends, and Mother loved every inch of the land. For her sake I intend to look into the matter thoroughly before I sign a contract."

"Gorry-me, you do?"

Puffer rubbed his hand up and down his unshaven cheek. The effect was not unlike the grate of radio static. His brows arched like the back of an enraged cat. He drawled:

"I'll donate one piece of advice, Rod. Don't trust

Calloway. Whatta mean is, that old trouble between you two is only smolderin'. Len's always been a queer mixture of terrible temper and a sense of justice. When he gets mad he sees blood-red. You know his mother was kinder—kinder—well, she had spells when she'd get so mad she'd smash things, then she'd be as smooth as the dove of peace."

"He's all right now, Si. He has been mighty fair and agreeable."

"Hmp. That's because he wants something. Butter wouldn't melt in his mouth when he aims to please. Just the same, don't let him have that timber."

Rodney Gerard paused in the act of applying a lighter to a cigarette. "What's the idea? You told me yourself that a lot of big stuff ought to come out for the good of the forest."

Puffer folded his jackknife and dropped it into his pocket. He picked his teeth with the finely whittled chip of wood.

"I did. There's thousands of feet of standing timber that's no longer growing, more than half of it decayin' an' likely to be destroyed by the first storm. Talk about frozen assets, you've got 'em there. I told you something else too—that you ought to have a forester here to mark every tree that was to come out, not leave it to the judgment of any man who can swing an axe, and that you ought to be here yourself when the cutting was done to see it was done right."

"I haven't forgotten, but, Si, they cut trees when the snow is on the ground. What would I do here in winter?"

Puffer shrugged his stooping shoulders.

"Folks have lived here through a winter, Rod, and slept and et like human beings. I calculate 'twouldn't hurt you none. Come to think of it, though, you couldn't sleep in a lumber camp in pink silk pajamas; that might disturb your rest some."

With a boyish shout of laughter, Rodney Gerard flung his arm about Puffer's shoulders.

"Si, stout fella, where'd you get that fool idea? Never wore the color in my life." His grip tightened, his voice sobered. "Don't you go back on me. I bank on you to stand by me as you have ever since you taught me to hold a gun. As to Len Calloway, I'll say 'nothing doing' to him now, and when I get around to it I'll have a forester give us a report on the trees."

"All right, Roddy." Puffer tossed away the chip and resumed operations on the interstices between his teeth with a straw. He prodded as he talked. "When you get the forester here, have him look over that wood lot of Miss Prue's. There's about five hundred acres along the rise that Austin Schuyler bought of Len Calloway's father. Old man Calloway died soon after he sold, and I've heard that Len was fit to tie when he heard of it—his father didn't consult him about the sale."

"Do I know the lot?"

"Sure. That stretch called The Hundreds between the highway an' the sky line. You an' I have been shooting over it year after year. It's the best stand of spruce and pine in the county. Her uncle was figuring on getting some of the money back on his investment that way—ought to bring that spunky little girl a nice bunch of cash; but I'm afraid if Len Calloway gets hold of Miss Prue before she knows its value, he'll make a sharp trade with her just to get even because Austin Schuyler bought the land without sayin' 'By your leave' to him. He's the kind of chap girls and women fall for—only the Lord knows why and he ain't telling—kinder mesmerizes them, I guess. He held me up in the fog last evening to ask when she was comin'. I didn't let on I had her in the back seat that very minute. Didn't want him to get in a lick till I'd warned her to watch her step. But he beat me to it. He's been to see her this morning."

"This morning!"

"Gorry-me, Rod, what's there in that to get so excited about? Every unmarried man in the county—I wouldn't put it past some of the married ones—will come buzzin' round the red brick house like bees around a honey pot, now that girl is there. I see Len coming away, head up, looking like he was the lord of the universe. He had I'm-the-big-man-of-this-town sticking out all over him. Somehow it made me kinder uneasy."

For a moment the shadowy barn was so quiet that two beadlike eyes appeared at the mouse hole; a brown hen sidled cautiously from an empty stall; the old horse poked an inquiring head over a gate and pawed for attention; a gay salty breeze shook a fragrant scent from the fringe of hay and danced on.

Rodney Gerard thoughtfully regarded a fish hawk sailing high above him. He was looking at a different world from the world he had known as he entered the old barn. The sky seemed bluer, the air more sparkling; his blood raced through his veins. He had the sense of a new beginning, as if again, as in his ardent boyhood, he set his compass by a shining star. Of course he had given to charities—money, not his time. Spending for a round of amusement seemed flat, when you saw a girl taking life in both hands and forcing a living from it. He colored as his glance came back to the quizzical eyes watching him.

"Look here, Si, don't let Miss Schuyler sign up with Calloway. She will listen to you. I'll have a forester here within a month if I have to buy one. It's up to you and me for the honor of our community to see that she gets a square deal. I was going to New York tonight—but I'll cut out the social stuff this autumn, stay here and attend to the timber."

Puffer strode after him as he left the barn. "Do you mean to say, Roddy, that you'll winter along with us and get out the logs? Mebbe I kin see you doing it?"

The not too thinly veiled taunt sent the blood in a red tide to Gerard's fair hair. He sprang into the low, long roadster, which had not a touch of color to relieve its shining blackness. He slammed the door and jumped the car forward.

"Mebbe, Mr. Puffer, you don't know as much about me as you think you do!" he flung over his shoulder.

Si Puffer's faded eyes were warm with affection as he watched the roadster skid round the curve.

"Got him mad, gorry-me, got him mad. Guess I

went to work the right way to wake that young feller up." He chuckled, prodded thoughtfully with the straw, before he reflected aloud:

"I wonder, though, how much I really had to do with his staying."

III

Dusk and Mrs. Puffer appeared simultaneously at the red brick house. Prudence was placing a fresh blotter on her brother's desk in the living room when the massive woman waddled in and set a crisp golden brown loaf on the table. Her purple and white striped print dress crackled with starch.

"That's for luck. My grandmother, who was Welsh, always carried along a loaf when she went visiting. She claimed it brought good fortune."

"It smells marvelous! Raisins—hundreds of them! I'm going to eat that crusty end this minute. Sit down. I'll be back in a jiffy."

When Prue returned with a wicked looking knife, Mrs. Puffer was wedged into a gaily cushioned Hong Kong chair. She approved throatily:

"Glad you like it; knew you wouldn't have time to cook today, so left some things in the kitchen for your supper. I wanted to come up and help, but Si said you had everything planned so fine that the moving went as if 'twas on greased wheels. Said you even took time to come out and hunt eggs at the noon hour. He thinks you're a wonder. Don't know but what I'll get jealous." Her small brown eyes, flecked with green, disappeared in rolls of flesh when she laughed.

Prudence dropped to a floor cushion beside the chair. She swallowed an especially plummy mouthful.

"Jealous! A woman who can make bread like this! You don't have to worry about keeping your men folk off the street. I'll wager they are on time for every meal."

Mrs. Puffer's eyes filled, her lips quivered. "Si is all the men in the family now—we had one boy." She touched a tiny gold star pinned on the breast of her gown. "This stands for a white cross in France."

Prudence laid her hand on the plump fingers. "Dear Mrs. Puffer. I can understand your heartache. I wasn't very old when David went across, but I remember Mother's eyes when the doorbell or the phone rang. They seemed to knife through my heart even when she smiled and talked in her beautiful voice. She had such gay courage."

"Gay courage! That's the sort. Most folks talk of grim courage. I guess that idea came from our Puritan ancestors. But your brother came back safe, dearie. They told me in the village that he wears ten bars on his Victory medal."

"Yes, for carrying ammunition to the Front of the Front in ten campaigns."

"They tell me, too, that isn't all you have to be proud of him for." She resolutely cleared her voice. "We're getting kind of solemn in the firelight. The boys in town don't give Si and me much chance to be lonely; they drop in round meal time—amazing how often business brings them to the house just as we're sitting down to the table. They look so surprised when I ask them to have a bite. Bless their hearts! I love boys." Her little eyes did their disappearing act. "Think I'm going to love a girl, too. You look real handsome in that dress, it's just the color of the shine in your hair, 'tain't red an' 'tain't yellow, it's like some of my prize zinnias—and those wax beads around your neck are awful pretty."

Wax beads! Julie's pearls! What would Mrs. Puffer say if she knew their value? The stout woman's eyes voyaged about the room.

"My, but you've changed this place! It seems alive and sort of young."

The copper and green and blue flames cast leaping shadows on the girl's hands clasped about her knees

as she critically surveyed the long room. Except for
the secretary, Franklin at the Court of France, the oil
lamps and Windsor chairs, the furnishings which her
uncle had used had been carried to an attic already
cluttered with intriguing sea-chests and boxes and
trunks. The contents of the New York studio living
room had been installed. Her brother's bookshelves—
empty—occupied wall space near his broad desk.
Vivid cretonnes hung at the casement windows which
were set deep in the bricks. She only would know
that the choice piece of Fortuny brocade on the dingy
wall covered a stain which looked like nothing so
much as a cubist flight of stairs, that the batik patch
of moonlight, turning a hill to silver and two stark
cedars to ebony, spread its charming self over an
unsightly crack. The few fine rugs glowed like jew-
eled mosaics on a floor beautifully dark, worn velvety smooth from the tread of countless feet.

Prudence nodded agreement. "It is nice. Everything is in place except the books. I didn't dare start
unpacking those for fear one might open and I would
stop to read a page or two. I'm a book addict."

"Guess you can do about everything, can't you? I
hear you make jewelry."

"Yes, I make jewelry, but I can't do 'everything.' I
thought I wanted to be a nurse, but when in my
twelfth month of training they picked me up off the
floor of the accident ward after I had expertly—get
the after and expertly, Mrs. Si—dressed a horrible
burn, the doctors kindly but firmly advised me to try
something else. Has Mr. Puffer told you that I intend
to farm? Will you show me how to raise chickens and
pigeons and ducks? I've got to get our living from the
place."

"Dearie, I'll do just that. I'll show you how to can
vegetables for winter, too; there are some late ones
coming along. There's a fine market here for small
fruits in summer and for lots of other things. Cater to
the city folks and you get top prices."

"What the economists call an effective demand.

Can I make money besides getting a living? I have a lot to learn, haven't I?"

"Don't pucker your pretty forehead over it. Most of us are still learning. Si and I will help. We're just aching to have someone kind of young to fuss over. Don't be afraid to ask him questions and don't mind if he grumbles. It beats all why men have to do just so much talking about everything, but they make up for it in other ways. I like men."

"Do you really? I don't. Some are such brutes and—"

Mrs. Puffer's surprise oozed in a fat gasp. "Lors, child! You say that, when they tell me your brother's about as near a saint as they make 'em in this world."

"He is! He is!" Prue's passionate confirmation brought tears to her brown eyes. "Of course I didn't mean David."

"Then judge men by the best you know; don't get bitter because some man has hurt you." Mrs. Puffer tried to edge forward in the chair, but it held her as in a vise. "Perhaps, though, I'm wrong advising you to judge men by the best you know. There are devils in this world; what's more, there's one or two smart Alecks in the village who'll do you, if they get the chance, just to keep in practice. Si's going to make this place hum next Spring; he and your Uncle Austin had planned so the farm would pay for running itself the first year. Selecting seeds will be entertaining for you during the long winter evenings."

A vision of one of those evenings, with sound effects, flashed on the screen of Prue's mind. Snow piled high, wind shrieking round the corners of the house, a shutter flapping, flitting batlike shadows on the ceiling, and she absorbed in a seed catalogue. Entertaining! She valiantly transmuted a groan into a laugh.

"I can't spend all my evenings poring over a catalogue; there must be some persons who will drop in for conversation. David will perish from mental starvation if there are not."

Mrs. Puffer's mouth pursed into a rosebud of contemplation. "Plenty of folks to talk, Miss Prue, whether they say anything or not, and something going on every night in the village. They had to set prayer meeting ahead an hour so's to give another evening for one of the clubs to meet." She hitched uneasily in her chair. The black and white setter pattered into the room, sniffed at her starched skirt, before he squatted beside Prudence and snuggled his cold pink-tipped nose into her lap. The girl smoothed his satin soft ear.

"What sort of man is Mr. Calloway, Mrs. Puffer? Something of an exhibitionist, isn't he?"

The stout woman's placidity was slightly shaken. "Dearie, you gave me a start. Si told me I must warn you about Len, and I was thinking how I'd best begin when you up and ask the question. He's born under the wrong combination of planets. Don't trust him."

Prudence chuckled. Mrs. Puffer's portentous voice was so out of character with her personality.

"Has he always lived here?"

"He was born in this house."

"Here!"

"Lors, Miss Prue, before you've lived here a month you'll think every person in the United States had a relative who was born in this house, or one who died here. There's been every kind from circus performers to people who kept a store in this room. Folks is everlastingly stopping to ask if they may look around because someone who belonged to them once lived here."

"Sort of a combination of maternity hospital and detention house for Heaven, wasn't it? It is almost dark. Let's have a light." She applied a match to the wick in the lamp on the table. "It's out! I'm clumsy. Wonder why Uncle Austin didn't have electricity put in. There! It's lighted!" She adjusted the green shade.

"I guess your uncle thought he'd spent enough on the old house for a start. If he'd had women folks, they would have struck for it. I've got everything electric from an ice-box to a sewing machine. Don't know that it gets me any more time, though." With difficulty she extricated herself from the chair. "I must be going. When's your brother coming, dearie?"

"Just as soon as I get the house in order. It won't be but a few days now. Do you think he will like it? David and I are all that are left of the family. Mother and Father died in my debutante year. He was so much older than I that he has taken their places. He has been everything to me—since I lost my sister. Oh, Mother Puffer, you think he will get well here, don't you?"

"Get well! Never knew anyone who once settled in this village to die of anything but old age. He'll be spry and dancing at your weddin' before you have time to turn around."

"My wedding! I married!" Prudence coughed in the vain hope of counteracting the bitterness of her exclamation. "I hope Dave gets well long, long before that. Thanks heaps for everything, Mrs. Puffer. Do you mind taking your basket when you go? It might be several days before we could return it. Goodnight! Come again soon!"

Prudence curled up in the wing-chair, confided to the fire:

"The long winter evenings! Seed catalogues for entertainment! Zowie!"

The dog put his forepaws in her lap, snuggled his chilly nose into her neck. She hugged him.

"Self-pity almost caught me that time, Happy. Did my voice tickle you? Don't wriggle your ears so; it cramps my style. I must talk to someone. Ingrate! Wailing over prospective long evenings, when, within my first twenty-four hours here, an all-conquering lumberman has called, and I have been snatched from a messy accident by a rich playboy."

She re-lived that episode. Shivered. Her realization of the smash from which Rodney Gerard had saved her had ripped off the shell of indifference to men in which she had encased her heart. She had told herself that she would go frigidaire should she meet the Gerard heir, doubtless a man from the world of penthouses, exclusive speakeasies, stage doors, and racetracks; instead of which she had clung to him like a limpet. She had actually liked him! Would she be able to harden again? Already the heavenly beauty and freshness of the place she had inherited was making life seem thrillingly worthwhile. The great spaces seemed as full of life as had the city streets crowded with pushing, dawdling humanity. So many persons there wore masks which gave slight clues, if any, to the mental processes behind them.

"Supper's ready, Miss Prue."

Prudence joined the woman at the door. "I'm hungry; that's why I'm low in my mind, Macky. Didn't Mother Puffer say that life could be awful dark and dreary on an empty stomach?" She linked her arm in that of the woman. "She's a dear to bring us things, and a wonderful cook."

Jane Mack sniffed. "She may be a wonderful cook, but she's a terrible talker. She said to me, 'What makes Miss Prue so bitter about men—a pretty child like her? Did her city beau turn her down because she lost her money?'"

Prudence bit her lips to steady them, blinked hard. Since the warning tap on her brother's shoulder, little hot, salty springs seemed in constant commotion behind her eyes.

"You didn't talk about Julie's husband and—and David's wife, Blanche, did you, Macky?"

"Me talk! When I started going from house to house sewing, Mother said to me:

" 'Janie, you'll hear and see things that the families you work for think is known only to them an' God. Drop the knowledge down a deep, deep well in your mind an' never let it bob up.' Me talk! Hmp! I know folks!"

Mrs. Puffer's question about the city beau returned to Prue's mind as several hours later she unclasped the string of pearls before the triplicate mirror on the chintz dressing-table. Si had had to call in reserves to help get the marble-topped atrocity it replaced to the attic, but it had been done. The rooms were in fairly good order. She was dead to the world, she was so tired from dragging and lifting and reaching, but the work was behind her—thank heaven!

She looked at the lovely, gleaming things which dripped from her pink palm. Her sister's pearls! Lovely Julie's, who had married the son of a multimillionaire, adoring him, believing in him. When after two years of marriage she had discovered his unfaithfulness—the treachery of her brother's wife—she had crumpled, her life had gone out like a candle, and with it the life of her baby. The tragedy had seemed to run back into the very roots of Prue's heart—if one's heart had roots—or the spring of her heart which threatened so often to bubble up in tears. It had killed the lovely shining belief she had had in people, taken the sunshine out of living.

Time had eased the ache, but it had not restored her faith. She had had men friends, but she had steeled herself against their protestations. There were plenty of safe, sane interests without staking her happiness on a man.

Men. The eyes of the girl in the glass narrowed a trifle. She had met two today. Mrs. Puffer had declared:

"There's one or two smart Alecks in the village who'll do you, if they get the chance."

Prudence laid the pearls in their satin bed and snapped the case shut. She tapped the velvet lightly with a finger as she reflected aloud:

"One of two smart Alecks. I wonder—I wonder if Mrs. Puffer was warning me against one or both of my new acquaintances."

IV

Prudence, perched on top of a grain bin in the dusty, shadowy barn, dangled her feet in their white and brown sports shoes. She nibbled a straw as she thoughtfully regarded Si Puffer, who, seated on a milking stool opposite, gazed back at her with fatuous admiration. The week of outdoor life in air which combined the incomparable tang of the sea and the heady essence of spruce and pine and cedar, had tinged her creamy skin with color. Her lips were vivid, her ruddy hair a riot of curls where the breeze had roughened it. With a corduroy skirt of leaf green, she wore a crêpe blouse of the same shade under a matching cardigan. A broad white collar rolled away from her rounded throat. She teased:

"What big eyes you have, Mr. Puffer."

He chuckled. "The better to see you with, Miss Prue. Whatta mean is, I was watching that dimple playin' tag at the corner of your mouth. You look most good enough to eat."

"I ought to. I'm milk and egg and chicken fed and salted by a daily swim. Marvelous water. It's like diving into prickly White Rock." The laughter in her voice and eyes changed to gravity. "What sort of man is Len Calloway, Mr. Si? He has called on one pretext or another every day since I took possession of this property. You don't have to tell me that he is a compelling person and good-looking. I know that. He's a little overdone, if you get what I mean. His eyes are too dark and flashing, too near-set; his chin a bit too assertive; his hair is getting perilously thin on top, isn't it? Already a shiny scalp glimmers through. He usually appears with an axe over his shoulder, and the first time I saw that ten-gallon hat he wears I had to cough frantically to choke back a laugh. Celluloid drama stuff, but still effective. Is he the whoop-de-doo lad of the village? Mother Puffer said that he was born in the red brick house. Has he always lived in this town?"

Puffer rubbed an unshaven cheek. "Grew up here. Went west 'bout two years ago after he'd met with a disappointment in love. Then his father died and he came back bursting with know-how and began contracting to cut timber. Len's been spoiled. Whatta mean is, from the time he could listen he's been told he was handsome; now he swaggers as if he thought he was a movie star. What's he been saying to you?"

Prudence slid from the bin. Hands in the pockets of her cardigan, she stood in the great doorway from which she could see two fawn color and white cows grazing in a nearby pasture, the shimmering, boulder-bordered bay, the hills of Mt. Desert, a lovely amethyst against a fleece-dotted backdrop of azure sky. Her brow puckered thoughtfully.

"He wants to buy the trees on the upper wood lot—the one Uncle Austin bought of his father. He didn't make a definite offer. He asked me to sign a contract giving him the right to cut all trees over ten inches and all wood necessary to get it out. Of course, I don't know anything about the business, but when he added that last clause the imp who regulates traffic in my mind flashed on a red light."

Puffer chortled. "You sure have your own way of saying things, Miss Prue. I guess that imp was on his job. Mind, I don't say Len would set out to cheat you, but he isn't in business for his health alone, and if you crossed him—well, don't have nothing to do with him. Then you're sure. Whatta mean is, he thinks he knows it all and a little more, an' he's the kind of feller that it's better to have for a friend than an enemy."

Prudence stooped to pick up the tortoiseshell cat rubbing against her green skirt.

"That last sentence classifies him. We've seen that type of man, haven't we—Cleopatra! That's a perfect name for you, kitty, you're so—so slinky. Calloway seems well educated and he's good-looking," she championed, with a mischievous desire to tease.

"You said that to get me to running on, didn't you? If you like him, that's your business. All I'll say is, handsome is as handsome does. Hulloa, here's Rod! Wonder if he wants to buy timber? He's been here every day too, hasn't he, since the morning you slid off the mow into his arms and daubed his suit with egg yolks? He was kinder solemn that day; haven't seen him like that since his mother passed away. Usually he's sort of devil-may-care."

He waved his hand to Rodney Gerard, who, with a spectacular flourish and fanfare of French horn, stopped his car in front of the barn. The sun lay warmly on his uncovered head; it accentuated the blueness of his smiling eyes, the whiteness of his even teeth.

"Greetings, Prue of Prosperity Farm! Morning, Si! Come for a ride, will you? It's a whale of a day." His eyes were on the girl.

"Terrible sorry I can't go, Roddy, but I've got to work on them poultry-houses. My boss is all-fired fussy. She's just read that 36,000,000,000 eggs were laid in this country last year, an' she don't like the way her hens are layin' all over the place." Puffer chuckled and vanished round a corner.

Prudence took possession of the stool her man-of-all-work had vacated. She shook her head as she answered the question in Gerard's eyes.

"If that invitation was meant for me, I can't go. I'm busy."

"You look it."

"Just because I'm sitting here with my hands in my pockets doesn't mean that I am not working. I'm thinking. The hens are approaching the season of diminishing returns—to put it conservatively, 'High yields and large profits' must be my battle-cry. Ever heard of an economic graph? Mr. Si and I have been tracing one."

"Come and think in the roadster. I promise not to talk."

"Don't wheedle. I can't."

"Won't, you mean."

"Won't, then, if you like that better. You seem to forget that I am a woman of affairs. I can't waste time playing with idle little boys like you."

"All right, I'm an idle little boy. Have a passion for the earnest worker, haven't you? Curious, just as money is the one universal want, belief in the newsboy-to-president urge—or its equivalent in achievement—is the one universal American faith. Why should I work? I don't need money; I put the best I've got into any sport I make a stab at; I like a good time and—there you are."

Prudence rested her elbows on her knees, her chin in her palms and studied Rodney Gerard curiously from under a fringe of lashes. He was the personification of smart gray-flannelled indolence at perfect peace with itself as he leaned against the side of the doorway. The breeze rumpled his light hair. His clean-cut face—she reluctantly conceded that it had an underlying strength—was care-free, debonair. Her memory flashed a close-up of Len Calloway. She compared the two. Rodney Gerard was as tall as the lumberman. He gave an impression of lithe strength where the other man was massive.

"What's happened to your ambition? Arrested development? Don't you care to accomplish things?" she asked gravely.

"Some things. Do you?"

"Adore it. I love trying to do what I have to do superlatively well."

He laughed and lighted a cigarette. "You are miscast. You don't belong in this age. You are a hangover from the nineteenth century when woman's place was in the home."

She colored faintly, indignation set little flares in her eyes, but she kept her voice in hand.

"Are you jeering at home making? I love it. I love planning appetizing meals. I would rather make the kind of home my mother made, which was an inspiration to everyone who came into it, made a tired man stand a little straighter when he entered it, than do anything else. It isn't the easiest job in the world, either. If trying and liking to make good dates me, then I admit I'm hopelessly old-fashioned. I made good as a craftsman."

"What sort of craftsman?"

"Silver and gold. When people began to sneak cautiously from their financial crash-proof dugouts, began to unhoard, I earned a fairly good income making jewelry and silver boxes. Then the back-to-the-land urge caught us, turned me into a farmer—and here I am."

"Giving up your craft?"

"Not if I can possibly squeeze in time for it. I adore it. You understand now, don't you, how little you and I have in common? From now on I shall be an extremely busy person; Mother Puffer is about to instruct me in the thrifty art of canning. You, doubtless, will soon return to that gay circle of society in which you must be a bright and shining light."

She hadn't known that blue eyes could be so flamingly black, nor that a fair skin could turn so darkly red.

"You've got that wrong. Do you know, sarcasm doesn't become you. I'm an extremely busy person too."

"You! Busy! About what?"

"Taking a medical correspondence course."

"What kind of medicine?"

"Don't look so skeptical. Perhaps it isn't medical, perhaps it's surgical. Trying to learn the remedy for hardening of the heart." There was a hint of seriousness underlying the light words. He regarded her steadily. "May be able to arrest the ossifying of yours. Is it true, as Mrs. Puffer intimates, that there's a white-haired boy in your New York stag line who's yearning to smash this farm obsession and carry you back to the city?"

Surprise hobbled Prue's voice. "W-what?"

"You know what I said. Don't side-step."

Indignation clarified her mind and loosened her tongue.

"Side-step! Why should I? There is, there was a man for whom I might have cared, but you have brought this on yourself by your question—he is of your type; wealth is an acid test few of the men I have known could stand—so I'm a perfectly safe person so far as you are concerned."

"What do you mean by that crack?"

"That wasn't a crack, it was reassurance. Mr. Si told

me that you were in terror for fear some girl would marry you for your money. I wouldn't marry a rich playboy if I loved him to distraction. I had to stand by helpless while my sister broke her heart over one of them."

Rodney Gerard caught her hands and pulled her to her feet.

"Si talks too much. I in terror about anything? That's his joke. Your heart wouldn't break for a man, would it?"

Prudence twisted free. "Not unless it split from fury because I had been so dumb as to believe in him."

"That's one in the eye for me, I take it. Boy, but you're bitter! I'm not in that class you detest. I'll make you take back what you said about my being of that type. I'll make you. It will be a no-quarter battle. Get me?"

She clasped her hands behind her back, leaned toward him smiling.

"Smashing climax. This is where a movie director who knew his business would shout 'Cut!' "

His eyes held her mocking eyes with steady inflexibility. "Si Puffer says that you are 'smart as a steel trap.' You may be, but apparently not smart enough to distinguish between the real and melodrama. I may be a lazy devil wasting opportunity, but I still believe in character, believe that there are levels below which—well, in the century in which you belong they called it *noblesse oblige.*"

His face was colorless as he turned away to his car. Prue's conscience smarted. Had she been unjust? She couldn't help liking him. She was beside him as he stepped into the roadster. She smiled apology.

"Don't go away angry. You asked a question. I answered it. Perhaps having seen the live nerve pulled out of two hearts has twisted my point of view. I'm sorry. Just because we live on different planets of ideals and ideas is no reason for our quarreling, is it?"

"How do you know we are so far apart?"

"Help! I've said the wrong thing again! I would love

to motor with you, really I would, but David is coming on the afternoon train and I have heaps to do before then. You don't know how you tempt me."

There was a reckless light in Gerard's eyes.

"Quote. 'Fly pleasure and it will follow you.' "

"Then I won't fly. Will you take me to the Puffers'?"

He swung the roadster door wide. Grinned engagingly.

"Taxi, lady?"

As the car shot forward, he inquired: "Who will bring your brother from the station?"

"Mr. Si. I have been too busy about the place to try out the car Uncle Austin left me."

"The road is still torn up. He would be jolted to pulp in that old machine of Puffer's. If you think a 'rich playboy' may be trusted, I will meet him."

"Don't be snippy. I have been dreading the trip for David, but if he could come in this wonderful roadster—he is so—so precious." Emotion broke up the sentence, menaced her voice. Gerard kept his eyes on the road bordered by mosaics of fall colors.

"Will you come with me?"

"If you don't mind, I would rather wait for him at home. I want to be sure that the fires are blazing, the kettle is singing, and everything is saying 'Welcome!' "

He drew an unsteady breath. She had been inexcusably thoughtless. Since his mother's death, there was no longer anyone he loved to keep home fires blazing, the kettle singing for him. She said quickly:

"I will accept your kindness only if you'll promise to come in and have tea when you bring David home."

There was a small-boy radiance in his face and voice which contracted Prue's throat.

"Mean it? Then of course I'll come. I'll drive this car as if it were a bubble with a grain of radium for passenger. Those are the most breakable and precious commodities I know. How are you, Calloway?"

The dark-eyed, dark-skinned man, passing, brought

his fire-department red car to a sudden stop and swept off his broad-brimmed hat.

"Good morning, Miss Schuyler. I've just been to your place, Gerard. They told me I was likely to find you somewhere round here."

There was nothing in the words which could be challenged. It was the implication. Rodney Gerard reddened.

"Come to High Ledges tonight, Calloway, and I'll let you know what I have decided about the timber."

"Can't you tell me now?"

"No, I can't."

"Perhaps Miss Schuyler will say whether she has decided to let me have hers—or—do you decide for her?"

"You're mighty impertinent," Gerard flared, and shot the car forward.

Prudence glanced back. Calloway was staring after them, a slight sinister smile twisting his large mouth. He waved his ten-gallon hat with a familiarity which set her cheeks burning. She faced about. The man beside her was looking straight ahead, his brows knit, his lips in a tense line.

"Oh dear! Have you made an enemy because of me?"

His laugh was curt. "The enmity between Len Calloway and yours truly is nothing new. He always gets my goat. Do you intend to sell your timber to him?"

"Mr. Si advises against it."

"Give me the contract to handle it, will you?"

"You?"

"Even I. Don't let surprise that I am interested in something besides sports shock you into insensibility."

She laughed. "How could it? Aren't you studying medicine?"

"Only the heart," he corrected evenly. "I have about a thousand acres of timber which have been on my mind for some time. I've decided to cut it this winter, and the more I have to cut, the better and more profitable job I can make of it."

"But—you'll have to live here!"

"All right. I'll have to live here. What a profound observation! Coming from a woman of affairs like yourself, it's a smash."

" 'Do you know, sarcasm doesn't become you,' " she mimicked. She stole a glance at his grave face. Her thoughts raced as swiftly as the fleecy clouds against the glaring blue sky. Had he had this in mind while she had been accusing him of indolence and indifference? Contrition warmed her voice.

"I should love to have you cut our timber, but, I warn you, I'm likely to be a pest I shall ask so many questions."

"Fire away. What say to forming a partnership?"

"Sounds grand—but that would take capital, wouldn't it? Why not sign a contract to the effect that the interest on your investment is to be paid before the profit is divided?"

"Hooey! I—"

"Unless that is done I'm off the partnership, Mr. Rodney Gerard."

"Oh, all right. I'm a lawyer—though I haven't done much at it. I'll draw a contract which will put skids under your fortune if you break it. Here we are at the Puffers'. Come on a little way. We have so much to decide, we are in business now, remember. We'll trace that economic graph you're so keen about."

Prudence swung open the door of the car. "Don't wheedle. I'll expect you for tea this afternoon. 'Morning, partner."

She turned to wave her hand before she entered the path to the back door. Its flower border was gorgeous with blossoms, pink larkspur, creamy roses, calendulas, and dominating all others were the chrysanthemums, yellow, tan, white, pink, carmine. Mrs. Si had a magic touch with flowers, Prue thought, as she opened a door in response to a soft, cushiony:

"Come in!"

The kitchen was gay with blue and white checked gingham curtains at the plant-filled windows, a blue and white linoleum on the floor, blue pots and pans arranged on the shelves. Spotless town, if ever there was one. A mass of chrysanthemums was in a yellow bowl on the table. The delectable smell of cookies baking was in the air. A long red curl of skin dangled from the knife with which blue-frocked Mrs. Puffer was paring. She looked up from a pan of rosy apples.

"Glad you've come, Miss Prue. I cut that bokay for you. Wasn't that Rod Gerard with you? I wonder what's keeping him in this part of the country so late in the season."

"He is looking after his timber."

"Lors! I hope he and Calloway won't get into trouble again. Len's been jealous of Roddy since they were boys, when little Milly Gooch, the circus folks' kid, was always turning down Walt and Len for him. Len thought 'twas because Rod's folks were rich and a fine family, but what did the child care for that? She just about worshipped Roddy. Then there was bad feeling between the two before Len went west, and since he came back he and Rod have had one set-to in town meeting. Rod pays the biggest taxes in the county. He believes in spending money to keep things up proper, and Len wants to squeeze all the improvements out of the summer folks. He gets terrible ugly if he's crossed. I'm afraid he'll get the best of Rod who's easy-going."

"Why not warn Mr. Gerard? He could escape before anything rough happens to him. It's good flying weather."

"Now, Miss Prue, don't you make fun of Rod. Si and I couldn't love that boy more if he belonged to us."

"I'm not making fun of him; on the contrary, I am thinking of engaging him as my legal adviser."

"Then you've got another think coming to you."

Prudence wheeled. Her eyes widened as they met the dark, near-set eyes of Calloway who was leaning against the door frame. He jingled coins in one palm as he dictated:

"Understand, Miss Schuyler, that if I cut your timber, I deal with you, with you and no one else. Gerard will keep out of my business or I'll know the reason why. He stepped between me and a girl once before—and it's for the last time."

Prudence regarded him from under sweeping lashes. "Just why are you inflicting me with the story of your young life?"

Even the bald spot of Calloway's head went crimson. "You won't get anywhere wisecracking with me. You'll come round sooner or later to wanting me to handle your timber—they all do—and when I do it, I won't stand interference from anyone. Get that?"

Prudence never before had realized her capacity for fury. "I get it. Did you think your methods too subtle for my Intelligence Quotient? I.Q. is the abbreviation, in case you don't know. Now get this. There will be no interference when you cut my timber, Mr. Calloway, for you won't cut it. I have already contracted with Mr. Gerard to do it."

"Gerard! Gerard get out lumber! That's a joke. Don't run away with the idea that because he can pilot a plane he'd stick to anything that was work. Dare-devil stunts are his specialty, but when it comes to sustained effort—nothing doing. He dances and games his days away. He'd run at the first touch of winter. As for managing a crew, his poor flabby muscles would make a fine showing in a lumber camp. They—"

"They are rather out of condition," agreed an icy voice behind him, "but flabby as they are, I don't take that wallop sitting down, they can chuck you out."

Rodney Gerard's face was white, his eyes were afire, as he caught the surprised Calloway round the waist and by sheer force of arms and knees rushed him outside.

He returned and banged the door shut. He leaned against it, dusted one hand against the other, and observed somewhat breathlessly:

"Saw his red car here and came back. Business seems to be opening with a whang, partner."

V

For the third time in ten minutes Prudence rear-
ranged the egg-shell cups on the butterfly table, lifted
the silver skittle-ball kettle to make sure that the wick
of the spirit lamp on its brazier-like stand would
flame at the touch of a match. She adjusted a blossom
in the mass of chrysanthemums in a jade-green bowl
on the old secretary. They put a soul into the living
room. Sweet of Mrs. Si to give them to her. Would
she ever grow flowers as perfect? Apparently she had
picked up the gardening bug—among others—since
she had come to the State of Maine.

She glanced at the banjo clock. Only five minutes
since she had looked before? Unbelievable. Time was
creeping on hands and knees. She crossed to the book
shelves. It had taken hours to fill them. A thankless
task, as doubtless David would rearrange his treasures
as soon as he was rested, he loved to handle his
books. She had put the poetry together. Shelf after
shelf of it from the Homeric poems through Chaucer,
Spenser, Marlowe, Shakespeare, to the pioneers in
Modern American poetry, Masters, Lindsay, Sand-
burg, Amy Lowell, Oppenheim, Untermeyer; on to
their successors, Millay, Wylie, the Benets. Except for
John Brown's Body she didn't care for them as she
did for the poets of an older tradition: she couldn't
get the same lift and inspiration from them; but Dave
knew them all. He could fit an appropriate line or two
of verse to any situation. She took down a volume of
Milton. The book opened as if from habit at a page in
Comus. Had her brother marked the lines:

> "That power
> Which erring men call chance."

She closed the book. David believed in that power; it wasn't merely a save-worry movement with him, it was a belief upon which he had built his character. The knocker? She glanced at the clock. Not time for her brother. Who could it be?

She went slowly through the hall. She ought to be prancing with eagerness at the prospect of a caller. She wasn't. Since the family scandal she dreaded to meet new people. That was the trouble with scandals, they didn't confine themselves to the principals, they boiled over and scalded the innocent unbearably. She opened the door.

She knew at once, from Si Puffer's description, that the tall woman facing her was Mrs. Walter Gerard. Large blue eyes, large floppy hat, large patterned gown, perfect accessories. The village women were right, she was a "nifty dresser." "All a-twitter" described her manner perfectly as she extended a white-gloved hand.

"Good afternoon, Miss Schuyler. I am your neighbor, Mrs. Gerard, and this is my darling daughter Jean."

She drew forward a thin little girl in a soft pink frock who had been standing behind her. The child curtsied demurely. She had puckish dark eyes, pale, unhealthy skin, short hair.

"Won't you come in?"

Try as she would, Prudence couldn't infuse warmth into her invitation. She hated the suave voice, hated the way the woman flicked her eyelids, hated her smile, hated the flutter with which she settled into the wing chair. The child sat primly on the ottoman beside her, her eyes darting about the room like a ferret's.

Even as she murmured platitudes, Prudence tried to remember what Si Puffer had told her about the girl. She had it! "Cute, but that curious that the folks lock up everything when they see her coming." At the moment, "darling daughter" was staring at the muffin stand with its intriguing doily-covered plates.

Mrs. Walter Gerard babbled: "So delighted to have

a woman of my own kind near. Of course, our house is full during the season, but that isn't like having a neighbor. We hope that you will come often to High Ledges. What is it, dear?"

She inclined her head for the child's whisper. "The idea! No. No, of course not, Jean. She wants to prowl, Miss Schuyler, to see things. She is so intelligent. My cousin, the Ambassador, says that she is the brightest child he has ever met. What an adorable skittle-ball kettle! Heirloom?"

Prudence wanted to snap, "No. Auction room." Mrs. Walter Gerard was so blatantly a person to whom family background would matter enormously in her estimate of a person, but she couldn't deny her father's great-grandmother.

"Yes."

Lorgnon in action, Mrs. Gerard bent over the kettle. "It looks like a Paul Lamerie."

"It is."

"But, my dear, don't you realize that it is a museum piece? That man's fame as a goldsmith has reached the ends of the earth. Fancy using it! I thought my cousin, the Ambassador, had the only example of Lamerie in this part of the country." She settled back in her chair. "As I was saying, my brother-in-law is a bachelor; in consequence, I am never at a loss for young company."

Her wink fired Prudence with an unholy impulse to scratch her.

"But he's such a butterfly. He flits from flower to flower, never settles to one girl. A quite natural attitude for a rich man who has been pursued all his life, don't you think so, Miss Schuyler?"

She was intimating what Si Puffer had said, that Rodney Gerard was in terror of being married for his fortune. Did the woman think that she needed warning? A crash saved Prue's reputation for courtesy. Jean had been investigating the sugar bowl. The child scowled down upon it.

"Gee, it made me mad to drop that!"

Her mother folded complacent hands. "Darling

daughter shouldn't touch things until she is better acquainted. She is interested in everything, Miss Schuyler. I am sure she is going to be a writer. My cousin, the Ambassador, says—"

"Uncle Rod calls me K.K., his K-urious Kid," Jean interrupted in a high voice. "He comes to see you every day, doesn't he?"

The elfish eyes interrogating her brought a wave of color to Prue's face, the rush as of many waters in her ears. Mrs. Gerard anticipated her answer.

"How amusing that you should have imagined that, darling. Your Uncle Rodney is an indolent, good-natured boy; perhaps he might allow himself to be monopolized—for a time. You have a brother, dear Miss Schuyler?"

"If she calls me dear once more I'll throw something at her," Prudence told herself furiously. Aloud she informed smoothly:

"Yes. I expect him at any moment." She deliberately looked at the clock. Never in her life had she been so rude, but never before had she had such occasion, she excused herself.

"Coming today! Happy girl! I'll run away, you must be busy. You will come to High Ledges when we return in the spring, won't you? We close the house soon, so I am afraid—"

"Uncle Rod isn't going," Jean announced as they reached the front door.

"Rodney not going!" Mrs. Gerard's suave voice shrilled. Her face reddened unbecomingly. Her blue eyes hardened; then she laughed and winked.

"This darling has the strangest fancies, Miss Schuyler. You won't forget me, will you?" She extended her white-gloved hand, showed her long teeth in a large smile, and started along the herring-bone brick path with a springiness bordering on juvenility. Her daughter lingered to whisper hoarsely:

"I know why Uncle Rod isn't going back to the city. He's goofy about you." She stuck her tongue in her cheek and ran.

Prue's eyes smoldered as she watched mother and

daughter enter the luxurious maroon touring car. A smartly maroon-uniformed chauffeur touched his maroon cap.

"Horrid woman," she thought passionately. "I wager that you are a scold, a hypocrite. I feel as if my heart and soul had stumbled into a nettle patch. They are all prickles."

She poked the fire with a vigor which sent sparks singing up the chimney. She looked at the skittle-ball kettle. It was almost priceless. She had questioned the wisdom of bringing it, but she loved it, and David had encouraged:

"If it gives you pleasure, why not use it?"

She crossed to the window and tried to concentrate her attention on the road by which her brother would come, but thoughts of her recent callers would intrude. Now it was her conscience which pricked. No matter how much she had disliked the woman, she should have offered her a cup of tea.

It seemed ages before Gerard's shining black roadster swept into sight. She darted between the brick gateposts as it stopped.

"David! Dave, you dear!" Her voice choked. Had her brother grown gaunter since she had left him? She sprang to the running board and laid her glowing cheek against his white one. He held her close for a moment. His eyes, so like hers, were warm and tender, his voice was humorously unsteady, as he admitted:

"Prue, I wouldn't have believed that I could have missed being coddled as I did. You've spoiled me. May I get out? This is a veritable armchair of a car, but I smell a wood fire and toast—don't tell me that you haven't grapefruit marmalade or I shall burst into tears. I'm ravenous for that toast, aren't you, Gerard?"

Prudence blinked valiantly. "David, I'm as temperamental as ever. I forgot everything when I saw you. Mr. Gerard, remember that you promised to have tea with us."

"Thank you. I'm all for it. Better grab my arm,

Schuyler. One is apt to be stiff after a long train ride."

Prudence put her arm under her brother's while Gerard steadied him on the other side. They led him to the wing chair in front of the fireplace. He sank into it and closed his eyes. Her breath caught in a strangled sob. He looked up and smiled.

"'And with difficulty they came into a place which is called Fair Havens,'" he quoted softly. "I doubt if even that port looked as peaceful to Paul as this room looks to me."

Prudence dropped to her knees beside him. "David, it is wonderful to have you here. You—you put the heart into the house. We'll have the happiest time, and you will gain in weight and health every minute with the milk and eggs and chickens fresh from the garden. I'm some farmer already, am I not, Mr. Gerard? Why, when did he go?"

"I suspect that he slipped out when you and I forgot there was anyone else in the room, Prue."

"I'll bring him back, pronto."

She straightened the foot-cushion, dropped a kiss on the top of his head, picked up the silver kettle. No sign of Gerard in the dining room. She opened the kitchen door. He was perched on the corner of the pine table, his hands clasped about one knee as he talked to Jane Mack. Wonder of wonders! Macky was smiling!

"Tea is served in the Club car!" Prudence announced in a stentorian tone, as she reached for the teakettle on the range from which to fill the silver one in her hand. Gerard seized it.

"Let me buttle. I'll feel like an outlander at this family reunion unless I can help."

Prudence stopped on the threshold. "Come with us, Macky. Something tells me that Mr. Gerard is tingling to hear his fortune."

In the living room she seated herself on a low stool beside her brother's chair. She answered his questions to the accompaniment of the purr of steam from the kettle, the crackle of the fire, the tinkle of silver on china. She concluded:

"The evening I arrived I racked my brain for a name for these acres we have inherited which would make our coming seem like a new deal. I seized a word which has been hiding in the dark recently, pulled it out into the light, and named the place Prosperity Farm. Get the psychology? Each time I say it my courage bobs up as if it were hitched to a balloon. I called the dog Happy, christened the car Success—so that it never will fail to get me to my destination—but I can't decide what to call the poultry. They've just got to lay eggs for me and I must resort to autosuggestion."

"What's the matter with Nickels?"

"Grand! Picture me scattering corn, calling: 'Nickels! Nickels! A little action this morning! Eggs, Nickels, eggs!' Macky, as a reward for Mr. Gerard's brilliant suggestion, tell his fortune."

"Miss Prue, I can't—I really don't—"

"No inferiority complexes allowed here, Macky. There ought to be plenty of signs and symbols in this tea. I didn't use the strainer."

"Come on, Miss Mack." Gerard's voice and smile brought a wintry gleam to the woman's worried eyes.

"If you want I should, I'll try. Any grounds?" He held out the cup of egg-shell china. She peered into it and nodded.

"Those will do. Now take it by the handle, swing it in a circle three times, turn it over on the saucer quick, and wish. Be sure you wish. That's right. Give me the cup."

Prudence smiled at Gerard as she leaned against her brother's knee, but he was intently watching the fortune teller's face.

"I see a journey," Jane Mack announced in an "Out, damned spot!" tone, which shot Prue's body full of tingles even though she had heard the prophecy scores of times before. She hadn't realized that she had engaged a potential Lady Macbeth as a housekeeper. "It is to be unexpected and will have far-reaching consequences."

"How about my wish?"

"Hst! Don't interrupt the oracle!"

"Far-reaching consequences," Jane Mack reiterated, with a *tragédienne's* disregard of the girl's theatrical reproof. "I see a piece of paper. It will have an influence on your wish. You'll have an unexpected present and a quarrel, but the journey is the most important thing I see. You'll make it within a two—two days—two weeks—two months—two—"

"But my wish?"

Miss Mack pursed her lips, drew her brows together. "I think you'll get it, Mr. Gerard—but there's a tall, domineering woman mixed up in your life."

Prudence swallowed a laugh. That hoarse, dramatic whisper was blood-curdling. Macky had missed her vocation. She should be barnstorming. She had seen her at an ell window intently watching Mrs. Walter Gerard's departure this afternoon. The oracle went on:

"That tall woman seems to have considerable to say about your doings. Watch her! You'll think she's out of your way and suddenly she'll pop up. I know folks. There's money here and a few tears. That means heartache for a man. Taken by and large, it's a lucky cup."

She handed it back to Gerard. He frowned at the grounds in the bottom.

"Lucky! A quarrel. Heartache. Call that lucky?"

"It takes a few clouds to make a glorious sunset," Jane Mack reminded oracularly, even as she prosaically collected china and spoons.

Gerard carried the tray to the kitchen. Prudence could hear the faint rumble of his voice.

"The impossible has happened! Macky's granite heart has been chipped at last, David," she confided, as on the cushion beside him she leaned against the arm of her brother's chair.

"Gerard certainly has an engaging manner. What do you know about him?"

"Nothing, except that even in the late era of frozen assets the bulk of his large fortune remained fluid. Mrs. Si is my authority. That woman is a regular Who's Who for this village. The fact that he is rich tells me all I want to know."

"All rich men are not alike, Prue. You and I have been unfortunate in some we have known."

"David, do you think that I will ever forget the result of Julie's marriage to a playboy? She was the sweetest big sister a girl ever had, and she died of a broken heart. Forgive me, Dave, forgive me," she pleaded, as his head dropped back against the chair and his eyes closed.

She caught his hands tight in hers. "Why, why did I bring that up! We'll forget it. It's behind us. What is that line about pressing forward? Wasn't Macky dramatic with her 'tall woman—watch her!'? She caught a glimpse of Mr. Gerard's sister-in-law when she called here this afternoon. I shall detest that woman. I feel it in my bones."

Her brother shook his head. His smile brought a tinge of color to his white face.

"Prue! Prue! Beware of snap judgment. It is your besetting sin."

She pressed her cheek against his arm before she retorted gaily.

"You are so wonderful that I have to have sins to keep the average normal. It would be boring to have two saints in the family. You've had a long, tiresome day, David, why not go to your room, and I'll tuck you into bed, and tomorrow you'll be rested and refreshed and I will show you everything."

"That program sounds good to me." He laid his hand on her shoulder and rose. He was tall and pathetically thin, but he held his head, with its thick, dark hair, with royal dignity.

"Bloody but unbowed." The words flashed into Prue's mind as she looked up at him. His deep-set eyes, his perfect nose, his sensitive lips blurred for an instant. As if he read her thoughts, his hand tightened on her shoulder.

"Everything's going to be all right now, Prue. Already I feel stronger. I will go up as you suggest. Say good afternoon to—here he is now," David Schuyler added, as Gerard entered. "I have been ordered to bed by my tyrant, so I'll say 'thank you' for bringing me from the train and obey." He offered his hand with cordial friendliness.

"Let me give you an arm. Those steep stairs look tricky. If she will promise to be good we'll let your sister trail along."

From the hall Prudence watched the two men as they slowly mounted the stairs. Tears blinded her. David looked so frail, so weary, as if too strong a wind might blow him away. She shut her teeth hard in her lips. It was her job to see that a strong wind didn't touch him. Could she prevent it? Could she! She had better cut out self doubt and cut it out quick. "Must prevent" were the words she wanted. One didn't stop to question when the most precious person in one's life was in danger; one did things. She wasn't much good if she couldn't stand between him and trouble.

Someone knocking! Another caller? Why had the neighbors started to be friendly today of all days when she wanted to devote herself to her brother? She opened the door. Her breath caught in a little gasp as she confronted Len Calloway. His huge hat was in his hand, his dark eyes were annoyingly confident.

"Good afternoon, Miss Schuyler. May I come in?" He entered the living room without waiting for an answer.

Prudence resented his assurance. He loomed above her, looking down with a tinge of indulgent amusement which made her feel absurdly childish, almost as if she were clutching a doll against her breast.

"I can't talk business now, Mr. Calloway. My brother has just arrived and I want to be with him."

"I won't detain you but a moment. I came to ask once more if you will give the contract for cutting your timber to me."

"I have already told you that I have arranged with Mr. Gerard to do it."

"Gerard!" Calloway shrugged his scorn. "You make me laugh! In the first place, suppose Gerard should stick to the proposition long enough to begin work—he won't, but we'll let it go for the sake of argument—where would he get a crew to log for him?"

"A crew! Hire the men, I suppose. Did you think he would conjure them out of his sleeve?"

"Wait a minute! Don't be so high-hat. Hire them! Sounds easy, doesn't it? But take it from me, you've got a lot to learn, young lady. There isn't a man in this town who would dare work for Gerard if I said 'No!' "

"What's that?"

The question rang like a pistol shot. Calloway shifted his eyes from the girl's face to stare insultingly at the man in the doorway.

"I can't seem to take a step without running into you, can I, Gerard? Try to put me out of this house, just try! You won't catch me off guard again. Perhaps you've appointed yourself Miss Schuyler's guardian, though?"

The sneering tone whitened Rodney Gerard's face. His eyes frightened Prudence. She took a quick step toward him. He shook his head. His smile was strained as he reassured:

"Okay. I shan't make a row when your brother is directly over this room. What do you want, Calloway?"

"What business is that of yours?"

"It is his business!" Prudence turned to Gerard. "He came to warn me that if he did not cut my timber no one else should."

"Boy! So racketeering has struck this small village!"

Calloway's eyes retreated into their caverns. "Call it racketeering, it's all right with me. The fact remains that you'll be unable to hire labor if I say the word. I'll give you and Miss Schuyler one more chance. Think it over. Contract with me to handle your tim-

ber and I'll treat you fair. If you don't—" He turned
away with a suggestive laugh.

"You've had our answer. I'll cut that timber. Try to
stop me. Just try!"

"Oh, I'll try."

Calloway set his hat at a rakish angle. On the
threshold he turned; his mouth had a merciless twist.

"Think it over! Think it over!" he advised, before
he banged the door behind him.

Prue's eyes were bright with indignation. "I felt of
as little importance in that contest as a cheer leader
without a megaphone, and I am supposed to be your
partner. Can he do it? Can he prevent you?"

"Can he! Just watch me, girl, watch me. 'Down
with the racketeer!' will be my battle cry. I have
made up my mind to get out that timber, and when I
decide to do a thing I do it. It will take something
bigger than Len Calloway to stop me."

There was a disturbing light in his eyes and a
vibrant note in his voice as he added:

"That isn't all I've made up my mind to do either,
but it is enough to announce for a starter."

VI

The last of September, with flames in the maples,
asters and goldenrod outside the garden fence, a
crisp, tingling breeze stirring the enormous Heavenly
Blue morning glories on the trellis. Station wagons
flying by trunk-laden. Somewhere a radio broadcasting a popular musical comedy song. A mother-of-
pearl sail on the horizon, frills on the cobalt blue sea,
a white ribbon in the wake of a speed-boat. A fish-
hawk sailing swift and strong in the infinite turquoise
of the sky.

Prudence Schuyler, in dark blue linen slacks and
short-sleeved green shirt, knelt beside the border of

the garden back of the red brick house. She filled her soul with the beauty of the world about her, her lungs with the sparkling air, and began to dig. A shadow fell across the earth. She called over her shoulder:

"Fill that pail with sand, will you, Mr. Si? The directions which came with the lilies stressed the importance of a handful under each bulb."

She measured a hole with a short ruler in her white cotton-gloved hand.

"Six inches. Correct. I wonder if the lily would refuse to come up if I short-changed on depth." She sat back on her heels as a pail was set down beside her.

"Thanks lots. These lily bulbs will be but a voice crying in a wilderness of bare ground, but it's a start. Thank heaven for my imagination. I'll wager I get as much thrill from visualizing what this border will look like as that physician got from isolating the pain nerve. Giant larkspurs, columbine, lilies in succession, holly-hocks, phlox, with mists and drifts of white gypsophila. Nice of me to treat you to a preview, isn't it? I'll make it a dream when my ship comes in and I can buy dozen of plants."

"No need of waiting for a ship to realize that dream."

Prudence looked up in startled surprise. "Just where did you drop from? I thought you were Mr. Si."

Rodney Gerard turned a bushel basket bottom side up for a seat. "You don't have to tell me that. 'Whatta mean is,' you never favor me with such cordiality. But we won't go into that now."

Prudence dug at the earth with a trowel. She met his clear, amused blue eyes with troubled brown ones. He was so darn likable. Almost he made her believe that a rich playboy might be honorable, might be true to that 'forsaking all others' clause in the marriage service. She demanded hurriedly:

"Why did you come? Is Calloway making more trouble for you? You really shouldn't have rushed him out of Mrs. Puffer's as you did the other day. He had as much right there as you and I."

"It was a kid trick, collegiate stuff, but he was bullying you."

"What a fire-eater you are! You can't fight my battles."

"Can't I? I'll make a stab at fighting your timber battles. What are you doing?"

Prudence looked at the holes she had dug, at the bulbs in the package.

"Mixing cake."

"Don't wisecrack. I know where you can get all the plants you want for this border."

"So do I. The nurserymen's catalogues are full of them."

"I don't mean buy them. I know a place where they are throwing them away this minute."

"Throwing—this minute!" Prudence was on her feet. "Come on, lead me to it."

Gerard caught her hand. Started on a run. Out of the garden. Around the house.

"Is it far—I'll tell—"

"Don't stop for anything or you may lose them. Action, girl, action!" He pulled open the door of his roadster standing at the entrance to the brick walk. "Hop in!"

"But I must tell Macky or Dave where I'm going. Where am I going?" Prudence demanded, with an excusable burst of impatience, as the car shot forward. Gerard called to David Schuyler standing in the hooded doorway:

"We'll be back in an hour."

Prudence looked over her shoulder and waved to her brother, before she inquired:

"Would it be committing a social blunder if I were to ask whither away, young man?"

Gerard laughed. "You pack more meaning into a word or two than anyone I know. We're bound for High Ledges. The nurserymen are there with bulbs and plants for the Glen. They always thin a lot of perennials—no reason why you shouldn't have them."

"Is that where—"

"Where my mother and father are buried. You won't mind going, will you? It isn't in the least depressing."

"Mind! Of course not. Mrs. Si has told me about it. She says it is beautiful."

"Mother planned it. I try to keep it as she loved to see it."

They drove the rest of the way in silence. As they passed the vine-covered stone and oak house, Prudence gave a fleeting thought to Mrs. Walter Gerard's reaction were she to see her on the place with her "butterfly" brother-in-law. Punctiliously she had returned her first call within the time limit ordained by etiquette, and had been overjoyed to be told that she was not at home.

Gerard stopped the roadster at the entrance to a dusky green trail. He led the way as it sloped gently down hill. The air, dry and soft and cool, was spicy with the breath of spruce and balsam. The sun shot long hazy rays through the branches, throwing intervening spaces into deep green shadow. The trees whispered among themselves, changing tempo like the rhythm of a low voice reading aloud. Startlingly near a quail called:

"Bob White! Bob White!"

At the top of three boulder steps Gerard stopped.

"Look! The frost hasn't touched it yet."

The sheer beauty of the garden below caught at Prue's throat. Such a garden! Regale lilies, crimson-spotted white; pink-tinged lilies; mammoth zinnias in pastel colorings; spikes of purple monkshood; plumes of pale blue larkspur, a second blossoming; snowy drifts of gypsophila; gladioli, pink, purple, mauve, white, amber, wine-red; clumps of Chinese forget-me-nots; sprays of pale yellow salpiglosis; tall dahlias, single, apricot colored.

From a towering anchusa, blue as the robe of a Madonna, rose a cloud of golden butterflies. They circled like fairies in a ritual dance, before they

winged aloft into the sunlight. White clematis cascad-
ed over rocky walls, above which spruces, hemlocks,
and pines kept unceasing watch. Their fragrance,
mingled with the perfume of Regale lilies, scented
the air; the light breeze through their branches
soughed in solemn requiem. Water rilled gently over
a ledge to tinkle into a fern-rimmed pool. An old-
fashioned wrought-iron seat was near it.

At the foot of the steps Prudence paused and drew
an unsteady breath.

> " 'The Lord is in His holy temple;
>   Let all the earth keep silence before Him,' "

she chanted softly.

Rodney Gerard parted the ferns and crimson gladioli which almost obscured a bronze tablet set in a
moss-grown boulder. She read the inscription. Whispered:

"How lovely! What profound silence! It sinks into
one's soul."

He said aloud: "The lilies wintered well. In the
spring the place is a riot of tulips, hyacinths, jonquils,
and narcissus."

"It is perfect now. Can't you imagine the spirits of
your father and mother walking here, hand in hand,
in the cool evening? The place almost restores one's
belief in faithfulness and love and—"

"There is faithfulness and love, Prue, lots of it. You
only hear of the heartbreaks. You must believe it.
I—"

"Don't! Please! Don't spoil it. Even the purple
shadows cast by the moving clouds pass more softly
here. See that white gull sailing high above us! How
far does the forest stretch?"

"On and on to the Canadian line. We'll go back and
I'll show you the direction in which The Hundreds
lie."

A few feet beyond the top of the steps he stopped.
"Your land lies to the east about half a mile from

here. It is nearer the pond road and the village than the woods I am planning to thin."

Prue's eyes followed the narrowing perspective of a trail, carpeted with velvet moss still damp from dew, splashed with gold dust which the sun was pouring lavishly through a filter of branches. It was bordered on each side by trees. Their breath was resinous, their green was almost black, their height incalculable, their grandeur gave a sense of eternity. She gazed at them in awed unbelief.

"Do I own trees like that?"

"Hundreds of them."

"Must those magnificent things come down?"

"Yes, for the good of the forest, I am told. The mature trees are taking the place of productive timber. Besides, there are a thousand bucks or more for you going to waste, so long as they stand."

"Practicality vs. sentiment. I'm not a practical person when it comes to beauty. I hear voices. Coming this way."

"The nurserymen."

"I'm going before they disturb the peace and beauty of this place."

"But the plants? Don't you want to select them?"

"Let the men save me anything they can spare. I shall love having them—from here." She looked down into the hushed garden.

"I don't know how anyone could be false or wicked with this heavenly spot to come to, Rodney Gerard."

He followed her along the trail, odorous of spruce and pine, dimly lit, throbby with unspoken thoughts. "You think too much of the frailty of human nature, Prudence Schuyler, it twists your judgment. Of course, I'm a man of affairs, but I'll try to find time to make you see the other side."

"Oh, yes?" She looked back at him. There was a hint of challenge in her brown eyes. "Perhaps I prefer—"

"Say, Mr. Gerard!"

The hail came from around the bend in the trail. Gerard stopped.

"Go on to the roadster, Prue. I'll give the men directions about the plants. I won't be long."

Prudence glanced at her wrist watch as she stepped into the shining black car. Almost noon. David would think her lost. She had so much to tell him about their trees. Magnificent things. They seemed like human beings. Some time he must see that heavenly garden. She would never forget it. It would help when she was engulfed in a tide of bitterness to think of the shades of husband and wife who perhaps walked there, hand in hand, in the dusky twilight. Where did people go when they departed from this earth? Did they know what was taking place in the world they had left? If that were so, there couldn't be much peace in the spirit world. Was Rodney Gerard's mother aware of what happened to her son?

Rodney was right—though she wouldn't admit it to him—she did dwell too much on the faults and weaknesses of people. The experiences of her brother and sister had made her incapable of seeing anything but unhappiness in love, the illusion of beauty and faith in romance had been wiped out—but—if, with his heart bleeding, David's tenderness and trust remained impregnable, if he could believe in human nature, she should be able to.

"The idea, Miss Schuyler! Didn't they tell you that I was on the rear terrace, snipping off a few dead blossoms from the boxes, when you stopped at the house?"

Mrs. Walter Gerard had appeared as soundlessly as a wraith beside her car. The woman knew perfectly well that she hadn't been at the house, it was her way of making her feel like a trespasser, Prudence concluded hotly. She must have been gardening in the hope that she would be photographed for the rotos; all her floppy hat needed to make it go Little Bo-Peep was long ribbon streamers. Over her good, but not thrilling, flowered frock she wore a gardening apron de luxe which had pockets for tools and a thickly padded border to protect her knees; her white gloves were immaculate. Prue had a vision of her own

warm, dusty self as Rodney Gerard had seen her
planting lilies. She was annoyingly conscious of the
dirt stains on the knees of her dark blue slacks as she
assured politely:

"It was a disappointment not to find you."

"But, my dear Miss Schuyler,"—Mrs. Walter
winked—"did you really—" She broke off as her
brother-in-law appeared on the trail. "Rodney, why
have the nurserymen come today of all days? I can't
have the Glen disturbed. I am entertaining some
Garden Clubs; women are coming from miles away to
see it. I told you about it a week ago."

"Boy! I forgot! I'll stop them, Annie."

He sprinted up the trail. His sister-in-law called after
him:

"I am expecting you to show my guests about,
Rodney—" As he disappered in the dusky greenness
without answering, Annie Gerard observed with a
hint of exasperation:

"He is so heedless. I hope that you won't detain
him, dear Miss Schuyler. I am depending upon him
to be host. If my cousin, the Ambassador—"

"Mother! Mother!" Jean, in a pink frock the shade
of a Radiance rose, dashed along the drive. "You're
wanted on the 'phone. 'Portant."

"The idea! I hope it isn't a regret at the last moment, it might mean rearranging the luncheon tables."

Without so much as a word to Prudence, Annie
Gerard fluttered toward the house. Jean dropped to
the bank and regarded the girl in the roadster with
her puckish eyes.

"I don't believe you've set your cap for Uncle Rod,"
she observed judicially. "What's setting your cap, anyway?"

Prudence shut her teeth hard to keep back a sharp
answer. The child was merely repeating something
she had overheard, something her mother had said
probably, she wouldn't put it past her. Lucky she had
said it, it would remind Prudence Schuyler of what
constantly she was forgetting, that she was to treat

Rodney Gerard with chill disdain. It was humorous, when you came to think of it, that she, who hated the thought of love and marriage, should be accused of pursuing a man. She said lightly:

"Speaking of caps, I love that floppy hat of yours, Jean."

The child pulled off the frail pink straw and flung it to the grass.

"The milliner who sold it to Mother said it did a lot for me. She knew her sales talk all right. What's the use of having pretty things if you never see other girls? Just because we're the Gerards of High Ledges, Mother won't let me have the village children come to play with me. I can't read and do puzzles all the time. I'd like to be with someone kind of young."

Poor, lonely little soul. Prue's heart warmed to her. Could she help? She had been submerged in her own problems for weeks. Time she snapped out of self-absorption and thought of someone besides David and herself. But Jean was so unattractive. All the more reason to help her.

"Come and play with me sometimes, will you?" Prudence invited as cordially as she could with the memory of the child's prying propensity pricking. "I'm not very young, but there's heaps to do. We'll feed chickens and play with Happy—Happy's my dog, you can teach him tricks—and Jane Mack will show you how to make cookies, and I'll teach you to use my tools—some of them—you can make a silver bracelet for your mother. Wouldn't you like that?"

Jean's usually pale face was radiant.

"That goes over big with me!" She called to Gerard who charged along the trail. "Oh, Uncle Rod, Miss Prue has invited me to come and play with her. May I go now?"

Rodney put his arm about the thin shoulders. "Not this time, K.K. I'll take you tomorrow. Be a good sport," he added, as the child's lips quivered. "You know your mother wants you at her party."

"Tomorrow, sure, Jean," Prudence called, as the roadster started. She looked back over her shoulder.

"I hate to leave her. She has that deserted look in her eyes that Happy has when I tell him he can't come with me."

"She'll be okay in a minute. It's mighty good of you to take an interest in her. I've been screwing up my courage to ask if I might bring her to the red brick house. You could do wonders with that kid. I was just in time to stop the men from digging up plants. Forgot Annie's party. They'll truck a load of stuff over to your garden tomorrow and set it out; all you need do is to boss the job."

Prudence suddenly remembered the refrigerating process to which she was committed. "But I can't let you do so much for me."

"Now you've gone icy again. Why shouldn't I send you a lot of worthless plants? Don't be pre-war. I've heard from Jim Armstrong."

"Who is he?"

"Didn't I tell you that I was importing a forester to advise us what trees to take out? Jim and I roomed together at college. He's a grand guy. He gets out and accomplishes things and makes a swell job of anything he undertakes, too. You'll like him, he's just your type—but—watch your step, I saw you first, remember."

She looked up between long, sweeping lashes with a gay challenge. Then something happened. It was as if she had caught her spirit rushing toward him, caught it, and dragged it back into the strong-room of her will. There was a hint of breathlessness in her voice.

"Taking the broad view of the matter, why should I watch my step? Have I a free and untrammelled soul, or haven't I?"

"I was referring to your heart." Gerard's voice was not quite steady. "When Jim comes we'll take a look-see at your property. You ought to know something about it before we begin to cut."

"Is it wild?"

"Yes. There are old lumber roads, grown up now, but we'll have those—I think the technical term is, swamped out—before we start, a sizable stream—used to be full of trout; and a log cabin."

"All mine?"

"All yours."

"Where does Len Calloway's land begin?"

"It adjoins mine on the west."

"What is the long building near the pond?"

"A cattle barn. My father had it full of blooded stock. High Ledges was an honest-to-God farm when I was a boy. Lots of horses and a smithy. It was a village in itself."

"Sounds fascinating. From what one reads in the papers it looks as if people were going back to the land, doesn't it? I read somewhere that farming will once again become a state of living and that prosperous farming communities are balance wheels to industry. How soon will you begin to cut?"

"As soon as Jim gets logging plans ready so that we may know what trees to take out."

"Won't you wait for snow?"

"It would make the work easier, but it is not necessary."

"Will—will Mrs. Walter Gerard stay until you get through?"

"She won't be asked to stay. As soon as I know when Jim is coming, I will tell Annie that she and Jean are free to return to the bright lights."

Prudence visualized Mrs. Walter Gerard's expression when she had cooed:

"Why! It's Miss Schuyler! Didn't they tell you that I was in the garden when you stopped at the house?"

She wouldn't leave her brother-in-law in the Maine wilds lumbering for a female neighbor in the early twenties—not a chance. As the roadster stopped before the red brick house, Prudence mused aloud:

"Something tells me that your sister-in-law won't go."

"Won't go! Of course she'll go. What would keep her when I want the house to myself?"

"Remember Macky's prophecy: 'You'll think that

tall woman's out of your way and suddenly she'll pop up.' " With an irrepressible laugh, she added:

"She's the popping-up kind. In the language of Jane Mack:

" 'I know folks.' "

VII

" 'The King was in his countinghouse
    Counting out his money;
    The Queen was in the kitchen—' "

Prudence, in a sleeveless white linen frock, broke off her operatic rendition of the nursery rhyme to address the tortoiseshell cat curled on the sill of the sunny window.

"I'm taking liberties with the text, Cleopatra. Adapting it, if you like it better. Do you know, I haven't sung before for two years, haven't wanted to. Never in my life have I had so little money. Not for a long time have I felt so lighthearted as I feel today. What's the answer?"

But the cat merely curled her plumy tail tighter around her, and with unblinking, slightly disdainful eyes regarded the girl moving quickly across the big, immaculate kitchen.

" 'Eating bread and honey.
    The maid was in the garden—' "

The musical voice trailed into a hum as Prudence stopped before the scoured pine table to regard proudly the shining jars of ruby beets arranged with the precision of an infantry squad on a mammoth white tray.

"I can't wait to see you on the storeroom shelf," she

said aloud. "Come on, I'll put you there." She lifted the tray. "Ooch, but you weigh a ton!

"Cleopatra! Behold! Am I one good little back-to-the-lander?" she called, as she started toward the cellar door. "A squirrel storing nuts for the winter has nothing on—"

A thunderous knock resounded through the house. Prudence took a quick step forward. The frightened cat reached the same spot in one leap. The girl tripped, the tray tipped, the jars of beets struck the floor with a crash calculated to make the pilot of the last word in bombing-planes pale with envy.

Ruby liquid flew in all directions. It dripped from walls and ceiling; it splashed the white frock; it trickled in crimson rivulets down Prue's cheeks; it did a modernistic design on her shoes and lavishly polka-dotted her bare arms. For an instant she stood in dazed consternation, then as she saw her face reflected in a small mirror, she laughed.

"Oh, you demon can—can—" The words choked into a spasm of mirth. She sank to a chair, dropped her head to her arms flung out on the table, and tried to control the peals of laughter which shook her. A hand caught her shoulder.

"Hey! What's happened? Quit laughing like that! You'll go goofy in a minute."

Lips twitching, nostrils quivering, eyes gleaming through tears, Prudence looked up at Rodney Gerard.

"C-canning trouble!" She choked on the words.

Where had he come from? She regarded him, lean, erect, bronzed, immaculate in light gray flannels, blue shirt, blue tie, spotless shoes; then her glance shifted to the spattered kitchen which looked as if it might have staged a supergory bull fight.

She opened her lips. Her words were caught up in a gust of laughter. Gerard administered an authoritative shake.

"Stop laughing! What happened?"

Prudence gulped back a giggle. "You ask! What's happened to your I.Q.?"

"Stop it! It's painfully evident that you are toppling

on the brink of hysterics. I know of only one sure remedy for that. I should hate to do it—but I may feel obliged to kiss you."

Prudence was on her feet. "Just naturally helpful, aren't you? You wouldn't dare—" She met his eyes and changed her tone. "I'll stop, Signor Mussolini. Only you could stand there like a graven image in the midst of this—this slaughter." She disciplined a gurgle as he took a significant step toward her. "You see, I've gone thrifty. I've been preparing for the l-long hard winter by canning young, tender beets—no t-taste to them when they g-grow up. I was carrying the jars on a tray when a thun-thunderous knock sent Cleopatra scurrying to cover—Cleopatra's the cat, in case you don't know—with the result of a f-foot-on collision. I—"

"Stop and get your breath. Hysterics will get you if you don't watch out." The hint of amused warning in Gerard's voice set Prue's pulses throbbing.

"They won't. I shan't need your prescription, thank you. Why are you here? It would be you, wouldn't it? What did you come for? My word! I believe it was your knock that brought on the catastrophe. You needn't groan, I didn't mean that as a pun. Are you responsible for this mess?" She indicated the smeared room with an accusing wave of her hand. "You won't be so popular with Macky—who is upstairs sewing— when she comes down and sees this kitchen."

"I'm sorry. Sure the glass didn't fly and cut you?" Gerard gently touched a streak like a sabre slash which spread from her eyebrow to her chin. "Does that hurt?"

She jerked her head away. "Only my pride. Of course it hurts to look like a comic strip in a colored supplement." She glanced in the mirror. "Sort of an Indian-on-the-warpath effect, isn't it?"

"You make the original painted chieftain look like a washout. Can't I help clean up?"

"You can not. Macky will be down in a few minutes, then we'll do it together. You'd better go while the going is good. Why did you come? I haven't time to talk even lumber business in the morning. I'm a working girl. Don't perch on that table! Your clothes will be ruined! I wish you'd go."

Even as Prudence frowned at him, she was thinking how Fate conspired to block her at every turn. The first time she heard of Rodney Gerard she had decided to treat him with frigid reserve, and the first time they met she had been hurled into his arms. After Jean's intimation that she was setting her cap for him, she had sworn to herself that she would chill him to the bone the next time he spoke to her; instead, here she was hysterical with laughter, friendly laughter. One couldn't be impressively dignified when one resembled nothing so much as an example of spatter-work done in beet juice.

Hands in his coat pockets, Gerard strode to the door, turned at the threshold.

"Stop scowling. I'm going. Hospitable, aren't you? As you seem so terribly interested in my reason for coming—that's biting sarcasm, in case you care— you'd better know that I didn't come to talk timber, I came to ask if you would have time to make a silver collar for that kitten of Jean's she's so crazy about. She has it with her upstairs. Mrs. Si arrived just as we did and they went up to talk with Macky."

"A silver collar! I'd love it! I've had an idea for one in my mind for months! I'll make time!"

Prudence seized a towel, wiped her hands, rubbed it over her face, thereby turning the sabre-slash effect into a rosy-dawn smear.

"Come on to the shop—I've turned Uncle Austin's office into a workroom—and I'll show you a sketch I made before I became a farmer."

She had not realized how she loved and had missed her craft, Prudence told herself, as she led the way to a room which opened from the front hall. A long bench by the window was laden with engraving and repoussé tools. Crucibles there were, several of them; anvils, at least two; an alcohol lamp; blowpipes, a dingy, battered collection; a charcoal brick; a pile of silver scraps, jagged, dented; a piece of gold partially tooled sunk in a pitch-block. Ranged with infantry precision on shelves against the wall were wide-mouthed bottles with glass tops, each one labeled.

Cannel-coal and shavings were in the grate beneath the simple mantel painted a soft green like the old trim in the room. Plants on shelves were in the bay window. The shabby paper was hidden on one side by a massive mahogany case with green glass-curtains. It had the opulent air of a made-for-the-room piece of furniture.

"It won't take me a jiffy to find that sketch." Prudence flung the assurance over her shoulder at Gerard who was looking curiously about the room. She pulled open one of the doors of the bookcase. A pile of papers showered to the floor.

"Darn! Wouldn't you know it when I'm in a hurry!"

"Hold on! I'll get them!" Gerard dropped to one knee beside her. "I don't wonder you can't find anything in that mess."

"It is a sight. I tuck everything I don't know what to do with in there. I adore order, but, as you may have observed from what you so politely call the mess, I'm not orderly. Here's the sketch! Now I'll find the stones."

Gerard laid the papers he had collected on top of a pile while Prudence manipulated the knob of a small safe. He stood beside her as the heavy door swung open.

"What are those white things?" He indicated the row of packets in one of the compartments.

Prudence collected them and crossed to the stool. Gerard pushed tools aside and perched on an end of the bench. She parted the packets with a pink-tipped finger as she read the labels.

"Stones. Some precious, some semi-precious."

"You must have a fortune there."

"Not a fortune, but more money than I can afford to have tied up in them. I'm a jelly-fish, I have no sales resistance when I see a lovely gem, I have an attack of what the economists call 'Buyer's delirium.' These are the most valuable, though I have a pigeon-blood ruby and a cabochon sapphire which couldn't be called grubby."

She opened a packet. With pincers she laid a large emerald in the center of a ring design on white paper, placed small diamonds. She indicated spaces.

"I want stunning baguette diamonds there and there and a platinum setting. When I've made my fortune on the farm, I'll make this ring for myself."

"That's a corking emerald."

"It is choice, it's flawless. It was my grandmother's."

"Won't that design make a huge ring?"

"I like them splashy, or not at all."

"What's that stuff in the bottles which looks like hunks of colored glass?"

"Enamels. Transparent and opaque. They are ground in a little water to salt-like consistency in that mortar, washed thoroughly before they are applied to metal, and heated until they melt. When I want them especially jewel-like I use them over gold leaf. I can't enamel here, worse luck. Can't get enough heat. Have to use bellows and a big blowpipe."

"Why the numbers?"

"Colors go by numbers. For instance, 19 is a gorgeous red; 48 a cool green; 25 sapphire blue; and so on."

"You sure know this job, don't you? What are you looking for in those papers?"

"Here they are!"

Eyes shining, Prudence opened a package and spread out a sketch.

"Here's the design for the collar. See those medallions between the links?" She looked up. "You're not listening! You're not looking!" She dropped the engraving tool she had been using as a pointer.

"I'm looking all right. Never realized before how much red there is in your hair. The sunlight brings it out. It's gorgeous, girl."

"My hair! I thought you came here for a silver collar."

"I did. Cross-my-throat-an'-hope-to-die, I did. I want a collar for the kitten, and you've been so sweet to Jean that she'll treasure anything you make all her life. She's a loyal little thing in spite of her glaring faults. You love this work, don't you? Your eyes are like stars."

"Of course I love it, but I get tremendously thrilled over whatever interests me. I never can do anything with the tips of my fingers, I plunge in up to my elbows. Exhibit A, the beets." She indulged in a reminiscent chuckle.

"You'll wear yourself out."

"Better to wear out than rust out."

"Meaning me, I suppose?"

"If the shoe fits, put it on. Do you realize that you are wasting my precious time? I thought you were about to give me an honest-to-goodness order."

Gerard laid his hand on the sketch. "Don't put it away. I do want the collar. From this moment my eyes and attention are glued to that piece of paper. You were explaining about the medallions between the links. Will they be silver?"

Prudence picked up the engraving tool. "Yes. They are to be carved and tooled with Micky Mouse episodes."

She poked at the stones spread on the white paper. Her voice, which had been cool and detached, warmed with enthusiasm.

"See these cat's-eyes glow and smolder? They are symbolic of health and long life. I'll set them in silver to alternate with the medallions. This pear-shaped piece of Korean amber—which is supposed to contain magic—will hang from the buckle in front. Like the idea?"

Gerard slid from the bench to his feet.

"You're a fraud. You ask that as anxiously as if you didn't know it was a knock-out. To me it sounds as complicated as taking an amendment out of the Constitution, but of course I like it." He carefully lifted the paper on which lay the emerald and the diamonds. "I like these, too. Any chance of your making this ring up to order?"

Did he want it to give to a girl? The thought

flashed through Prue's mind even as she shook her head.

"Not a chance, even if I had money to invest in baguette diamonds, which I haven't. It has been one of the dreams of my life to wear that ring. Unless Prosperity Farm plunges so deep into the red that we can't pull it out, I'll hold on to the emerald."

She thoughtfully nibbled the point of the engraving tool.

"The silver collar for the kitten is likely to be rather expensive. I can't set a price because I have no idea how much time it will take."

"That's all right. I'll give it to Jean for Christmas. Think you'll have it done by then?"

"Christmas! I hope so, but, of course, if I have many more morning interruptions—"

"I accept your delicate hint. I'm off. It won't interrupt your work, I hope, if I stop to collect Jean and the kitten and speak to your brother, who is lying on the grass patch in the middle of the garden?"

"David on the ground! I left him—"

Prudence fairly flew through the house. She heard Gerard behind her as she raced into the garden, which showed borders of brown earth stuck full of little sticks and cut-back plants. Dave on the ground!

He pulled away the soft hat over his face as she dropped to her knees beside him.

"Dave! Dave! Did you fall?"

With a murmur of concern, he sat up and put his arm about her.

"Prue! Prue! Of course I didn't fall, dear. After a while the chair seemed hard and the grass inviting, so I flung the rug on the ground and stretched out on it. I've been asleep." He tightened his hold. "Look here, my dear, if you have me on your mind every minute, I'll go off by myself somewhere. For heaven's sake, what have you been doing? Slaughtering poultry?"

A little cyclone of relief and laughter swept Prudence. She met Gerard's warning eyes and sobered.

"Nothing more serious than canning beets, Dave."

"You look as if you'd been caught in an explosion of red corpuscles. Give me a hand up, Gerard. I've been lying here so long that I'm stiff."

Rodney Gerard linked an arm in his as he stood up. Prudence was conscious of the tension about her mouth as she looked at them. David's face was so pale in comparison to that of the man beside him. She achieved a fair imitation of a laugh.

"Have you on my mind every minute, Dave! You'd be surprised if you knew that I haven't thought of you once since I tucked you into that steamer chair. Now who's coming?"

The gate in the white picket fence which enclosed the garden creaked on its hinges. A grotesque figure turning cartwheels with incredible rapidity hurtled through the opening, came right-side up, scratched a chalky ear which protruded through his white skull cap, and made a sweeping bow.

Jean, who had been standing in the kitchen doorway with a coal-black kitten pressed tight against the breast of her pink cotton frock, raced to her uncle.

"A clown! Uncle Rod, a clown! Where's the circus?"

Had Rodney Gerard gritted an exclamation between his teeth, or had she imagined it? Prudence looked from his narrowed eyes to the smeared blue eyebrows, the lips like a bloody gash in the whiteness of the chalk-face of the man who was looking back at him. A peaked cap tipped rakishly over one ear. The regulation white suit of the sawdust ring, polka-dotted with black, showed traces of travel. Hands in his pockets, enormous shoes planted far apart, the clown stretched his pantaloons till the effect was that of a mammoth V.

Jean's eyes were like stars. Her precociousness had disappeared. She was a child eager with excitement. She dropped the kitten, squeezed Gerard's arm, hopped up and down.

"Oh, Uncle Rod! Isn't he a peach! You will take me to the circus, won't you?"

"How do you know there is a circus?"

"Jean knows that where there is smoke there's a

fire, where there is a clown there's a circus." David
Schuyler spoke from the steamer chair to which he
had retreated. He held out his hand and smiled.

"How are you, Chicot? Must be two years since I've
seen you. Where did you drop from?"

The clown shook Schuyler's hand. He blinked and
swallowed. Sunlight accentuated the harsh color of
the triangle patches of vermilion on his white cheeks,
the paint on his lips. He turned his cone-shaped cap in
chalky hands.

"Never expected to see you here, sir. They told me
at the Rescue Mission that you were sick somewhere.
I'm with Sassoon's Smashing Show. It's stuck in a
nearby town, and when the boss found I—I'd once
lived in this region, he thought I might have a drag
with folks and sent me out on a motorcycle to drum
up trade. Saw this garden, took a chance on it—I'll
try anything once—and here I am."

His eyes shifted to Rodney Gerard. "The little girl
would like the show, Mister. No harm could come to
nobody from goin' to it. It's a swell show. Milk-white
horses with spangles; lions roaring; a tiger that minds
a lady; elephants—say, you never seen such elephants; balloon men—and how!"

"Uncle Rod, you will take me, won't you?" Jean's
lips quivered with eagerness. "I've never seen many
horses! I've never been to a circus! Mother thinks
they're cheap. Oh, Miss Prue, ask him to take me,
please—he'll do it if you ask him."

Significance shone through the amusement in Rodney Gerard's eyes as they met Prue's. Only an instant
their glances met, before he parleyed indulgently:

"Take it easy, Jean. You've got me all excited.
You've started something, Chicot. You said the show
was stuck in the next town. What's the trouble?"

Again Prudence had the sense of an undercurrent,
a dramatic undercurrent at that. Gerard's curt question seemed to set atmospheric high-potency waves in
motion. Was he angry? Annoyed was a better word.
Whatever his mood, it tightened her nerves—much as
she felt when she waited for a crash after a flash of

lightning. The clown crushed his cap in one vein-knotted hand.

"It's this way, Mister. The twenty-four-hour man—he's the fella who goes ahead to make sure all contracts for hay and provisions will be filled okay—wired that the next town we were billed in had been cleaned out by fire; it was the next to last stop for the season, we're travelin' later than usual tryin' to make up last year's losses, the Cattle Fairs cut into our business terrible. Our show keeps up with our paper, rain or shine, floods or knee-deep mud, but when the town itself goes blooey, what have you? That throws us out. So the boss says we'd lay out the show in the burg I've come from. As we weren't billed there, he sent us clowns scouting for business. It's a good honest show for the little girl to see, Mister."

He pulled at a painted forelock, looked at Prudence with haggard eyes, stretched the red gash in a grin.

"An' for big girls too. We've had to turn away crowds all season, and the parade—whoops, you should see the parade! Horses and clowns, bare-back riders—all the headliners out—and the calliope. Sounds this-a-way—"

Chicot gave an imitation which set the echoes jangling. It brought Si Puffer from the barn on a run. His wife and Miss Mack spilled from the kitchen door. The clown doffed his cap and cut a pigeon-wing. Mrs. Puffer clasped fat hands on her black and white striped bosom.

"Lors! I haven't seen the likes of him since I was a girl and Si took me to the circus. I remember the lemonade, pink as the roses on my floppy hat, and the fresh clown who—My soul and body! I believe—"

"You said the show was in a nearby town, Chicot. How near?"

Prudence caught the swift glance between Rodney Gerard and the woman as he asked the question, was aware of the sound as of gas escaping from a punctured balloon, before she closed her lips and retreated, pulling Jane Mack with her into the house. Did the clown's presence mean something to her too?

"Sure it's nearby. Only fifty miles, Mister. What's that in these days when a slick car'll eat up the road, like an elephant drainin' a water bucket. I wish all you folks would come. We like to get quality a-watching us—it pleases the performers, especially the girls ridin'."

Rodney Gerard took a step, as if tired of the man's explanation. The clown went on eagerly:

"It's a good show. The ridin's worth goin' a long way to see, an' there ain't nothin' better in their line than the Cascamari aerialists. The little girl would get a great kick from it."

"Oh, Uncle Rod—" Jean's voice broke from excitement.

"Take it easy, Jean, we'll go."

"Will we see the parade?"

"Sure, we'll see the parade. That's half the fun. What time does it start, Chicot?"

"Nine."

"We'll be there. Prue, Jean and I are counting on you to keep us company. We're really grand pals when we get going."

"I'd love it—if—" Prue's eyes flashed to her brother.

"Of course you'll go, Prue. You haven't been away from this town since you came, have you? Jane Mack will look after me." David Schuyler answered her unspoken question.

The clown twisted his cap. "I wish you'd come, sir. It's a good show."

"Can't make it, Chicot. Glad you have your job again. Watch your step—this time."

"Thank you, sir. I will, sir. There ain't no occasion for me not to, sir. Well, folks, I'll be seeing you."

He pulled his cap hard over his ears, and departed on his hands, his legs in the air. Jean ran beside him, pelting him with questions, going into girlish giggles of laughter. The black kitten scurried along at her heels. As the clown disappeared through the gateway, Rodney Gerard and Si Puffer followed without one backward glance.

Prudence looked around the garden. It was as still

as if a masked Harlequin had flashed through, shaking his magic wand to clear the verdant stage of actors. Only her brother lay in the steamer-chair, a slight frown between his brows. She dropped to the grass beside him.

"Strange that you should have known that clown, Dave."

"All sorts of men came to the Rescue Mission, Prue. Chicot was in great trouble about a granddaughter who had been running wild. Unusual for that class. Circus performers as a rule are a fine lot. They have to be. He beat up one of her followers—to hear him tell it, she had a lot of them—and lost his job for a while."

Prudence appeared absorbed in her search for a four-leaf clover in the rusty grass.

"Dave, did it occur to you that Mrs. Si knew that clown, that Rodney Gerard knew him?"

Schuyler swung his feet from the chair and rose. His sister sprang up and linked her arm in his. The lines between his eyes deepened as he answered gravely:

"I'm sorry to say that it did, Prue. Confoundedly sorry."

VIII

Jean Gerard regarded the desk in the gun-room at High Ledges with pursed lips and angry eyes.

"Gee, but you make me mad!"

She addressed the piece of furniture as if it were maliciously responsible for her frustration. She wriggled a hairpin in the lock of the top drawer. This was the third attempt she had made to open it. Curiosity throbbed in her veins, tingled in her finger tips. In all her experience in prying—and it had been a rich and varied experience—never had she met anything so obstinate as this.

She looked about the room, at the guns in racks, at the rods, at the baseballs in their glass case, each one marked with the date when Rodney Gerard had pitched it in a college game; none of them suggested an implement which might help. She seldom came here. Not only was it the room in which her Uncle Rodney conducted the business of the estate; it was her father's retreat in the rare visits he made to High Ledges, he used the desk at which she was jabbling. To her the room echoed with his petulant:

"Run away, Jean. Never come in when I am here. Isn't there one spot in this ark of a house where I can get away from my family?"

He was in New York now, thank goodness, and she could go where she liked. Uncle Rod never shooed her off. He was a lamb. He wouldn't mind if she forced open that drawer. Wouldn't he? She thrust down the question. She would open it anyway.

With teeth set, she grasped the handles, jerked with all her strength. The drawer came out with a suddenness which sent her sprawling and scattered three letters from the desk onto the floor.

"Good old hairpin!"

Ruefully she rubbed the back of her head. She knelt beside the drawer and eagerly examined its contents. There were several photographs of a pretty girl. One showed her in smart street costume peering mischievously from behind a huge muff; one in bouffant tulle on the back of a horse. Jean's eyes dilated.

"Circus rider!" she crooned. "Goody, I'll see one like her tomorrow." She turned the photograph over. On the back was scrawled:

> "Miraculous escape. From calico
> and Calloway to liberty and lo—
> Fondly, Milly."

"Why didn't she finish writing that word?" Jean sat back on her heels and scowled at the pictured face. "She's a cutey all right. I—" She gulped as a shadow fell across the photograph. Who had caught her this time? Uncle Rod wouldn't—

"Where's your uncle?"

The photograph fell from her hand and lay with piquant, smiling face upward as Jean stared at the scowling man who loomed over her.

"I—I—don't know. Shall I try to find him, Mr. Calloway?"

Len Calloway removed his glance from the pictures and letters on the floor long enough to glare at her.

"Tell him I want to talk with him. Scram!"

Frightened at the greyness of his face, Jean fled. She scurried through the different rooms. Called. No answer. None of the servants had seen her uncle. She had better go back and tell Mr. Calloway.

As she entered the gun room, one of the long French windows banged.

"He's gone. I guess that's that."

She dropped to her knees beside the drawer. Better put it back before anyone saw it. She scrambled up the contents. Where was the picture of the cutey circus rider? She went through the photographs again. Gone. Had Mr. Calloway taken it? Why should he want it? Would her uncle be mad with her for having touched the desk?

"I'd better get a move on."

She hurriedly replaced the drawer, picked up the letters. Only two! There had been three when they fell. Had Mr. Calloway snitched one? What would he do with it? "Gee, have I started something?" she thought, and looked anxiously about the room to be sure that no trace of her prying remained to betray her, before she tiptoed to the hall.

In the library after dinner, Rodney Gerard glanced at Jean speculatively as she bent demurely over a book. Her absorption was out of character. She was too quiet. She had been prying with rather frightening results; he recognized the symptoms. Usually she would be sprawled on the hearth-rug making miserable the lives of the two black Field spaniels, now peacefully toasting their backs before the fire.

He glanced about the room as he refilled his pipe.
Good room. Big, yet not too full of things, mellow,
dignified. Deep-seated chairs cushioned in *toile de
jouy*, which repeated the rust-color tone of the
damask hangings drawn across the long windows; old
portraits; no ornaments, save a mammoth copper
bowl of small yellow chrysanthemums and a slender
crystal vase holding one perfect talisman rose beside
the photograph of his mother on a drum table. The
flower glowed against the pine-paneled background,
which blended with the leather of the book bindings
in shelves on each side of the mantel. A small grand
piano reflected the dancing flames of the fire. A restful room from its absence of detail. Not too bad a
place in which to spend part of a winter. He glanced
at his sister-in-law knitting rapidly in the light of one
of the softly shaded lamps. Not so restful. He was in
for a battle. He'd better go to it.

As if she felt his eyes on her, Mrs. Walter Gerard
looked up. She laid down her knitting.

"I have planned to close the house on Thursday, if
that suits you, Rodney. The days are getting so
short."

Gerard thrust his pipe into the pocket of his dinner
jacket, rose, and backed up to the mantel.

"You needn't bother to do that, Annie. I shall remain here for part of the winter. I have decided to
thin about a thousand acres of woodland and it will
require my personal oversight. Judkins has a sister—
Mrs. Patch—who will come with her husband to keep
house for me; he says she's a grand cook, and the man
will be the butler. They haven't had a break for two
years, and Judkins says they won't mind the country.
He has promised to stand by. With three to look after
me I'll be comfortable enough, so you and Jean toddle
along to New York as you planned."

"The idea! Of course I shan't desert you, Rodney. I
can stay, at least until after Christmas; then my cousin, the Ambassador, has asked me to visit him."

Gerald buckled on his armor of determination. He

hated to hurt her, but he couldn't, he wouldn't have her under his feet, and that's where she would be.

"I appreciate your kindness, Annie, but Jim Armstrong, one of my roommates at college, who is a forester, will arrive soon to look over the timber and advise me as to what should come out. I hate like the dickens to say it, you have been so kind to keep house for me this summer, but I would prefer not to have you here."

Jean hurled her book to the floor with a force which brought the black spaniels up standing. She flung herself at Gerard.

"Hey there, Kurious Kid, go slow. Want to push me into the fire?" He tried to loosen the skinny arms which threatened to squeeze him breathless. The girl's grip tightened.

"Uncle Rod, please let me stay with you, please! I'm not going to school this winter anyway. I hate New York, and Mother and Father are always fighting, and I love to be with you, and I'll be a perfect lady, honest I will. Please let me stay. I'm—I'm always sort of peaceful with you."

Gerard's eyes were tender as he looked down at the pleading face. Peaceful. Poor, lonely kid. She did have a tough time. Not much fun living with her parents. Walter rarely came to High Ledges now. Was it too dull for him, or were there other reasons? Should he let Jean stay? Judkins' sister could look after her, and he was fond of the funny little thing. Prue Schuyler was taking an interest in her; she was making her happier, more human than the impish child she had been. He smiled down into the tear-drenched eyes.

"What say, Annie? Will you let Jean stay with me until after Christmas? No," he anticipated, as his sister-in-law started to speak, "it will upset my plans to have you here; besides, you should be in New York with Walter."

"Walter doesn't want me either."

For the first time since he had known her, Rodney heard Annie Gerard acknowledge defeat. Mighty hard on her. Walter was a bad egg, of course, but she had a cruel tongue and was so affected. That didn't excuse Walt; a man should be true to his wife no matter how she developed—but—the gods be praised, the problem of being true to Annie wasn't his.

He shook his head doubtfully at the girl who still clung to him.

"Look here, K.K., if I let you stay, will you solemnly promise not to pry into my affairs or—or the affairs of the—the neighbors?"

Joy glowed beneath the tears. "I promise I'll be the finest girl ever, Uncle Rod."

"I'll give you a try. May she stay, Annie?"

"If you want her, Rodney. The doctor said she should live out of doors this winter, so perhaps she'll be better off here in the country."

"Then hustle to New York, send down warm clothes for her and the bills to me. Take the servants with you. I'll pay them for lost time."

Mrs. Gerard thrust her needles into her knitting with a force which made them click.

"I'll hustle. Will the first train in the morning be soon enough?"

Gerard ignored her bitterness. "Fine. Jean and I will be off early, perhaps before you start."

"Off! Where?"

"There's a circus in the next town and we—"

"A circus! the idea! I don't approve of circuses."

"This one can't possibly hurt Jean. We—we are going in a party."

"A party! I see. I think I know who the party will be. I wasn't born yesterday, Rodney."

How he detested her wink, Rodney thought, as he watched her leave the room. Jean slipped her arm through her uncle's.

"She's mad!" she observed in a strident whisper.

"Cut that out, K.K. Never criticise your mother. I've taken on a big responsibility keeping you here. You make good or you'll be packed off to New York on the first train. Get me?"

"I will, Uncle Rod. Cross-my-throat-an'-hope-to-die. I don't mean to pry, but—but Mother watches me so, and tells me what to do every minute, that sometimes I feel as if I would fly into little pieces if I didn't—didn't do something wicked. What time will we start for the circus? I'll be ready. I won't go to sleep for a minute tonight."

"I'll bet you won't. I'm not so old that I've forgotten the nights before your father and I went to the circus. Go to bed. Get going."

He watched her as she ran to the door. On the threshold she stopped to throw him a kiss. He returned it absentmindedly.

"You sure have taken on responsibility," he reminded himself.

The first frost of the season, delicate as silver gauze, veiled the world the next morning as Rodney, with Jean snuggled in the roadster beside him, stopped before the red brick house. Ferns bent under its sparkling weight, pine trees glistened. Gay leaves drifted across the shining black road. Glorious air. He filled his lungs with it. Decidedly fallish.

Prudence was waiting at the gate. Her brown sports coat and beret accentuated the ruddy light in her hair. Gold flecked the velvet of her eyes; her vivid lips were curved in a radiant smile.

"Good morning, Jean. I'm thrilled! My heart is so light it's bouncing along on balloon tires. Will there be room for me on the front seat, Mr. Gerard?"

"Cut out that 'Mr.'—Gorgeous. It doesn't click with a circus. Rod—to you. Of course there's room in front. We'll make a sandwich of the Kurious Kid, nice tender little chicken. Hop in."

Jean bounced in her seat. "Hurry up, Miss Prue. Let's go, Uncle Rod."

They drove along glistening black roads bordered with rusty ferns and berry bushes whose leaves had turned bright yellow and red. Asters purple as Persian amethysts swayed against a background of trees among which waved maples like tongues of flame, under a sky of pure azure. They talked gaily of the inducements Chicot had offered to lure them to the circus, confidently of the success of their timber project; wondered which of the plays opening that week in New York would pull the S.R.O. sign from the Success Bag, agreed that there was nothing—unless it were a book—so unpredictable.

The main street of the town was already lined with crowds when they reached it; it boiled with children, echoed with the cries of fakirs, blazed with mammoth black and red posters:

RAIN OR SHINE
SASSOON'S SMASHING SHOW

Gerard parked the roadster on a side street. Jean's feet barely touched the ground as between Prudence and her uncle she was swept along in the hurrying crowd. She stopped short in front of a poster showing an equestrienne in rose-color tulle skirts and a brief bodice, with the caption:

MADEMOISELLE MILLEE

"Why, there's my cutey—"

Gerard looked at her sharply as she bit off the next word.

"What do you mean, K.K.? You—"

"Buy the kid a balloon! Buy the kid a balloon! Say listen! What's a circus to a kid without a balloon?"

The hatless man with an unkempt mane of black hair and a flock of colored balloons straining at their leashes, blocked the way. Jean's eyes were like dancing stars.

"May I have one, Uncle Rod?"

"Sure. Choose the color. Have one, Prue?"

"Of course. I want that fat green one which looks as if it were about to burst from its own importance. I'm crazy about the red you've chosen, Jean."

What fun she was! How friendly she had been on the drive over. Had she buried the hatchet she seemed always to have up her sleeve for him? She was so alive mentally and physically. Life never could get one by the throat if one had a girl like her with whom to travel through the years, Rodney thought, as he dodged the tugging, bobbing, red and green globes over his head.

"Pop—corn! Pop—corn! Here, you nickel squeezer, buy two bags for the girl friend."

The youth in cheap clothes, hectored by the vendor, grinned sheepishly and produced a dime.

Rodney presented a bag to each of his guests. Jean's skinny fingers dove into the fluffy, slightly greasy contents. She stuffed a handful of puffy white corn into her mouth, expertly tucked in an elusive kernel, mumbled:

"Gee, Uncle Rod, isn't this s-swell? I didn't know there was so much f-fun in the world. Mother never lets me—"

"It's coming! The parade's coming!" Prudence gripped Gerard's arm. "Hear that bugle, Jean?"

Rodney pushed Jean in front of him. Crushed his arm against his side to keep Prue's hand there. He craned his neck until it hurt, rose on his toes till the ankle muscles creaked. Far down the street was a restless sea of waving plumes, shining helmets, brilliant flags. Music billowed forward. Snares. Drums. Cornets. Clarinets. He said to Prudence:

"The thrill of the Big Top. It's got me. I'm as excited as any kid in the crowd."

The girl's brilliant eyes met his.

"It's got me too. I'm shaking with excitement. Here they come! I wonder if we'll see Chicot."

"Here they come! Here they come!" The murmur of the crowd swelled to shouts of acclaim.

Music nearer now. A band in brilliant red coats, tall shakos on their heads, passed playing, "Stars and Stripes Forever." Countless feet tapping the rhythm. Countless throats humming the tune. Outriders resplendent in red and gold, pennants waving, mounts prancing. Hollow resonance of axle flanges against steel rims. Wagons of amazing magnificence—circus magnificence. Cages closed. Cages open. A giraffe's head with enormous soft brown eyes, sticking through bars. Prowling lions. Frisking monkeys. Chariots bumping, swaying. Cotton velvets. Paste jewels glistening sumptuously. Cream-color horses. Six dappled grays drawing a red boxed wagon. Long white reins. Spangles glittering on the habits of equestriennes. The Goddess of Liberty perilously perched a-top a gilded coach. A closed, heavily barred wagon—to tickle the imagination. The throb of drums. Boom! Boom! Boom! A woman in a cage, a tiger crouching near, a whip across her knees. The crowd breathed raggedly. Suppose the beast should spring! The sound was like the soughing of the wind.

Everywhere the glitter of rhinestones among sequins. It was as if all the jewels in the Prince of India's cave had been spread on saddle-cloths and howdahs to catch the sunlight and give it back in a million rainbow sparks. Jockeys in gray silks. Acrobats in pink fleshings and crimson trunks twisting over a horizontal bar. Aerialists in bespangled tights. Everyone gay. Everyone smiling. The parade was hitting on all cylinders.

"El-e-phants are coming! Hold your horses!"

From far down the street came the shout. The crowd's repetition surged to a roar. Above the tumult sounded the strident steam voice of the calliope:

"There's a long, long trail a-winding—"

An enormous elephant led the herd, the scarlet coated man on his head seemed like a midget, the keepers strutting at his side mere pigmies. Carefully, ponderously the huge creature raised and placed his feet; the piglike eyes bulged; the great ears flapped.

Gerard felt Jean's fingers tighten in his, heard her quick breath of relief as the unwieldy beast passed. Prudence caught her free hand and smiled. Had she sensed the child's fear?

"See, Jean, how the elephants dwindle in size. The two last ones are babies. Aren't they funny dressed in poke-bonnets? See the camels hump along. Here come the clowns!"

"Where? Where?" Jean's voice was drowned by an able-bodied wail from the calliope.

"On top of that red wagon. Hear the wheels squeak!"

A kernel of corn lodged in Gerard's throat and did things to his voice. He pointed in lieu of speech to a clown with a bulbous crimson nose, stringy black hair, red brows smeared high on his forehead, who was endeavoring to sew a patch on the seat of his pantaloons. The crowd cheered wildly. A monkey-faced clown commenced to beat up a gigantic police-clown. Jean wailed:

"Chicot isn't there. He said he'd wink at me." Her eyes were deep wells of disappointment. Gerard squeezed the thin fingers sympathetically.

"Take it easy, K.K. He'll come. There he is now! See him? See him?" He caught her under the arms and lifted her for an instant. "He's on that funny little bicycle. See him?"

She nodded excited assent. He set her on her feet. "See how the big fat-faced clown on the motorcycle behind him keeps butting into his hind wheel? Chicot has a balloon. A red balloon like yours, K.K. He'll see you in a minute."

Prudence laughed up at Gerard. "Chicot must have a magic charm for attracting hearts. Jean is positively tearful over him, and I warmed to him at once."

"If he has touched your shellacked heart, I'll offer him a fortune for his—"

"You are missing the comedy," Prue reminded crisply.

The crowd hooted as the motorcycle clown butted the wheels of the bicycle without effect. Sulking, the fat fellow lingered behind to upbraid his deriders. As Chicot came abreast of Jean, his balloon popped. With heart-rending sobs he shook the bit of rubber toward the girl.

"Well of all people! If here isn't the new lumber firm of Schuyler and Gerard eating pop-corn and watching the el'phants!"

Calloway's taunting voice at his shoulder sent the

blood in Rodney Gerard's body rushing to his ears in blinding, black anger. He dropped Jean's hand to clutch Prudence Schuyler's arm as she started to speak. His furious eyes met the mocking eyes on a level with his.

"Shut up, Calloway! You—"

"Take mine, Chicot! Take mine!" Jean's excited voice cut into her uncle's. She darted forward. Rodney grabbed for her. Missed. The motorcycle clown, looking back in a parting wisecrack, shot forward at full speed. The crowd shrieked. Chicot caught the girl. Flung her back with all his force. The panic-stricken cyclist crashed into him.

Aeons after, it seemed to Rodney Gerard, the physician, bending over Jean's limp figure on the black haircloth sofa in a nearby house, straightened.

"She's coming out of it all right. Prolonged faint from shock. She looks out of condition anyway, delicate child. Better get her home as soon as she can sit up."

Prudence Schuyler, who was tenderly smoothing back the moist rings of hair on Jean's forehead, whispered:

"Don't look so agonized, Rodney. See, her eyelids are quivering. You had better loosen that string." She nodded toward the red balloon which, tethered to the girl's wrist, was swaying with every breath of air from the opening and closing door.

"I'll cut it. I'm all shot to pieces over this. I—I didn't know how much I cared for the Kurious—" Gerard choked on the words.

The circus boss, checked as to suit, dazzling as to tie, eyes red-rimmed, slid into the room. He cleared his throat twice before he produced his voice.

"Fatty, the clown, is batty about the accident. He's pulled that speeding-up trick a hundred times before an' it's gone great. He'd just graze the bicycle an' the crowd would go crazy. Poor old Chicot was near through anyway, he was getting old, likely to get the axe any minute, didn't fetch the laughs. He'd gone through hell with that granddaughter of his, an' he was getting stiff, but—the little girl—" he looked down at the still figure on the couch—"say, I got two of my own."

"Don't! Don't—please! The doctor says she will come out of this all right."

"Sorry, I didn't mean to blubber, Miss. Say, I can't tell you how glad I am. Poor old Chicot saved her, didn't he? Can you pull him through, Doc?"

Across the room on the floor where they had dropped him lay the clown. The painted eyebrows gave the effect of ludicrous surprise; the red smirk added a last ghastly touch to the chalky face; a little breeze from the open window stirred the ruff at his throat, as his breath might have stirred it. Rodney Gerard bent over the twisted body, laid his hand on the dirt-streaked shoulder.

"You saved her, Chicot. Can you hear? You—"

"Let me in! Where's Grandpop? Let me in!"

A girl, in the cotton velvets and plumed hat of a circus-rider on parade, burst into the room. Patches of rouge stood out like fever spots on her colorless face. Her black eyes were distended with fright. With a shriek she flung herself to her knees beside Chicot, put her arms under the old clown's shoulders, and lifted him until his head rested against her breast.

A spasm of pain contorted the grotesque face. The lids under their painted brows opened. He tried to put his hand over hers. It wavered futilely and dropped. His whisper seemed to fill the still room.

"Be a good—girl, Milly. You'll be a—great—rider— if you keep at it. I've kept you—with me—you're safer—now. I—must—get up. Time—for—my act—"

The last faint word fluttered in a sigh. Chalky lids drooped over dull eyes. The crumpled figure settled lower in the girl's arms.

IX

"Grandpop! Grandpop! Don't leave me! I can't bear it to have you hurt! First I hurt you and now—"

A sequin on the red velvet habit caught the sunlight and glittered like a yellow eye. The physician gently loosened the girl's arms and eased the body of the old clown to the floor. Rodney Gerard laid his hand on her shoulder.

"Nothing can hurt him again, Milly. You—"

"So, I've run Milly Gooch to earth at last! Mademoiselle Millee! And with you, Gerard! She would be!"

With a smothered imprecation, Rodney wheeled to face Len Calloway who leaned against the side of the door. With difficulty he kept his voice low.

"Don't you see what has happened? If you can't keep your dirty mouth shut, get out."

The sound Calloway made was more a snarl than a laugh, though an expression of sardonic mirth doubtless had been his intention.

"I'm going."

He turned to Prudence who, white and still, knelt beside the couch on which Jean was stirring restlessly.

"Any ten-year-old child would get wise to what's been going on between those two, Miss Schuyler."

Rodney Gerard shut his teeth hard into his lips. Prue could deduce anything from Calloway's voice and implication. What would she think?

Milly Gooch caught his hand and with a choking sob laid her cheek against it.

"What shall I do, Roddy? Grandpop's gone and I have only you now."

Half of her appeal to him was genuine grief, half was staged to irritate Len Calloway who was glaring at her from the threshold, Gerald decided, Milly was like a cat with a mouse. She didn't care a hang about the man at the door, to whom she once had been engaged, but she couldn't resist poking him with unsheathed claws.

With a suggestive laugh Calloway departed. The physician touched Gerard's shoulder.

"You'd better get that youngster home—quick."

"I will."

Rodney bent over the girl crouched beside the crumpled body of the clown. He freed the hand she still clutched. "I'll see you tonight, Milly. Pull yourself together. Your grandfather knows, wherever he is, that the Show must go on." He laid his hand on the bowed head before he turned away.

"Come, Jean. I'll carry you, dear."

Jean rested listlessly against Prue's shoulder as the roadster made its slow way through the crowd. The sun blazed among swaying tree tops. Fakirs were shouting, boys were jeering and yelling, pop-corn and balloon vendors were plying their trade. Drums were throbbing, Boom! Boom! Boom! A mammoth black and red poster announced to a waiting world that

RAIN OR SHINE
SASSOON'S SMASHING SHOW

went on. "In joy or tragedy as well it goes on," Gerard though. Shrill and high the calliope steamed:

"There's a long, long trail a-winding—"

Jean roused. "Oh, Uncle Rod, can't we—stay for the circus?"

"Not today. I'll get you to High Ledges as soon as possible."

"But I don't want to go home," she whimpered. "Mother may be there, and she'll stay—and stay—and then—you and I won't have any fun."

Gerard had thought of that and had been ashamed of the thought. He remembered Annie Gerard's sharp:

"The idea! I don't approve of circuses!"

What would she say when she heard what had happened?

The town behind them, he sent the roadster forward along the smooth road between its gay borders of fall shrubs. Once he looked at Prudence. He had the feeling that only her body was beside him, that she had removed her spirit to a distant planet and an icy one at that. She had her face against Jean's hair; the child's long lashes lay like finges on her pale cheeks. He said gruffly:

"What a mix-up! A town burns up. A circus is thrown off schedule. A clown sent scouting. He took a chance on your garden—he'd try anything once—and then—a man who hates me lays his hand on my shoulder—and this for Jean—and tragedy for Chicot."

"Remember that line from Milton's *Comus?*

" 'That Power
Which erring men call Chance.' "

"It wasn't all chance, Prue. Chicot's daughter, her husband and child lived in the red brick house when Milly Gooch was a little girl. He visited them. That was what he meant yesterday when he said that he had lived in this region."

"I suspected you had seen him before."

"And because of what Len Calloway implied, you have me tried and sentenced, I'll bet."

She did not answer, only pressed her cheek closer against Jean's hair. He kept both hands tight on the wheel. If he said what he wanted to say, he would smash the fragment of friendship between them, which was as perishable as gossamer at the present moment. Why had he let her invade his life? Why had he allowed her to make him madly happy or so infernally miserable by a look? Rapture and agony. He knew what the words meant now.

"I'll drop you at your gate," he proposed curtly.

"No. I will go on to High Ledges. I won't leave Jean until I see her with her mother."

Jean opened her eyes and lifted her head from Prudence's shoulder.

"I'm not going home until Mother has gone. There's nothing the matter with me except that I feel kind of dizzy; it helps steady things to keep my eyes closed. You won't mind if I stay with Miss Prue for a while, will you, Uncle Rod? Her house is so peaceful and—she—she has such grand eats."

"Miss Prue is a woman of affairs. She doesn't want you."

"Don't you, Miss Prue?" Jean's eyes filled and her lips quivered.

"You should be with your mother, dear."

"I'm not going to be with my mother, so that's that."

"Getting back to normal fast, aren't you, K.K.?"

"Course I am, Uncle Rod. Let me stay with Miss Prue today, that's a peach. I'll wait on Mr. David. I love him. Perhaps he'll pat my hand when I bring him things and say as he does to Miss Prue:

" 'You're the light of my eyes.'

"When I do anything for my father he says:

" 'Stop fidgeting, Jean, you get on my nerves'."

She began to cry.

"Let her stop with me," Prudence pleaded.

"No. She's going back to High Ledges and I hope I land her there before her mother gets away. Annie was to return to New York today with the servants. I had persuaded her to leave Jean with me; it is only fair that she should know what happened, what a flop I am as a guardian."

Except for an occasional query as to Jean's comfort, Gerard said nothing during the long ride home. He was living over those last minutes of the parade. Poor Milly. Of course he would do what he could to help her, but what a hector she was. Even in her real grief she couldn't resist stirring up her one-time fiancé. Did Prue believe Calloway's implication? He gave her an oblique glance. She looked white. Her heart wasn't bouncing along on balloon tires now. The laughter and sparkle with which she had greeted him this morning were gone. He put his arm about Jean and drew her against him.

"Your shoulder will be stiff, Prue, if you don't rest it," he said in explanation.

Jean straightened. "I don't have to lean against anyone. I'm feeling great."

As if to prove her words, she sat almost erect until they reached the red brick house. Gerard opened the door of the roadster. Without meeting his eyes, Prudence suggested:

"At least let me go home with her."

"No. Jump out. Make it snappy. Jean and I are in for a scene. We'll keep you out of it. Sorry our grand party was such a washout."

He thought she answered as he stepped into the car, but he was too hurt by her evident suspicion of him to listen.

Jean drew a long sobbing breath as the roadster started forward. Her uncle looked down at her.

"Pull yourself together, K.K. If you and I are to be on our own, we've got to go forward like soldiers, not whimper when we have to do things we don't like. If things are too easy for us, we'll be like those squab chickens we had for dinner last night. Bones out, muscles gone, all ready for someone to gobble. Get me?"

Jean straightened, wiped her eyes, gave him a watery smile.

"Sure I get you, Uncle Rod. I feel fine now, really I do." She slipped a hand under his arm. "Perhaps, perhaps Mother has gone already," she whispered hopefully.

In his mind Gerard echoed the hope as they approached the house of stone and oak which his grandfather had built. Window boxes crowded with slightly frost-bitten bloom, woodbine already showing crimson, awnings, softened the outlines. Corking house. Not too large in these days when the trend was to contract one's living quarters. Pity he couldn't enjoy it without having Walter's wife under his feet. He stopped the roadster at the front steps.

Judkins appeared as if by magic. There was a faint

light of excitement in his slaty eyes; his black tie had slipped out of place the fraction of an inch; his thin lips twitched at one corner. What had happened to disturb his usual frozen calm?

Gerard sprang from the car, lifted Jean out. He kept his arm about her.

"Where's Mrs. Walter, Judkins?"

"She went soon after you left, sir. She decided to motor to the city. She took the big car and sent the maids by train. They have just gone."

"Oh goody—"

Gerard clapped his hand over Jean's lips. For an instant Judkins' eyes met his. Had they gleamed with sympathy? Boy, how they all dreaded Annie!

"Aren't you back earlier than you expected, sir?"

"Yes, We—we didn't stay for the show." Rodney stopped on the great tiger skin in the wood-panelled hall. "Better go up and lie down, K.K."

"I don't want to lie down, Uncle Rod. I feel swell."

"Do as you are told. Go up with her, Judkins. Have Patch and his wife come?"

"Yes, sir; they've been staying in the village so's to be ready to step in when the others stepped out."

"Preparedness. Ask your sister to take a look at Miss Jean, will you? I want to phone."

"Yes, sir. Mr. Armstrong arrived soon after you left."

"Armstrong! So soon! Where is he?"

"He went for a walk. Mrs. Walter was just going, and things were in kind of a stir, so he—" He coughed discreetly behind his hand.

"So he stepped out. I get you. Go up and lie down, Jean, and if you are good and feel fine, you may dine with us. Don't put out my dinner clothes, Judkins. I must leave the house at seven and I'll go as I am. You'll like Jim Armstrong, K.K., he's a great old boy."

Jean stopped on the lowest stair. Her eyes shone. "I won't move from the couch all day, if only I may have dinner with you just as if I were grown up, Uncle Rod. Will I sit at the head of the table the way Mother does? Do you suppose Mr. Jim will like me?

I wonder—I wonder if he will fall in love with Miss Prue—too."

Gerard felt his face warm with color. He pulled a cigarette from his pocket and lighted it.

"That last wisecrack has shown me that you are back to normal, K.K., quite back to normal. Now listen, one more like that and you'll spend the winter in the bosom of your family—in New York City."

He phoned the village doctor as a measure of precaution. The medico came and reiterated what the other physician had said, that the delicate child—too delicate—was suffering from nervous shock only. The assurance had taken a big load from his mind, Gerard told himself, as after an early dinner he watched Jean as she sat on a low stool beside the fire. Elbow on her knee, chin in one hand, her eyes were on Jim Armstrong who was spectacled, sinewy, with an out-of-door bigness.

"It's corking to have you here, Jim. You haven't changed, unless you've grown heavier," Gerard commented. The two black spaniels on the hearth rug looked at him, yawned, stretched, and flopped down at his feet.

"It's grand to be here, Rod. I won't say that you haven't changed in the last two years though. If you were to speak to me in the dark, I wouldn't know your quick, determined voice. Where's that lazy drawl which drew the female of the species after you in squads?"

"I chucked that when I decided to become a lumber king. I'm in business now, as I wrote you. At least I'm making a stab at it. At present I've struck a snag. There's a guy here named Len Calloway, also in the lumber business, who threatens to boycott any man who works for me."

"From what I saw of the country when I was prowling about this morning, I should say that there was plenty of work for two concerns. For the first time in years the demand for lumber is way ahead of the supply. The markets have been flooded with pulp from foreign countries. At last our dealers have gone,

'Buy American.' What has stirred this chap Calloway up?"

"I beat him to it in persuading Miss Schuyler to engage me to cut the timber in a five hundred acre tract she owns."

Jim Armstrong paused in the process of filling his pipe.

"Who is Miss Schuyler? She doesn't belong by any chance to that family—"

Gerard glanced at Jean whose ears were fairly standing out in eagerness to hear.

"She is a sister of David Schuyler. Know him? He was a New York lawyer."

"I've heard of him. Poor—"

"As I was saying, Miss Schuyler inherited a tract of woodland, along with a house and other land. She came here to farm—her brother's health had broken down. Immediately the aforementioned Calloway—"

"Hate him pretty much, don't you, Rod?"

"It isn't a chuckling matter, Jim. Si Puffer, who worked for the new owner's uncle and is a sort of handy man for her, told her not to let Len cut for her. I decided that I would cut for her and myself—that's when I sent for you. Calloway was furious as—well, we've had trouble over another matter."

"Is Miss Schuyler—young?" Armstrong quizzed, as he lighted his pipe.

"Yes, and so pretty," Jean chirped eagerly. "Mother Puffer says that her eyes are like brown pansies and that her voice would coax the birds off the bushes." She reproduced the stout woman's thick, deep tone to a note. "When she laughs her eyes are all gold spangles."

"K.K., you've been so quiet I had forgotten you were here. It's time you went upstairs. Toddle along now like a good girl. Mrs. Patch will look after you."

"All righty, Uncle Rod." She kissed him, and with a little curtsy said good-night to Armstrong. The two men rose and waited until she had left the room. A log crumbled and indulged in pyrotechnics. The hiss of sparks roused the dogs, who opened sleepy eyes, stretched, and closed them. Back in the luxuriously cushioned chairs, Gerard and Armstrong smoked in silence. The forester dropped a question into the quietude and calm.

"Has this man Calloway by any chance a sentimental interest in your neighbor?"

"He'd better not have."

"Why the growl? Why the deep, dour frown? What's the matter with him? Is he short an eye or an ear, moral sense, or any little handicap of that sort?"

"He's all right so far as appearances go, Jim; in fact, he is something of a looker, he is the eligible man of the village and knows it. He has a devilish temper." Rodney Gerard rose impetuously and stood back to the fire. "But—here are my cards face up on the table. I'm mad about Prudence Schuyler. I will marry her if I have to move the world to do it. Get that straight?"

"I'll say I get it straight. I can read a 'No Trespassing' sign when I see one, believe me. Does the lady with the spangled eyes realize that she is posted, Rod?"

"It's no joke to me, Jim. I suppose it seems like lunacy to you. You know that while I was at college and law school I was off girls; fussing over a plane or baseball practice meant more to me than the heaviest date you boys could make for me."

"Your worst enemy wouldn't accuse you of being a philanderer, Rod."

"No credit to me, never could get mushy. I guess the old song's right, 'Love has a meaning all its own—' to different people. Mine is the one-woman brand. The first time I met Prue—I can't explain it to you, you will think I've gone goofy—I felt as if—as if the universe had been made over and I was reborn—with an ambition to grab the world by the tail and a determination to make that girl love me."

"Raring to go off the deep end, aren't you? What has become of your obsession that you might be married for your fortune?"

"Did I ever think that? I should prefer to be mar-

ried for love, but I will take Prue any way I can get
her."

"Any progress?"

"No, practically static. She detests men of my
type."

"Um. Pretty serious jam you're in, Roddy."

"It darn well is."

Armstrong laid his hand on Gerard's shoulder. His
eyes, magnified by the strong lenses of his spectacles,
were warm with affection.

"Buck up! I don't know how any girl could resist
you. You generally get what you want. To return to
our muttons. Contracts made to sell your lumber?"

"Not a contract. I have been so, what Si Puffer calls
het up, with this fight with Calloway that I hadn't
thought where I would dispose of it."

"You'd better get busy on that end. You mustn't cut
beyond the point where reasonable prices may be
secured. Timber has been cut as recklessly as if the
supply were unlimited. The lumber market has had a
blood transfusion from the rejuvenated building business. You'll get better prices than at any time during
the last three years—if you can get the right people
sold on your proposition. I'll give you a list of going
concerns: then you'd better hustle after business."

"I'll hustle all right. I will put this enterprise over if
I never do anything else in my life."

"Do we start our investigation of the timber tracts
tomorrow?"

"Yes." Gerard glanced at the clock. "You'll excuse
me, Jim, if I break away? Something important I've
got to take care of tonight. You needn't grin, not that
kind of a date, worse luck, someone who needs my
help—perhaps. I'll let you know as soon as I get in if
it isn't too late. Ask Judkins for anything you want to
drink. I don't keep it round. Long ago I decided
between machines and liquor—Death too often
crowds himself in as a gruesome stowaway when they
travel together—and chose machines."

"Think I'd like you for a pilot, Rod. I shan't keep
Judkins very busy. How about the wood roads? Those

I saw need to be cut out before we can see much."

"Si Puffer is engaging men to go along with us tomorrow to cut."

Puffer appeared in the doorway. His eyebrows looked shaggier than usual in contrast to his slicked-down iron gray hair.

"Here he is now! Come in, Si. This is my old friend Jim Armstrong who has come to tell us what trees to take out."

Puffer removed the sliver of wood from between his teeth.

"Pleased to make your acquaintance, Jim. Gorry-me, Rod, I'm plumb discouraged. Don't know's we're goin' to need a forester."

"Why not? What has happened?"

"Now don't fly off the handle like that just because I hint we're in for trouble." Puffer drew near the two men who were facing him, backs to the fire, and lowered his voice.

"Whatta mean is, I've been all over the village tryin' to hire men to cut for us tomorrow. They all had some fool excuse. I cornered one of 'em an' jest squeezed it out of him that Len Calloway had let it be known that none of them would get any more work from him—ever—if they hired out to you."

"Hooey! if he boycotted them, what would he do for men later?"

"Well, he's got 'em scared. He pointed out that you might start out big, Rod, but you wouldn't stick; that this was just a fad of yours, an' where would they be when you quit?"

"I! Quit!" Gerard's blue eyes were black. "Go back and tell those men that there isn't room in this town for Len Calloway and me and that I am staying."

X

His challenge to Calloway had been good theatre, but could he back it up, Gerard asked himself, as a few moments later his car shot into the highway between the two great iron gates set in stone posts at High Ledges. He glanced at the illuminated clock on the dial board. He was late in starting. He wanted to reach the show grounds before Milly went on for her act. Of course she would go on, the world of the circus didn't even slow up for the death of an old clown who no longer "fetched the laughs." Perhaps he couldn't help her, but if he didn't, she might turn to someone not so disinterested as he.

Eyes on the black road which lured with enticing smoothness, his thoughts turned back to the first time he had seen Milly Gooch. Her father and mother had hired the old, out-of-repair red brick house for almost nothing and had lived there one summer while out of a circus job. He, at High Ledges from Prep School for vacation, Walter, on an indefinite leave of absence from college, had spent every available hour with the family listening to their stories of the innermost life of the Big Top. The father had been a ring-master. He was dark haired with richly colored skin. The day he had appeared in his white riding breeches, black coat, patent leather boots, and high silk hat, smiling and revealing gleaming white teeth, Rodney had then and there decided that he would join a circus and work and work till he could snap a long whip in the ring.

He recalled the mother, as fragile as a figurine and as beautiful. She had been his first love. He smiled as he remembered how his fifteen-year-old heart had jumped each time he saw her. She was an equestrienne of no small reputation. He thought of little Milly

as he had seen her on the back of an old white horse
in an improvised ring in a field behind the barn,
learning the toe-to-pommel, the foot-back, the foot-
around, and the foot-on-the-neck. In memory he
could hear the thud, thud of cantering hoofs, see the
grandfather—he was not old then—acting as her
clown, her Joey, they called him in circus parlance. It
had been his proud privilege to dust rosin on the back
of the old horse before the young rider began her
practice. She had been a tease and a hector even
then. It had seemed as if the little girl were being
ruthlessly trained, but now he thought of what old
pain-racked Chicot had said:

"You're good enough for the biggest show."

She was good. After the Gooch family left the red
brick house for the circus, Milly had come each year
to visit the Puffers to get "fed up" and some red blood
into her, Mother Puffer had told him. He had seen her
rarely, but, as she had grown into a stunning looking
girl, her long, narrow eyes and her expert use of them
had caught Len Calloway. Had it been just an exciting game with her? She had become engaged to him.
Next he heard of her he had received a wire:

ROD. MUST SEE YOU STOP SHOW IN YON-
KERS SATURDAY STOP DON'T FAIL ME
                              MILLY GOOCH

He could recall even his amazement at the sum-
mons. Why had she sent for him? In that far away
summer Walter had been more of a friend than he;
he had been fascinated by her mother. Of course he
would go. He had liked the poor little over-worked
kid. He had written to her and sent her flowers when
he had heard that her mother had been killed in a
fall from her horse after her husband's death from
influenza.

He visualized the "Back Yard" of a circus as he had
first seen it, remembered his amazement at the effi-
ciency. Acts going on. Acts coming off. Hardly the
sound of a voice. Low whistles. Constant movement.

No confusion. Flashlights winking and fading like mammoth fireflies. Then Milly at the door of her tent, Milly in the bouffant tulle of an equestrienne.

He remembered the defiance in her big dark eyes, the whiteness of her face under its make-up. The clutch of her fingers on his arm, the spice of mischievous satisfaction in her voice as she had whispered:

"I—I've walked out on Len, Rod."

He recalled that he had laughed at her—it was unbelievable that Calloway would release anything he once had held. She had perched on the edge of a chair in front of her tent. Grooms led frisky ponies to the little horse tent as she had retorted:

"Yeah, it isn't a joke. I—well, your brother Walter's been my boy friend. I just burn him up. I'm sick of riding, riding whether I'm feeling bum or not, and having Grandpop out of a job half the time. I'm going to be a lady and be taken care of and take care of him."

"Walter!" Gerard felt again the shock that had brought him up standing. "Walter! Walter has a wife."

He remembered her laugh. "Say, Big Boy, where have you come from? Been asleep since the Puritans landed?"

He had caught her hands tight in his. "Look here, Milly, you can't do that. Walter isn't worth it."

"Listen, is any guy worth what a girl gives up for him? I've got their numbers. Course I can do it. I'm going to, too."

"Then why send for me?"

He remembered her eyes as they met his. There was no mischief in them. They were like those of a wounded deer which had looked up at him, the first and last he had shot.

"Because—because you're not like the others. You're such a square-shooter, Roddy. You always were as a boy. You give Walt his income, don't you? Somehow I couldn't take his money—your money— without you knowing."

The memory brought the same lump to his throat

her words had brought that night in the Big Yard. He had had to clear his voice before he said:

"Who's a square-shooter now? If it's money, why not marry Calloway—"

"I wouldn't marry Calloway for all his jack. Walter is a grand fella! I like him. He—Time for my act."

Rodney remembered that he had caught the girl's hand as she stood up.

"Milly! Milly! Promise that you—you won't—until I see you again."

Quite plainly now he could see her shining eyes as they had met his.

"Listen, if you care what I do, I promise, Roddy."

Gerard sent the car ahead in a burst of speed. He remembered the limpness of his relief that he had extracted that promise. He had become familiar enough with the inner life of a circus in the months which had followed. He had given Milly an allowance—a fool thing to do; if it were discovered, his motive would be misconstrued. She wouldn't accept it unless he brought the money himself or sent it in a letter. If he had been disappointed in her that she would accept it at all, he had crushed back the thought. If anything he could reasonably do would keep her straight, he owed it to her mother. And she had kept straight; of that he was sure.

He had run into Calloway once when he was leaving her in front of her tent. He remembered the flaming incredulity of the man's eyes, then the sardonic twist of his mouth. Of course, he thought he had been cashiered on his account. It had not seemed important then, rather a joke that he should think so, but now, Calloway's implication to Prue this morning— had it been only this morning, it seemed a lifetime since he had seen poor crumpled old Chicot on the floor—had made him realize that there was more, much more than a contest over timber beneath the lumberman's enmity. He was in for the fight of his life. He had had a premonition of trouble when the clown had appeared in the garden of the red brick house. He thrust back the thought. Time enough for that later.

Corking night. A sort of luminous darkness slipped away into a faint crimson afterglow. Occasionally the shape of a building stood out sharply.

A string of wagons was leaving the show grounds as he entered. That meant that the audience was in the big tent. Cook-house equipment, the range and steamboiler wagons, wagons carrying the dining tent canvas were moving. He had watched the exodus many times when he had been waiting to speak to Milly.

Inside the big tent a band blared. A breeze blew the flames from the squat cans of kerosene which served as torches about the show grounds. Wreaths of black smoke swirled and mounted like the smoke from a magician's pot in the Arabian Nights; one could easily imagine a hideous jinnee taking shape within it. A breeze, which flapped the scalloped canvas eaves of the Big Top, was laden with the mangled smells of corn popping, hot dogs frying, hay, animals, and sweating humanity.

Two ghostlike horses plodded within the glare of the torches; their hoofs struck an occasional yellow spark; lead-bar rings jingled. Inside the Big Yard Gerard passed red and white tubs, red and white pedestals in orderly piles, mysteriously shaped tables, barrels gayly painted, golden coaches gleaming in a dim corner.

He glanced at the huge dressing tent as he approached the row of square tents used by the headliners. Before it a clown and a groom in scarlet and gold were intent on a game of backgammon. A woman in the fleshings and blue satin of an acrobat sat in front of a small tent sewing, a Siberian sheep dog at her feet.

Gerard could see heads above the wall of the Big Top when the breeze lifted the canvas edges. Must be a crowd. How still it was inside! Aerialists doing their stuff probably. A thunder of applause. The crash of the band. Two men in crimson satin tights, their faces beaded with sweat, dashed out of the show tent and on a run disappeared into one of the small dressing tents. Six white Shetland ponies dragging a miniature silver coach trotted across the yard to the entrance to the Big Top. A polka-dotted clown in enormous shoes clopped after it. He dropped to a tub to bend the sole of one foot and then the other between his chalk-white hands.

Gerard stopped before the tent on the wall of which MADEMOISELLE MILLEE was stamped in black letters. As if she had been waiting for him, Milly Gooch stepped from behind the curtain drawn across the front of it.

Never had he seen her look lovelier. Her dark hair was curled close to her head; the mascara on her lashes increased the brilliance of her narrow, sloe-black eyes; the crimson of her lips accentuated the ivory pallor of her skin. Layer upon layer of the fluted rose-color tulle of her skirt—the top one starred with brilliants—stood out crisply. Brilliants bordered the low-cut satin bodice, twinkled with every movement of her supple body. In one hand she carried a slender silver whip. Her great dark eyes glittered with tears.

"You sure are a dependable guy, Roddy." She perched on the top of a pedestal. "Take that chair. Say, wasn't that a terrible deal Grandpop got this morning!" She put up a Chinese-red nailed finger to remove the moisture from her eyes before it should ruin her mascara. "And wasn't it like Len Calloway to put on his act at just that minute! That bozo's grown old."

"When did you talk with him last, Milly?"

"The day I gave him back his ring. I've felt his eyes on me times enough, couldn't see 'em, just felt them. Look out for him, he has it in for you, Roddy. Doesn't he know that it was Walter, not you, who made me break with him?"

There was a lull in the activities of the yard. In the comparative silence Gerard could hear the roar of a lion.

"Forget him, Milly. I came to see if I could help about your grandfather. Won't you need money?"

"Not from you. The management takes care of that. Who was the kid Grandpop saved?"

"Walter's little girl, Jean."

"Say listen, are you fooling?"

"No."

"Well, of all the breaks—Grandpop passing out for the kid of the man he hated." She laughed, laughed until the sound cracked in an hysterical sob.

"Milly! Milly! Stop! You won't be able to ride if you don't. Remember, your grandfather told you this morning that you would be a great rider. You can't let your public down. Here, look up." He pulled a handkerchief from his pocket. "Let me wipe your eyes. I won't hurt your make-up. Now smile as if I were a Johnnie in the front row."

She looked up with an attempt which twisted his heart.

"That-a-girl! All set now?"

She choked back a sob. Caught the handkerchief.

"All set, Roddy. May I have this?"

"Sure, but what the dickens will you do with it? Haven't any pockets concealed in the ritzy costume, have you?"

"It's so fine, I'll tuck it in here." She thrust it under her low-cut bodice. "See, it doesn't bulge. The feel of it will sort of keep me steady through the act. You know—Grandpop always went on as my Joey." She gulped back a sob. "Lucky, only one more date and then we're through; it's a ham show, anyway."

"What will you do this winter, Milly?" Gerard's eyes were on the performing elephants crossing the yard to the ring. Two rodeo riders, still whooping, dashed from the Big Top, leaped from their mounts, and hurried toward the main dressing tent. He heard the sharp buzz of a whistle, the blare of the band. The elephants were making their entrance.

The girl crossed and uncrossed her silver shod feet before she answered his question.

"Hollywood. Two big shots from a traveling talkie

studio saw me ride a month ago. They followed me into the Big Yard when I came off after my act. Say, did one of them have a line! He handed out that 'Where-have-you-been-all-my-life?' dope. They gave me a test. Okay. I'm booked for the Coast right after Christmas to do a circus picture."

"Did your grandfather know?"

"I had put off telling him, knew he'd blow up about it. What do you think? Mother Puffer and old 'whatta mean is' Si came to see me this afternoon! I blubbered good on her fat shoulder and then I felt better. She wants I should spend Christmas with them. What say, Roddy?"

"Why ask me?"

"Why shouldn't I? Haven't you been my best friend since the day of your fifteenth birthday party? Remember how the kids of the summer folks high-hatted a circus performer's kid? Of course, you, being you, led the march to supper with the freak, so she wouldn't be hurt. Gosh, I must have been a sight in one of Ma's tulle riding skirts cut down to fit and a sky blue sash that hung to my heels. Remember?"

"Not your clothes, but I'll never forget your cheeks, which were as red as MacIntosh apples, and your eyes big and black as shiny marbles. If you visit the Puffers you may run into Len Calloway."

"What if I do? I'll give him a little whirl for old times' sake." The cat and mouse look narrowed her eyes. "You don't think I'm afraid of that big noise, do you? I've traveled some since I sent you that S.O.S."

"And traveled straight, Milly?"

She met his eyes squarely. "Sure thing. Didn't I promise? I'm off men, they're just a game, anyway. Say, who was the girl with the kid this morning? She was classy, all right. Any relation to Walter?"

"No. She is Prudence Schuyler. Her uncle died and left her the old red brick house."

"Well, what do you know about that! That ruin we lived in? We used to set tubs to catch the rain which dripped through the roof."

"It's been repaired since then. Prue—Miss—"

"Time for your act, Milly."

As the maid spoke behind them, a groom in rose-color velvet with silver trimming led a milk-white horse bridled with rhinestones to the tent. The pale blue saddle glistened with brilliants. The maid produced a box of sugar. Milly put a white cube in her pink palm and held it out to the horse, withdrew it to tease him. He nuzzled her hand until she opened it. He nibbled daintily.

"Silver looks for that the first thing—the old sweetie!" The horse rubbed his nose against her soft shoulder. "He knows I'm feeling low."

"The last elephant is out. Better get over to the door. You're on in a minute," the groom reminded. He started across the yard with the horse. A man, who might have been his twin, joined him carrying a silver pedestal and paper covered hoops.

"Will you be here when I come off, Roddy?" Milly asked wistfully.

"No. I've left a friend at home who is a forester; he has come to put me wise to timber values. Did Mother Puffer tell you that I had gone into business with a capital B?"

"For the love of Mike, you haven't lost your money, have you? I've got some—"

"Don't be foolish. Of course I've taken some terrific losses, who hasn't, but it won't break me. Be a good girl, Milly, and write if you need anything. Sure now."

She caught his hands and looked up at him. "Sure, I'll be good. I promised you, didn't I? There's only one person who could tempt me not to be, and he— he doesn't know I'm on earth. He—"

A hiss. A flash cut off the word.

"What was that?"

"Don't be so jumpy, Roddy. If you traveled with this show you'd get used to that sound. Flashlight. Publicity, of course. Some reporter writing up the show wants a picture." A whistle blew. "That's for me. I'd better get going."

The maid came from the dressing tent with a cape

of glistening silver sequins over her arm. Milly settled a sparkling shoulder strap, gave a slight twist to her lithe body which set her bouffant skirts a-swirl.

"Bye-bye, Roddy. Don't—don't send me any more money—ever—I won't need it—now that I've gone Hollywood. Perhaps you'll be at High Ledges at Christmas—if Miss Schuyler stays."

What had she meant by that, Gerard wondered, as his eyes followed her in her rose-color tulle and glistening satin across the yard. Was his feeling for Prue so evident? He lingered to see her make her entrance. She was a good little sport, he thought, as he watched her. Near the back door of the Big Top she handed her silver whip to the maid, stretched her slender arms above her head as if about to dive, then brought her open hands to the ground in a long sweep. As her palms touched, her feet shot up. Palms up and feet down, feet down and palms up. A half dozen times she limbered her already supple body, the brilliants on her costume twinkling like a million iridescent sparks at every motion.

A whistle blew. The blare of the band eased into a sensuous melody. Milly put one silver shod foot into the hand of the groom and sprang to the back of the white horse. She turned and flung a kiss over her shoulder; then the sparkle and radiance went out as Mademoiselle Millee passed through the entrance into the Big Top.

As he started across the yard to the exit, Gerard heard the tumult of applause which greeted her entrance, heard the music increase in pace. Well, that was that. Milly hadn't needed his help, wouldn't need it again probably, she was going on to bigger things. Hollywood. What would it do to her? Who was the man who didn't know she was on earth? Crazy about him evidently. He wasn't afraid for her. One couldn't look into her eyes when she promised and doubt her.

Near the exit he stopped as a voice shouted: "Take it away!" He looked back. A whistle sounded, and as if by magic, a side wall of canvas slipped to the ground. Instantly, with jangle of traces and clump of hoofs, waiting teams were hooked to tarpaulined dens. Another whistle, and once more the circus menagerie had begun its nocturnal trek.

Music and shouts of acclaim shook the canvas of the main tent.

"Milly must be going over big. She's a good little sport," Gerard thought again, as he stepped out into darkness which only a short time before had been a bedlam of voices, a sea of light and a hive of activities. Fakirs and side-shows had, like the Arabs of poetic memory, folded their tents and silently slipped away leaving behind them a sombre air of desertion.

One foot on the step of his car, Gerard stopped and stared. Had a red roadster shot out of the parking place just ahead, or was Len Calloway so much on his mind that he had imagined it?

XI

Prudence pulled at the wire netting at one side of the poultry yard.

"Darn!" she gritted between her teeth, as the elusive thing wriggled away from her. "Mr. Si, I'm not so good as I thought. Give me a hand, will you?"

Puffer dropped the tools with which he had been hacking at a weathered granite boulder, seized the netting, and pulled.

"Grand! Hold it a minute till I get this brad in; two more and it's done. Those pesky hens got out yesterday and scratched in my garden border. There! I'd like to see them get through that!"

"The pesky hens ain't the only things that escaped yesterday. Hear 'bout the convict who dug himself out of prison?"

"Jane Mack heard the announcement on the radio and told me. She's all excited about it. He isn't likely to come to this small town, is he?"

"Gorry-me, he'd be running his head into a noose if he did." Puffer shook the wire netting. "That's a good job you've done. They ought to have you down to the prison to do their repairin'. I guess there wouldn't be no one breaking out then."

Hammer in hand, Prudence sank back on her heels and smiled at the man looking down at her with eyes which made her think of the favorite glassies of her youth. He pulled a whittled sliver of wood from his pocket and prodded between his teeth and words.

"You sure can handle tools, Miss Prue. Whatta mean is, I've never seen a girl nor woman before so handy with 'em. The way you made that handsome gate for the front—ain't nothing like it in this county— an' took the top off that busted sewin' machine you found in the attic made my eyes pop. What did you want the old wreck for?"

"For polishing silver. I fastened a buffer to the wheel. With my foot on the treadle I can make it hum. I've been using tools for years. Love them. I ought to be skillful."

He grinned. "Got your union card?"

"Not yet, but I may have to join something if I keep on tinkering with repairs in our old house." She drew a deep breath. "What a day! I can't believe that this is the middle of November in the State of Maine. It's glorious. There is still a lot of color in the woods, heaps of it, exhilarating color, and by the roadside— and look at it in the bay! Streaks of cobalt, sapphire, jade, and malachite, even a swirl of amethyst. Look at the red, white, and blue of the Stars and Stripes floating from the schoolhouse in the village against that turquoise sky!"

She filled her lungs with the sparkling air. "Do you know what color does to me, Mr. Si? It sends my courage shooting above par, gives me the-world's-my-oyster feeling—know it? Makes no difference where I see it, in a shop window or a gay gown. Color does to me what the touch of the earth did to the giant Antaeus—sends new life, vitality, courage, initiative surging through me. Sometime the scientists will discover that color is a renewer of life."

Si Puffer's laugh was like the rumble of distant thunder. "You got color enough in your eyes an' cheeks. Glad you're feelin' set up. Mother an' I've been kinda worried about you. Whatta mean is, you've seemed as if something was troubling you. You haven't been like yourself, as we first knew you, since the day you went to the circus. Didn't know but what you was troubled about Walt Gerard's kid."

Prudence kept her eyes on the ground she was industriously thumping with the hammer. Troubled! That was hardly the word to express what she felt. It was relief. Relief that she had found out what Rodney Gerard was in time. She had begun to believe in him, to think he could be trusted, and then—the memory of the circus rider in her cheap, spangled velvet on her knees beside the crumpled figure of the old clown, with her painted cheek snuggled against Rodney Gerard's hand, flashed on the screen of her mind, as it had flashed countless times since she had seen the original. She felt Puffer's eyes on her, and assured hurriedly:

"Nothing the matter with Jean. She comes here every day."

"Thought so, but I didn't know of anything else to trouble you now that your brother seems so much better."

Prudence sprang to her feet. Her eyes shone, her face was radiant.

"Then you've noticed it too, Mr. Si? It isn't just my imagination?"

"Sure, I've noticed it. So's Mother. Whatta mean is, his color is better, his voice is stronger, an' he moves quicker. That giant Ant—Ant—well, the one you was speakin' of, isn't the only fella that draws strength from the earth. Comin' to live in the country is jest settin' David on his feet. Rod's noticed it too."

An expression, which suggested the first thin film of ice on water, dimmed Prue's exuberance.

"Oh, he has! I haven't seen Mr. Gerard lately so I

didn't know." She avoided Puffer's eyes as she remembered the many times of late that she had fled to the barn loft so that she would not see Rodney Gerard when he called.

"Gorry-me, you haven't seen him? Seen Jim Armstrong?"

"No. Dave has, but—but I was out when he called."

"Well, of course, Rod was away to the city most three weeks trying to get some firms to sign up for the timber you and him are goin' to cut. Since he come back he's been terrible busy cruising the woods. Jim's tellin' us what trees to take out, an' trying to engage a crew to cut when the time comes. Rod isn't used to havin' difficulty gettin' what he wants; things have always come easy for him. This lumber business 'pears to be gettin' on his nerves. Jim was tellin' me this morning that Rod snapped at everyone who come near him yesterday. Perhaps it's that newspaper picture of him and Milly Gooch holdin' hands in front of her tent at the circus that come out in the local paper the day after the show was here that got him mad. Seen it?"

"Only three copies."

"Gorry-me, you jest spit that out, didn't you? You—well, if here he isn't now! What you gum-shoeing round like that for, Roddy?"

Prudence was furious at her own start of surprise. Had Rodney Gerard seen it? He did look troubled. There were lines between his nose and mouth she never had seen before; he had lost some of his bronze. Perhaps it was the brown of his suit and the matching tie against the beige of his shirt and collar which made him appear colorless. His eyes seemed deeper and darker and bluer in contrast.

"Well, will I pass? Perhaps you weren't sizing me up, perhaps you were just wondering how it happened that I had caught you, Prue of Prosperity Farm."

"Don't bite, Rod." Si Puffer flung himself into the breach. "Now that you've got company, Miss Prue, I'll go an' chop some wood. What does the Mack woman do with all she uses—eat it?" He laid his tools on top of the partially hollowed boulder.

"For Pete's sake, what are you doing to that stone, Si? If that's all the work left to be done at Prosperity Farm. I'll find a man-sized job at High Ledges."

Puffer scratched his head and scowled from under shaggy eyebrows, which looked like miniature gray mustaches in revolt.

"Can you beat it, Rod? Miss Prue wants that stone hollowed out an' put in the middle of her garden so the birds can wash in it."

"A bird bath!" Gerard looked at Prue. "How will you fill it?"

"There are such things as pails, you know."

Puffer stuffed his hands into his overall pockets, feet akimbo, and grinned.

"Terrible communicative, aren't you, Miss Prue. I can see you're just bustin' to tell Rod all about it. I'm so busy, I ain't got time to listen." He moved away with surprising quickness.

"Mr. Si!" Prudence started after him, but Gerard caught her arm and held it.

"You're not going until you tell me why you have been dodging me."

"I dodging! How absurd!"

"Is it? Drop that hammer. It makes you look blood-thirsty." As she still clutched the tool, he loosened her fingers until it dropped to the ground. "That's better. I want to talk to you before Armstrong and Jean get here. Have you seen that infernal picture?"

"Picture?" Prue echoed the word with breezy indifference, but her breath caught as his eyes darkened and he took a purposeful step toward her.

"Don't bluff. You know perfectly well that I'm referring to that fool snapshot of Milly Gooch and me at the circus."

"Oh, that! We are as God and the rotos make us," she paraphrased flippantly.

"Stop wisecracking and listen. I had gone there to—"

"Really, I'm not interested."

"Look here, you've got to be interested. I'm willing to bet my roadster that Calloway had a hand in that. I saw his red car shooting out of sight as I left the grounds. It would be like his methods—"

"Don't abuse Len Calloway. It would be disloyal for me to listen because"—Prudence hoped that her eyes and voice were as maddeningly provocative as she intended them to be—"because, you see, I've decided to have him cut my timber."

"What!"

Never had she seen eyes blaze as Rodney Gerard's blazed in his white face. She remembered what Si had said about his mood the last week. She shouldn't have tried to torment him—but—hadn't that hateful picture hurt her too? He caught her by the shoulders.

"You didn't mean that, Prue, about letting Calloway cut for you."

"Go slow! Go slow!" whispered the sprite perched on the hillock of her commonsense. She ignored the warning and rushed into the fray.

"Of course I meant it. The more I think of it the more I go bullish on the idea. I'm beginning to like Len very much. He's so forceful, so—"

"Forceful!" For a pulsing instant Rodney Gerard hesitated, then he caught her in his arms. "Forceful!" He crushed his mouth, hard, ardent, upon hers. "If that's what you like—Gorgeous—" He kissed her again.

Prudence wrenched herself free. She clamped her teeth into her lips to stop their quivering. Every pulse in her body was throbbing unbearably. How had he dared! Was that the way he kissed the circus rider? She dragged her voice back.

"Don't ever speak to me again! Ever! Do you think I'll let you cut my timber now? Suppose Len Calloway does cheat me in money; at least I shall be safe with him."

"Prue! You can't do it! You knew what you were doing when you looked at me like that. You're no child. Be a sport. You deliberately smashed my control, and now you make me pay for letting myself go. Well, I'll take my medicine, I will keep away until you want me, I'll never kiss you again until you ask me to, if—"

"I ask you! That's the funniest thing I ever heard."

"All right, it's the funniest thing you ever heard. But the promise stands. Don't, don't hurt yourself by turning that timber job over to Calloway. I—"

"Hi! Rod!"

The hail came from the garden. Prudence dashed toward the gate and collided with a big, spectacled man with heart-warming eyes. She saw them narrow as they looked from her face to Rodney Gerard behind her. His glance came back. He smiled.

"Miss Schuyler, isn't it? I would recognize you anywhere from Jean's description. One so seldom sees 'spangled eyes.' I'm Jim Armstrong, and I am happy to report that you have a nice little bunch of money in your wood lot."

Prudence extended an eager hand. "Have I really! I'm so glad you've come. Now I can learn a lot about trees. Will you take me on as a pupil?"

From the corner of her eyes Prue noted with satisfaction the set of Rodney Gerard's jaw. She would show him that he couldn't kiss her after he had been holding Milly Gooch's hands.

Jim Armstrong laughed. "Sure I'll take you along if Rod says the word. He's my boss. I'm a whale of a teacher. I'll train you to estimate the number of board feet in a standing pine; so many board feet at so many dollars figures into real money. Already Jean can tell a white pine from a balsam."

"Where is K.K.?" Gerard demanded curtly.

"In the house. Rod said you had a plan of your wood lot, The Hundreds, Miss Schuyler. May I see it?"

"Of course. It's in my shop. I'll bring it to the living room."

Prudence was conscious of Gerard watching her as a few moments later she cleared a place on her brother's desk and spread out the blueprint. As she and Armstrong bent above the map she heard Rodney and her brother talking. Jean danced in from the kitchen, her hands full of cookies.

"Uncle Rod, we must go. You know it makes Mrs. Patch furious if we are late to lunch."

She crossed the room to speak to David Schuyler seated in the wing chair. As Armstrong joined them, Rodney Gerard detained Prudence at the desk.

"Wait a minute! Look here, Prue, you didn't mean what you said about letting Calloway cut that timber. You mustn't do it."

The sternness of his voice sent tingles through her veins, but she kept her lids provokingly lowered.

"I can transact my own business, thank you. When I need help I shall appeal to Mr. Armstrong. He impresses me as being such a reliable, self-controlled person."

"And I'm not. I get you. All right, let me cut your timber and you will have no fault to find with me again—ever—I'll be the original ice man."

He turned on his heel. Prudence swallowed hard and forced a smile as the forester approached.

"Thanks lots for your encouragement—Mr.—may I call you Jim as Jean does? Come in for tea quite by yourself any afternoon. David and I are always here. Bye-bye, Jean. I'll be seeing you."

As the outer door closed, she crossed to the fireplace and head on her hands resting on the mantel looked unseeingly down at the red coals.

"Is Armstrong an old friend, Prue?" her brother asked. His long fingers tapped the arm of the wing chair.

His tone brought the color to her face. "No. I've never seen him before today. Why?"

"You seemed to twinkle, twinkle with excitement when you spoke to him. I concluded that if you hadn't met on this earth you had been affinities in some previous incarnation."

She dropped to the floor cushion beside his chair. "Humorous, aren't you? Perhaps I did rather overdo the welcome-to-our-city act, Dave, but—"

"But it was done for Gerard's benefit, wasn't it? Like him a lot, don't you?"

"Like him! No. He leaves me cold."

"Too fervid for one so cold, Prue. What have you against him?"

"You said yourself that you were confoundedly sorry that he—he knew that circus clown, Dave."

"If I had any suspicion of him then, I haven't now. I think him one of the finest, cleanest, straightest, most likable men I ever have met, and you will admit that I have had some experience."

"That's what we thought about Julie's husband before they were married."

"I never thought that. He was irresistible and charming but—he had a bad eye. I tried to make Julie understand, but she wouldn't listen. Often since I have wondered if deep in her heart she didn't feel, as I felt about my marriage, even in the first rapturous year, that there was something lacking to make it soul satisfying. I never have bared my heart to you before, Prue; never will again. I am doing it now to beg you to listen to your instinct when it sounds its warning tocsin. And, on the contrary, be mighty sure that your aversions are just. Remember that my wife, Blanche, and Julie's husband belonged in the post-war decade when men and girls acquired habits of thought and action which got an octopus grip on them. Your generation has learned from their tragic mistakes; you wouldn't let yourselves be shackled to habits as they are."

"How could we, when we see them wrecking their own lives and hurting everyone who cares for them? As for me, I shall never love any man but you, Dave darling. I shall remain Prue of Prosperity Farm and make your life a burden by camping on your trail."

"Go slow. No armor ever has been forged which is invulnerable to love. You are shaking your fist in the face of Fate when you use 'never' like that, Prue, and Fate resents being defied. Real love, no matter how unworthy the object, is a glorious adventure. It bursts the shackles of selfishness. One's world is bigger, broader; one's sympathies are amazingly more tender. No matter what the result, if you haven't really loved, you haven't really lived. As for having you camped on my trail, I wouldn't have pulled through if it hadn't been for you—and I have pulled through. I feel like a new man. I have a brand new outlook. I know now that I got the signals mixed. I surrendered to heartbreak and weakness when I should have accepted them as a challenge."

"Dave! Dave! How marvelous! There's the knocker. Who has come, I wonder. You've had visitors enough this morning, so I'll close the living room door. A pedlar probably."

Prudence was thinking of her brother's realization of his returning health as she crossed the hall. Her eyes were radiant with relief and happiness as she opened the front door. Len Calloway confronted her. She was conscious of her change of expression to blank amazement—she hoped that her jaw had not dropped—as she stared at him.

Without speaking he passed her and entered the shop. His assurance crisped her voice.

"What do you want?"

He sat on the end of the bench and tossed a coin in his palm.

"Same old request. I want the contract to cut your timber."

"Same old answer." Prudence mimicked his diction to an inflection. "I have made arrangements with Mr. Gerard to cut it."

"Gerard again. See here, I'll warn you once more not to rely on him. I have to laugh when I think of him cutting timber. He was away from the village three weeks. Do you still think he is serious about this woodsman stuff? He—well, you saw that circus rider who calls herself Mademoiselle Millee, the day the old clown passed out. Her right name is Milly Gooch. She was engaged to me. Threw me over for Gerard and he—"

"That's a lie like some of the other statements you

have made, Calloway." Her tone lashed his color to dark red, hardened his eyes.

"Oh, it is! See this?"

He held out an envelope. Involuntarily she read the address. She had not intended to gratify him by looking at it. Mr. Rodney Gerard.

"Get that? Now listen." He pulled out a card. "And get this:

" 'Dear Roddy—
    Thanks for the check. Don't mail it again. Bring it as usual. I've kept my promise. Nobody knows.
                                    Milly.' "

"I found that on the floor near Gerard's desk. Now will you let me handle your timber?"

Furious with herself that she had stood like a lump of putty and listened to the note, an unbearable realization that it confirmed her suspicions of Rodney Gerard's philandering roughened the voice in which Prudence scoffed:

"You must be the original if-at-first-you-don't-succeed-try-try-again lad. But this time you have thrown sand in the machinery. It won't work. Rodney Gerard and I will get that timber out."

Calloway's eyes burned red. They reminded Prudence of the hot embers in the living room fire.

"You and Rodney Gerard! That's a joke. Try to get men to cut. Just try, that's all. I suppose you are trusting to your partner for that?"

"If you realized how homely you are when you sneer, Mr. Calloway, you would cut it out. Anger is frightfully unbecoming to anyone, but to your features it is devastating."

Prudence swallowed a nervous chuckle. His expression was that of a wrestler she had once seen who had received a punch in the middle. Blank amazement. She added sweetly:

"You have guessed it. I am trusting to my partner to engage the men to cut. Good-morning."

He looked like a man who was still dazed from a

body blow as he departed. Once his lips moved, but Prue banged the door behind him before he could speak.

She leaned against it. Her lips twitched in a smile as she visualized Calloway's expression. Amusement flamed into rage. Timber! She hated the word. Hated it! Had Calloway found that note of Milly Gooch's in Rodney Gerard's room? "Don't mail it again." Apparently there had been other cheques. Why hadn't she asked the man why he had been snooping at High Ledges? Another cutting afterthought which came too late. Her mind bulged with them. Not that she cared who wrote to Rodney Gerard or what he did with his money. Mrs. Walt had been right. Her butterfly brother did flit from flower to flower. He had thought that she—Prudence Schuyler—would allow—

A sob of fury shook her. She brushed her hand savagely across her lips.

XII

With sighs of relaxation Gerard and Armstrong, in the tweeds in which they had come from a long day in the woods, settled into deep chairs before the fire in the library at High Ledges and lighted their pipes. Jean, in a slim little frock of white wool, flitted from one to the other, supplying ashtrays, adjusting footstools, like a motherly bantam intent on the comfort of mammoth adopted chicks.

"That's a great piece of woodland of yours, Rod," Armstrong commended, as he stretched his long legs nearer the blaze. "It is more nearly virgin than the average in these parts and has little space given over to forest weeds. The firm or firms that get that lumber will get a prize."

Gerard rapped the tobacco from his pipe. "But what a fight I put up to sell to them! I had supposed that lumber was just lumber, but boy, aren't its uses infinite! It was my first experience as a salesman, but I hung on. I didn't know what else to do. Gave each of my prospects a hop in the plane; even invited one of the wives up. It took me three weeks to put the deals across. That trip must have been the unexpected journey with its far-reaching consequences Miss Mack saw in my teacup, for having once felt the thrill of winning out in a business project, I'll never be content with all play again. Those men must have been infernally fed-up with me; perhaps they signed on the dotted line to get rid of me."

"I can't see any of that hard-boiled crowd doing that. They would have chucked you out first. Now that the logging plan is made to take out trees over twelve inches only and we have decided on the number which will leave a good basis for a second cut, we ought to get going. For the restocking of the open spaces I believe in depending on natural seeding."

"I'll say I started something when I set out to thin my woods! I thought that all that was necessary was to chop down a few trees and there we were. Now it seems that I have embarked on a life work."

"You are lucky to own timber in a state which has thorough fire protection and the intelligence to fight blister rust. The breaks are with you about hauling, too. Some owners have to construct railroads; we will snake our logs down to the pond road and haul them to that old granite wharf on your shore, big lumber boats will load them—and there we are."

"Just like that! After we get our crew, you mean. Puffer was to report on the labor question this afternoon. There he is now! Hear that thunderous rumble in the direction of the gun room? That's Si's voice when he is excited. It doesn't sound good to me. Come in, Si."

Puffer stood in the doorway. His face, which had been puckered in a worried frown, relaxed in a broad grin as he looked at the two lazy figures before the fire. He chuckled.

"Howdy, Jim! Don't have to ask how you two are,

Rod. Kinder beat out, ain't ye? You're lookin' pretty as a picture, Jean.'"

Gerard pulled himself stiffly to his feet and drew an inviting chair nearer the fire.

"Sit here and be comfortable, Si."

"Gorry-me, I guess not. Whatta mean is, if I was to set in that I'd go plumb asleep and forget what I come for. I've something serious to report an' I want my eyes and my wits goin' on high. This looks hard enough to keep me awake." He perched on an end of the piano bench.

Gerard backed up to the fire. "All right, old-timer, shoot."

"No use beatin' 'bout the bush. I've been to every village within a hundred miles an' I can't get a man to work for ye, Rod. They all say as how they've got too much to do for themselves. That's jest guff. They're afraid of Calloway, he's put the fear of God into them. I guess we're up against it, all right."

"We can't be up against it, Si. That timber must be cut. I don't want to import labor if I can help it, too many people round here needing work—no matter what they say to the contrary—but the timber will be cut. I'll find some huskies somewhere who haven't sold out body and soul to Len Calloway. Do we need skilled lumbermen, Jim?"

"No. Skilled labor would save time and money, but with you and Puffer and me to boss a crew we could get the wood out."

Patch, the butler, lean, straight, with eyes washed colorless from worry, appeared at the door.

"Miss and Mr. Schuyler."

Gerard doubted his ears. Prue here! He heard Jean's ecstatic, "Oh goody!" as he crossed the room to welcome the girl and her brother. His lips tightened at the hostility in her eyes as they met his. It was abundantly evident that he was still in disgrace for his passionate outburst of yesterday. Seeing her here was like fresh brush thrown on a smoldering fire. With difficulty he kept his voice steady.

"This is a clear case of thought transference. How

did you know that we need your advice and your brother's at this very moment, Prue? Patch, take Mr. Schuyler's coat. Come over by the fire, Dave."

He dumped a spaniel from a chair and drew it nearer the hearth. Schuyler laughed.

"How you all conspire to spoil me! We are not so neighborly as we seem. We were driven here for shelter."

Gerard watched the faint color tint Prue's face. She was avoiding his eyes. That meant that she knew he was in the room. He had a hunch that he would have the fight of his life to get her, but some day he would have her in this very house to stay. She had said she loved home-making. Would she love doing it for him?

"Dave and I have been to the village to barter eggs and poultry for groceries. Curious how that old-fashioned word has come back into use, isn't it? I'm getting good at bargaining. Just as we reached this drive, Success belied her name and passed out. I didn't dare let Dave sit in the cold car—it is beginning to snow—while I probed for internal disturbances; he flatly refused to leave me in the dark road—he had the escaped convict on his mind—so here we are. Now that he is warm and comfy, perhaps you will come out with me, Jim, and help diagnose the engine trouble."

Gerard spoke to the man who had been laying wood on the fire.

"Patch, tell Judkins to look over Miss Schuyler's car. When he has it in shape, let me know. Tell him not to hurry," he added in a low tone.

"Very good, sir."

"But I don't want Judkins to bother with my car. I can perfectly well—"

"No, you can't." Gerard met her stormy eyes steadily. "It is a part of his present job to tinker disgruntled engines. Take off your coat."

If she hesitated for an instant before allowing him to help her remove her swagger-coat of nutria, no one but he noticed it, the three men were deep in conversation. He whispered to Jean who was hovering about

David Schuyler. She listened with an expression of blissful importance on her thin face and slipped out of the room. He turned to Prudence seated in a low mahogany slipper chair, which had been one of his grandmother's wedding presents.

"Your arrival is uncannily opportune, partner. Jim, Si, and I have struck a snag."

"All is not serene on the logging front?" Prudence asked anxiously.

"Calloway again? I hope you haven't permanently incurred that man's enmity because you are helping us."

"That's only a little gas spilled on the fire, Dave. Len is drunk with the idea of his importance in this community. He has had it in for me since—since I beat him on a tax expenditure at Town Meeting. You and Prue are the victims."

"Don't worry about Prue, Gerard. She did her best to pull wool over my eyes, but I know that she came to the State of Maine expecting that her days would be an endless round of recurring monotonies. Instead of which she finds herself embroiled in labor troubles. Between you and me, she's fairly lapping up the excitement."

"I'll bet she gets the troubles," Puffer agreed with a throaty chortle.

Hands clasped on her knees, Prudence leaned forward. The firelight danced in little reflected flames on the two copper buttons on her brown wool frock, on a broad bracelet of the same rich-toned metal; it stole up even to the earnest eyes that reproached her brother.

"Dave, you're a traitor. I'm not lapping up excitement, but it makes me see fiery pinwheels in frenzied revolution when I think of Calloway's power. He will find that I won't stand being dictated to."

Gerard's relief left him limp for an instant. Yesterday she had been strong for Len. Had she been putting up a bluff to defy the man who had kissed her, or had Calloway chopped off his own head by a stupid move? Whatever the explanation, the fact remained that she was still relying upon the original plan for getting out her timber.

"Jim, suppose no one here will work for us? What shall we do?"

Gerard's recent satisfaction burned up in anger. She was deliberately ignoring him. He cut in:

"Just a minute, Prue. Jim knows nothing but trees. I'm your best bet as to labor information. It is my job to cram Calloway's threats down his throat and also to produce a crew to cut. We'll have to hire men from outside the state. I'm going to New York tomorrow to try my luck there."

"New York!" David Schuyler repeated thoughtfully. "You'll win out, Rodney. Nine times out of ten, when one is backed up against an insurmountable wall, a gate will open behind one if one puts up the fight of one's life."

"I'll put up a fight, all right. On that table, Patch."

The butler set down the heavy Sheffield tray with its silver tea equipment. Jean, holding the muffin stand she had brought in, looked at her uncle with expectant eyes. He smiled and placed a chair.

"Pour for us, will you, K.K.? We won't need you, Patch."

Radiant with importance, Jean adjusted priceless Sevres cups, inquired preferences, tempered the tea to individual tastes. David Schuyler approved:

"You are the first person, Jean, besides Prue, who ever has given me a satisfactory brew when I asked for hot water with a dash of tea. I like your thin bread and butter and fruit cake, too. Life looks brighter and that balky engine outside seems of no importance. Wasn't it Cervantes who said. 'All sorrows are less with bread'? I'll drop in on your parties whenever I am invited. Prue, see that piano? I'm hungry for your music. I have regretted daily that we leased ours with the apartment. If Rodney and the others don't object, play for us."

"Object! We're all for it. There is music in that cabinet," Gerard suggested.

Prudence shook her head as she crossed to the bench which Si Puffer had hastily vacated.

"It's a horrible confession to make, but I don't read music, I play by ear. What will you have, Jim?" The notes ripped under her supple fingers as she smiled at Armstrong, who, beside Puffer, was at the other end of the piano.

"Something gay. I'm a lowbrow when it comes to music."

"Play something we can sing," suggested David Schuyler, who had joined the other two men. He stood with an arm about Jean's shoulers.

Rodney Gerard felt as if he were a foundling left on an unfriendly doorstep as back to the fire he watched the group about the piano. He wasn't missed, certainly not by Prue. Her eyes were alight with laughter, her cheeks were slightly flushed as she looked from one pair of admiring eyes to another and swung into a popular song: "May I have this waltz with you, Madame?"

Rodney remembered Si Puffer's dry comment:

"Every unmarried man in the county—I wouldn't put it past some of the married ones—will come buzzin' round the old red brick house like bees round a honey pot now that girl is here."

This was a new side to her. How versatile she was! She played with verve, crispness, sparkle, exuberance, and warm sentiment. Once she threw a fleet glance at him. Between half closed lids, under the sweeping gold-tipped lashes, he caught the glint of her eyes. There was mockery in them, certainly nothing of friendship.

Even as he stood unconsciously tapping his foot in time to the rhythmic sway of her music, he was wondering if she would ever forgive him for yesterday, wondering why out of the whole world of women her eyes had been the eyes to strike a spark in him that had leaped into flame as he had held her close in his arms that first day in the barn.

She stopped playing and glanced from one face to the other of the men grouped about the piano.

"Is the hitch in our billion dollar industry making you all look so solemn?" She struck a few chords. "Together now!

> " 'Pack up your troubles in your old kit bag and
>   Smile, smile, smile.
>   While there's a lucifer to light your fag
>   Smile boys that's the style.
>   What's the use of worrying
>   It never was worth while, so
>   Pack up your troubles in your old kit bag and
>   Smile, smile, smile.' "

Armstrong joined in lustily; Si Puffer pounded out an accompaniment on the shining rosewood of the piano; David Schuyler carried the air in a baritone which caught at Gerard's throat. Jean's contribution was young and shrill, Prue's was a slightly husky contralto. With the crashing finale she rose.

"The concert is over. Jean, refill my cup, please. After leading that outburst of song I feel the need of refreshment."

As she returned to the slipper chair with her cup, her brother inquired:

"What sort of men do you need for the work in the woods, Rodney?"

"Husky lads. Jim will do the head work and Si and I will drive the crew," Gerald answered, as he picked up a plate from the mahogany stand. "Cake, Prue?"

"No, thank you."

"We need men who can swing an axe and cut as we direct," Armstrong elaborated.

"You said you were going to New York to look for them. I have been thinking—"

"If you have a suggestion, for Pete's sake, don't hold out on us, Dave!"

"It may not be worth the breath to state it, Rodney. I was wondering if some of the men at the Rescue Mission might not fit in. Not the panhandlers who drift in and out, but those whom I call my regulars. They're a rough lot, but there are about twenty of them who are devoted to me. If they have jobs they are mighty uncertain. If they came, I could keep them straight while they worked, I think, but where would they live? The villagers wouldn't take them in; I wouldn't ask it."

Gerard did a sum in lightning calculation. "They could live in the big cattle barn down by the pond. It hasn't been used for years. I'll have bunks built, wood stoves would heat it, and get a cook from New York to feed them."

"That expense would cut into your profits."

"Into mine only, not my partner's. I'll charge it up to showing Calloway where he gets off when he attempts to dictate to the lumber firm of Schuyler and Gerard. The more I think of your suggestion the more I'm for it, Dave. Whoops! I believe you've solved the problem! I'll pay any wages you say—providing, of course, my partner approves the plan."

Prudence shook her head. "The plan is all right, it's as good an idea as putting women into politics that they may attend to municipal housekeeping, but will it work any better than that did? Perhaps those men will incline their ears to the siren rustle of greenbacks—but—if said rustle spells w-o-r-k, I doubt it. You must make allowance for the fact that Dave believes that his boys like 'all God's children got wings' when they are exposed to right spiritual conditions."

Her brother's thin face was flushed, his fine eyes were alight with enthusiasm.

"You're wrong, Prue, they have more sporting spirit than you think. Most of them never have had a chance. I admit they are not the sort who can pull themselves up by their own bootstraps, but, give them a boost, and who knows but that a job, a few months in this grand country and a new deal would remake them? Suppose we set three or four permanently on their feet and incidentally get the timber out. Wouldn't that be worth while? What say, Gerard?"

"I think it's keen. Give me a letter to the head of

the Rescue Mission and I will go to New York tomorrow."

"I'll go with you."

"David!"

"Don't spike our plan, Prue, with fear for me. I must be sure that the boys understand the proposican. Remember Malone's Opportunity?

" 'They do me wrong who say I come no more,
        When once I knock and fail to find you in;
    For every day I stand outside your door.'

"I hear old Opportunity knocking. He is giving me a chance to help my boys. I'm going."

"But, Dave dear, Mr. Gerard can do it. He is a lawyer. He can appeal to them in his most impressive gentlemen-of-the-jury style. His eloquence might prevail when yours wouldn't."

Gerard ignored the tinge of sarcasm. "My eloquence wouldn't be a patch on your brother's, Prue. His idea of going himself is a winner. I'll take great care of him. We will fly down and back. I'll send Judkins along by train to make him comfortable in my rooms. I have a closed car in the city. I swear that his feet shan't touch the earth roughly once."

"Don't make an invalid of me. I'm through with that. What has to be done always can be done. I'm going."

"Of course, if that's the way you feel about it, Dave, who am I to stand in your way?"

"Glad you realize your unimportance, Prue." Her brother smiled at her.

Schuyler seemed like a different person, Gerard thought, as if he had shed an outworn garment of care and disillusion and heartbreak and had left it behind him forever. After all, there was nothing like an absorbing interest to make one vitally alive from head to feet. If anyone knew the truth of that, he did.

"Shall we go tomorrow, Rodney?" David Schuyler's voice had the eagerness of a boy's about to fare forth on an adventure.

"Yes. Armstrong will drive over for you, take you to the plane field, and—"

"Do you approve of this wild scheme, Jim?" Prudence demanded.

Armstrong looked down at her through his big lenses. "Sure I do. The idea is worth trying. I know Rod's expeditions. Your brother will have the time of his life and return all pepped up and ready to shoulder an axe himself."

"Perhaps you'll come and see us off?" Gerard's eyes were on Prudence. Jean caught his arm.

"You couldn't take me, could you, Uncle Rod? This house will seem aw-awful big without you." She swallowed hard.

"Let Jean come and stay with me."

"Oh, Uncle Rod, may I stay with Miss Prue while you're away? I'll be as good as gold."

"Do you really want her?" For the first time since she had entered the room Gerard felt that Prudence looked at him. "Just a moment, K.K. Do you really want her, Prue?"

"Of course I want her."

"Sure? If you are alone, it will be your chance to get in a lot of work at that bench of yours."

"My bench! I shan't look at my tools nor open my safe while Dave is away. I will paint and paper the living room. I have been dying to get at it."

"You would be. Heaven won't be heaven to you, Prue, unless you change the color of a celestial room or two," David Schuyler teased. "Better let Jean go, Rodney."

"Okay then. Come over and see off your brother, Prue, then Jim will drive you and Jean back to the red brick house."

"The car is in running order, sir," announced the melancholy Patch.

"Then we must go at once, Dave. Jane Mack will think we have been held up by that prisoner who escaped day before yesterday. That is her current cheery obsession. I wish you success, Mr. Gerard, but just wait till you see Terry McGowan and Shance

O'Shea. I prophesy that you will go slightly bearish on the proposition."

The hint of old-time friendliness in Prudence's voice set Gerard's heart racing.

"Prue, that's rank gratitude. Haven't all my boys bowed and scraped to you, and wouldn't they do anything—but keep sober—for me?" David demanded.

"Shure, an' 'twould be the devil of a shame if they didn't, Mr. Schuyler," Prudence retorted. "You will recognize that as a Shance O'Shea imitation when you see and hear that red-headed Irishman, Mr. Gerard. I tremble to think what the villagers will say when they see that colorful and hear that profane aggregation which you are planning to hurl into their unsuspecting midst."

"I guess if you an' Rod can stand for them, Dave, the rest of us can," encouraged Si Puffer, still leaning on the piano. "Most of us are all-fired sick of Calloway and his tootin'. He's gone kinder goofy with the idea of his own community, but the son—well, whatta mean is, I don't wonder that Milly Gooch—" His eyes met Gerard's. "Gorry-me, I guess I better get a move on and measure that cattle barn right off so's we can get those bunks in."

"Hold on, Si. What's the rush? Do it tomorrow."

"Rod, some day you'll realize that when folks get into the sixties an' have an important thing to do, they don't stop to pick daisies by the roadside, they get it done. Whatta mean is, they don't do no puttin' off till tomorrow."

"Right as usual, Si. Measure the barn, but don't let on why you are doing it or our plan will be a washout. Get me?"

"Sure. I've forgotten already what we was talkin' about. All I kin remember is that piana playin' of Miss Prue's. She's a wonder. I'd better get goin' or Mother'll think that Mack woman's escaped prisoner has got me."

As he left the room, Gerard turned to look at Prudence who was talking gaily with Jim Armstrong.

Something in the bend of his friend's head tightened a band around Rodney's heart. He picked up her coat.

"Hate to have you go—but if you must—"

She flashed an unfriendly glance at him before she slipped her arms into the sleeves. As Armstrong crossed the room to speak to David Schuyler, Rodney's hands tightened on her shoulders.

"Just a minute, girl. I know why you are flirting so outrageously with Jim, but has it occurred to you that what may be fun to you may prove a knockout for him?"

Prudence twisted free and asked with suspicious sweetness:

"Suppose I am not flirting?"

When Rodney returned from seeing off the Schuylers, Jim Armstrong, standing back to the slim tongues of scarlet and flame licking up chimney, remarked sombrely:

"Whoever let that girl's eyes loose on a defenseless world has a lot to answer for."

XIII

"Dark, isn't it? Pitch-black roads must be a State of Maine specialty," Prudence commented, as she bent forward to look through the windshield against which an occasional big snow flake splotched and melted. "You won't fly to New York tomorrow if this storm keeps up, David."

In his turn her brother peered at the road ahead.

"This won't last. Too early in the season. The clouds are breaking now. Of course we'll go. There are still railroads. Nothing but what the Hollywoodians call an 'Act of God' will stop us now, and I doubt if He blocks our plan. Isn't High Ledges an interesting house? It has an atmosphere of tradition, yet, judging by the architecture, it has been built forty odd years only. Did you get that impression of generations of ideas and ideals behind it?"

"Yes. Entering the great hall was like stepping into a different world, a world of soft-toned wood, of dusky portraits of men in high stocks and women in powder and brocades who had lived and labored in the new world when it was young. It spoke of world contacts. It fairly bulged with tradition. I felt like an immigrant once removed as I stood there."

"An immigrant! Ridiculous. Our background isn't what might be called grubby."

"Oh, I know you're a Cincinnati and I'm a Colonial Dame—but—the old red brick house is shabby even with that stunning Fortuny brocade doing its bit for the crack in the wall. That and Mother Puffer's immaculate cottage are the only other houses I have entered since I came to claim our inheritance."

"It is your own fault, Prue. You have shut your real self tight behind bars. You have snubbed the summer residents when they have tried to be friendly with you in the village. I can't bear to see you withdraw into yourself so. Go among the people here. Broaden your outlook by a broader understanding of them."

"I can't bear to meet people. I'm so sure that when they see me they are remembering—"

"Aren't you overrating your own importance? I am trying to put the past behind me. From now on I shall have no time for yesterday, I'm concerned with today and tomorrow."

"Dave, you're marvelous!" Prudence steadied her voice. "I'm all for your new program. Tomorrow! Tomorrow you will be winging to New York. Jean and I will hie us to the post office daily for letters. Send us an occasional postcard of the Lenox Library lion or the Empire State Building or the Bronx Zoo, will you?"

"We'll keep you informed as to progress. I'm glad you asked Jean to stay with you. That girl is growing a soul. It's an acute, painful process for a child who has grown up with a snooping, tattling complex added to a determination to outsmart, if she cannot escape, her mother's espionage. If only Mrs. Walter could be made to realize that the wings of her daughter's individuality have begun to sprout. It should be the business of a mother to subtly instill moral and spiritual lessons without stuffing them down a young throat."

"Curious that Jean has so little love for either of her parents. Usually a child adores one of them."

"Have you heard anything about her father which sounds lovable? As for her mother—"

"You don't like Mrs. Walter Gerard any better than I do, do you, David?"

"Perhaps I'm unfair. I met her once only. She is the type of know-it-all female who fires me with a desire to hurl something at her, preferably something that will squash. Know the urge?"

"To a quiver. It's wonderful to hear you laugh again."

"It is a sound to which you will get accustomed from now on. I told you that I had put my yesterdays behind me. When I opened my eyes this morning, it seemed as if I emerged from a smothering fog into light and life—full, vigorous, courageous life—with a renewed assurance of the indestructibility of the human soul. Through the corridors of my mind echoed the fragment of a verse I haven't thought of for years:

" 'Lengthening roads that wind through dust and heat to hilltops clear.' Hilltops clear! I awoke on one this morning."

"I knew you were better—but don't go too fast, Dave, darling. Don't think of going back to work for months."

"Not until spring, at the earliest. Perhaps I needed to be knocked down and out for a while. I haven't been much of a fighter, and you've got to fight to get anywhere in this world. If it hadn't been for your habit of plunging straight through the breakers, with or without a surf-board of encouragement, Prue, I wouldn't have made this come-back. You've done the trick."

"Don't forget Uncle Austin's legacy. It seems a miracle that it should have come just when we needed it."

"I have a firm belief in miracles. How is the book-keeping coming on?"

"It isn't coming, it's going. Since you started those double-entry books for me, I've lost my mind. Prosperity Farm has belied its name; from my figures it seems to be operating exclusively in the red."

"I'll keep the books."

"No, Dave. Not so long ago I boasted that I was a woman of affairs. I won't be stumped by an aggravating lot of figures if I am more artistic than mathematical."

A woman of affairs. With the words flashed the memory of the sunny morning when she had vaingloriously flung them at Rodney Gerard. With straight gazing eyes she looked into the dusk. The snow had stopped. A young moon, looking for all the world like a chaste sliver of a silver globe, moved serenely behind skittishly dissolving clouds. Faintly came the swish of the tide against the great golden-brown boulders, the distant moan of a buoy; the breeze shook out a tang born of shore-tossed kelp. A leafless oak was silhouetted stark and black against the crimson and orange afterglow. A woman of affairs! Those early days had been friendly days. Now the mere thought of Rodney Gerard was like the prick of a splinter in her finger, and the trouble was that the prick was incessant, she couldn't keep the man out of her mind. It was maddening; it was humiliating; it was outrageous.

"Far be it from me to attempt to pry into the secrets of a lady's mental processes, but why that impassioned 'Darn!'?" David Schuyler inquired lightly.

"Did I say it aloud? Perhaps I was thinking of Len Calloway and what a mess he can stir up for a totally disinterested person because he and Rodney Gerard want the same girl."

"Who is the totally disinterested party?"

"I am, of course."

"Um, I see. Here we are. Those lighted windows in the red brick look like brilliant eyes watching us. Nice old house."

"I love it. Always feel like patting it as I pass."

David Schuyler turned as he stepped from the car.

"It helps to hear you say that, Prue. You don't know how troubled I have been that for me you gave up your friends and work in the city to come into the country. If you had been discontented—"

Prudence laughed. "I discontented! Somebody once said, 'Tragedy is chic but discontent is dowdy.' Now, I ask you, can you think of me as being dowdy?"

"I can think of you only as being the best little sport on earth," her brother commended gruffly.

David wouldn't think her the best little sport on earth if he knew how tight and choky her throat was at the thought of his making the trip to the city. Suppose it were to undo all the good that life in the country had accomplished, Prudence asked herself the next morning, as, before breakfast, she ran down the stairs. She stopped in amazement as Rodney Gerard, David, and Jane Mack stepped from her shop.

"What in the world—have you changed your plans?" she demanded, and drew a quick sigh of relief. "What has happened? You three look—"

"Can't Rodney come to tell me of something extra to pack, Prue, without turning your eyes into huge interrogation points?" David Schuyler demanded with assumed indignation.

"Of course, but—"

"I'll be seeing you, Dave. Prue, be sure that he wears his warmest coat. Keep me posted, Miss Mack." With the last request Rodney Gerard closed the front door behind him.

Prudence looked from her brother's amused eyes to Jane Mack's flushed face.

"What are you to keep him posted about, Macky?"

Jane Mack drew herself erect.

"Mr. Gerard knows that I'm kind of anxious about that prisoner who's on the loose, an' with no man in the house—"

"Forget it!" David Schuyler interrupted. "Look over my bag and see if I have everything I need, will you, Prue? It's so long since I've traveled that I'm all excited."

Excitement over the trip was certainly doing David good, not harm. His eyes were brighter, his face less careworn, Prudence decided an hour later, as standing between Jim Armstrong and Jean she watched Rodney Gerard's plane take off from the landing field which had a double runway, east-west, north-south. The huge flying machine was a perfect materialization of her conception of a pre-historic darning needle as it lumbered along. Suddenly from a sluggish waddle it skimmed into speed—she could hear the rush of the wind against its mammoth mother-of-pearl wings— lifted buoyantly, climbed into a sky of cloudless blue. Barely breathing, she watched till the plane seemed hardly larger than a gull dipping and soaring above the bay.

"'The captains and the kings depart,'" she quoted theatrically. "Come on, Jean. Let's get back to the red brick house. I've planned to paper and paint the living room while Dave is away."

"Paint it yourself?"

"Of course, Jim. I'm a demon painter. If I have time I'll do a few pieces of furniture. You'll help, won't you, Jean?"

"Gee! I'm crazy about it!"

Jean slipped an arm in Prue's and one in Armstrong's as they crossed the field which bordered a pond. Reflections of leafless trees blurred as a breeze ruffled its gleaming surface. Its shores were like Persian rugs woven of dull reds and greens, browns and purples, its canopy a turquoise of exquisite, infinite blue. A long building stood out sharply in the clear air.

Even as Prudence photographed the beauty of the scene on a memory film, she told Armstrong that she liked his o.d. breeches and puttees much better than the ugly plus-fours men had been wearing; asked Jean if she was bringing her kitten to Prosperity Farm, assured her that Happy would treat the black guest like a host and a gentleman; made a date with the forester to tramp through The Hundreds to inspect her timber; commented upon the lure of ponds in general and this one in particular.

"What a place to skate!" she exclaimed in conclusion.

"It's a bear!" Jean agreed. "I came here on a Christmas when Grandmother Gerard gave a big party for a lot of Uncle Rod's friends. I was just a kid, but I remember it perfectly. Big fires on the shore, people skating and shouting and singing. Hot coffee and doughnuts in the blacksmith shop—see it squatting near the road? Perhaps Uncle Rod will have a skating party for us. Ask him, will you, Miss Prue?"

"That's the thought of the month, Jean, but we'll wait until the timber is cut before we ask for parties. Am I right, Jim?"

"Sure you're right. Let Rod get his feet on solid ground as to labor before you ask for festivities. You understand, K.K., don't you, that the object of your uncle's trip to New York is to be kept a deep, dark secret?"

Jean scowled. "Do you think I'll tell? Do you think I didn't know it was a secret when you and Uncle Rod stopped talking whenever I appeared? I'm not dumb if I'm not pretty."

"Who said you were not? Pretty—"

"Don't get off the slush about pretty is as pretty does, Miss Prue. I—well, for crying out loud!"

They had approached the front door of High Ledges. Patch, of the washed-out eyes, was placing bags in Gerard's roadster. Prue's eyes followed Jean's as the girl stopped short to stare at the man at the top of the steps.

He was of medium height and slimly built. He might be forty-five, though he looked thirty-five. His sleek black hair was gray at the temples; his eyebrows were not much heavier than his clipped dark mustache; the lips of his eyes drooped to hide half of the pupils behind them. High cheek bones added to the impression of enormous eyes. His lips were full and red. He wore, somewhat theatrically, a gray suit of excellent cut with sartorially perfect accessories and a carnation in the lapel of his coat. Jean sniffed.

"Wouldn't you know it! Wouldn't you know he'd appear just as I was getting ready to have some fun!" She looked at Prudence through tear-filled eyes. "In case you don't know, that's my father. He's not going to spoil my visit, he is not!"

"Of course he's not, K.K. Probably he is here to see your uncle, and when he finds that he has gone he will go too."

She had been right in the first part of her conjecture, Prudence discovered, when Walter Gerard had urbanely introduced himself. She noted the puffiness under his eyes, the unsteadiness of his hands. Evidently he had celebrated before he left town in the best Metropolitan tradition. She recognized his type. She had had one like him in the family.

The coolness of his greeting to Armstrong was exceeded only by that gentleman's response. Apparently unaware of her latent hostility, he tweaked his daughter's short hair, explained that he had come to see Rod on business, that when he discovered he had gone he had planned to follow him to the city.

"But now," he looked at Prudence and twisted one end of his slight mustache with brilliant-nailed fingers, "but now I realize that I'm in need of a week in the country. I'll camp here until Rod returns."

Armstrong touched Prue's arm. "Jump into the car. You were in a hurry to get home, weren't you?"

Prudence caught Jean's hand. "Your daughter is coming to stay with me, Mr. Gerard. The visit was planned before we knew you were coming. You won't need her here, will you?"

Jean brought her foot down on Prue's with a force which set stars skittering before her victim's eyes. Walter Gerard smiled.

"Of course, I shall miss my dear little girl, but I wouldn't deprive her of what I know will be a pleasure. Jump in, Jean, I can see that Mr. Armstrong is in a hurry." There was a malicious glint in his eyes as he stepped back from the roadster, an ironic note in his voice as he called:

"*Au revoir.* Don't feel badly about leaving me, Jean. I'll drop in to see you daily."

The car shot forward. After a mile or more of road had been covered, Prudence broke the silence.

"You are giving the best imitation of a thunderhead I ever have seen on a human face, Jim."

"Great Scott! How I detest that rot—" He broke off and concentrated on driving. Jean, snuggled between him and Prudence, sighed with content.

"Don't be afraid of hurting my feelings about my father, Mr. Jim. You couldn't say worse things than I think of him. Mother says he's the world's worst phil-philanderer. I looked the word up in the dictionary. I went all through the f i l s. I couldn't find it. What's a philanderer, Mr. Jim?"

"It's a—a—What's that noise in the rumble? Something scratching?"

Jean bounced in the seat. "It's my kitten. I told Patch to put him in his basket. I forgot him when I saw Father. What did you say philanderer meant?"

"Look Jean! Happy is here to meet us!" Prue exclaimed, as the roadster stopped at the entrance to the red brick house. As Jean flung her arms about the black and white dog, Armstrong, lifting a bag from the rumble, said in a low voice:

"If that f i l anderer annoys you by coming here, Prue, give me a ring. I'll see that he doesn't repeat."

"My word, Jim, don't scowl so. How can you stop his coming to see his 'dear little girl'?"

"Piffle! He's lost his job I'll bet a hat. Rod would lose his mind if he knew Walt was in the neighborhood."

"Then he mustn't know. Curious that he should appear just as Rodney left. I wonder—I wonder—"

She looked up at Armstrong's spectacled eyes without seeing them.

"Do you know, Jim, something tells me that Calloway pulled the wire that brought Walter Gerard to High Ledges."

XIV

As the week traveled forward, Prudence's suspicion that Walter Gerard and Calloway were in some underground fashion allied strengthened. Not that she had seen them together or that Jean's father in his daily visits ever mentioned the master lumberman.

Why did she think it, she asked herself, as perched on a stepladder she carefully wielded the brush in her white-gloved hand. She applied soft yellow paint to a window frame in the living room of the red brick house to the accompaniment of her thoughts. She called the hunch intuition; perhaps it was merely a fantastic product of an always overactive imagination.

Another splash of yellow on her blue smock. The one before had trickled from her suspended brush an hour ago when she had heard a plane flying over the house. For an instant she had thought that her brother and Gerard had returned from New York; then she realized that it could not be they, they wouldn't come without the men from the Rescue Mission—supposing that the men decided to accept the offer of work. She would look like a poster ad for a paint concern if she didn't keep her mind on the job. Lucky this was the last strip to be painted.

She glanced at the sample of wall paper on top of the sheet-shrouded desk. Perfect match. What a break that David should have gone away for a few days and given her this chance at the décor. He so hated to have a room upset even for a simple cleaning— having no vacuum, Macky did rather stir things up.

When he returned, he would feel as if he were step-ping into a room glowing with tempered sunlight. The hangings from the New York studio would com-plement the walls perfectly. Perhaps the paint was an extravagance—she had made a terrible dent in the five thousand dollar legacy already—but what did that matter? What did anything matter so long as David was getting back his health and strength and courage? She could always—

"Miss Prue! Miss Prue!" Jean, in a white apron over her green wool frock, followed her voice into the room. She waved a mixing spoon coated with dough. "Mr. Jim is here! Uncle Rod is coming tomorrow!"

"Tomorrow!" Gloved hand clutching the handle of the paint pail, Prudence perched on the top of the steps. "Tomorrow!" she repeated, as Armstrong en-tered carrying a long, white cardboard box. "Are they really coming tomorrow, Jim? Look at this room!"

He peered about in his short-sighted way. "It is upset, isn't it? Can't you get it straightened out before they come?"

"Straightened out! The paper isn't on."

"Who's going to hang it?"

"A man from the village."

"No hurry. You'll know why when you hear Rod's letter. That is, if you want to hear it. It came by plane—with this."

He held out the white box.

"For me?" Prudence looked at it without touching it.

"If your name is Prudence Schuyler. It is, isn't it? Take it. Come off those steps. Don't look at it as if you expected it concealed a bomb."

As Prudence set the box on the table, untied strings, and removed wrappings, Armstrong ex-plained:

"It came in Rod's plane. He sent the pilot with a letter and the box. The man was instructed to deliver both to me and take back an answer to the letter."

"Oh-o-o! How beautiful!"

Prudence clasped her hands in ecstasy as she looked down at the long-stemmed roses in the open box. Their crimson was rich and velvety, their fragrance exquisite, their foliage perfect and smooth and green.

"Templars!" she explained breathlessly. "Did you ever see such gorgeousness; their beauty sets the sir vibrating!" She lifted two of the lovely blossoms to her face.

"Rod certainly has said it with flowers this time," Armstrong observed gruffly.

"Said what?" Prudence demanded, and promptly wished she had not asked the question.

"Your innocence is good but not good enough, Prue. Want to hear this letter? I'm in a hurry."

"Of course I want to hear it. Jean, dear, take the roses to Jane Mack and ask her to put them in vases. Then come back," she added, as the child looked at her with wistful inquiry. "Come to the shop, Jim."

Armstrong followed Prudence into the room across the hall, a room filled with sunshine and the smell of potted plants in the bay window and of a wood fire scented with pine. As she perched on the stool in front of the tool-littered bench, he frowned at the open safe.

"Do you leave that unlocked? You need a guardian. It would be easy for someone to pick up those unset jewels you told me you owned."

"Who knows they are there?"

"Even the average intelligence—rated at twelve years, isn't it—might suspect that a safe held something of value. People don't cart them about the country because of their beauty. And—of course it's none of my business, but I think you should put those pearls you wear every day in a safety-deposit box in the city. I don't want to frighten you, but that escaped convict is still at large."

"He wouldn't dare come to a small town like this. One would think from your expression that this was the center of the crime belt." She touched the softly gleaming gems at her throat.

"It's swank to wear a string of pearls even with shorts and tailored shirts on the Lido, I hear, but that isn't why I wear mine. Contact with the skin increases their luster and they—they seem so much a part of my sister that I feel as if she were with me." She steadied her voice. "It may ease your mind to learn that you and David and Jean—and one other, I did tell Rodney Gerard—are the only persons who know I have those unset stones."

"Four! It's four too many. There's bound to be one broadcaster in the bunch. Keep the safe locked. Is Walt Gerard still putting on the devoted father act? He has, as I suspected, lost his job. Why is he hanging round this town? I don't like his eyes. They are furtive. I'll bet he is being hounded for money and is waiting to pounce on Rod and get it from him the minute he arrives."

With an engraving tool Prudence poked thoughtfully among a lot of tourmalines spread on a white paper. Shades of pink from true pink to salmon, greens in varying tints caught the light and blinked like colorful eyes.

"He is here on one pretext or another every day. He pretends that I am the lure—I've heard his obvious line before—but I know that I'm not. And it isn't a paternal urge which brings him, I'll wager my best bit of jade. What's his racket?"

"Racket! That's easy. You are here, aren't you?"

"Don't be foolish. I'm not hobbled by an inferiority complex, but imagining that every man I meet is in love with me is not one of my obsessions."

"Does he annoy you?"

"Don't roar. He annoys me by taking my time which I want to devote to work. I have several Christmas orders besides this necklace I'm making for Jean of these stones—and I haven't touched my tools since David left until this minute.

"Come in, K.K. Set the vase of roses on the bench where I can feast on their color."

"I left another vase just like this in the living room.

Jane Mack looked for a card, but there wasn't one, Miss Prue."

Prudence remembered Armstrong's "Rod has certainly said it with flowers." Why should his supposition send the color to her hair? Doubtless Rodney Gerard had sent every girl of his acquaintance flowers. She felt Armstrong's eyes on her, and reminded:

"Now, Jim, the letter."

For an instant there was no sound in the room but the tick of the clock, the dog's heavy breathing. Sunshine set a thousand little reddish lights glinting in Jean's dark hair as she crouched on a floor cushion; spotted the dog's back with golden coins as he dozed and blinked with his head in her lap; sent little discs of light dancing on wall and ceiling as it struck the lenses of the distance spectacles which Armstrong had pushed up on his forehead as he began to read.

" 'Dear Jim—

" 'Have waited before writing for something definite to report. Hate letter writing as you know, but don't dare wire or phone for fear Calloway will get on to our plan, so am sending this by plane. We had a quick trip down. Schuyler is none the worse for the activities of the last week—we've kept on the move—on the contrary, the interest and excitement have quite set him up.

" 'While he rested the first day, I dropped in on the lumber firms. They are still keen for our output; guess you've put them wise to the quality, haven't you?

" 'Enough about lumber. On to the Rescue Mission! When Schuyler and I arrived there, he received an ovation which set the radiator rattling in its lair. I've met individual down-and-outers, but never before have seen them *en masse*. There was a cold, hard rain outside and hot water heating doing its darndest inside. The place smelled to heaven of damp wood and unwashed humans. I confess that for a minute I flinched, but not David Schuyler. He was in their midst, beaming, encouraging, but never, apparently, condemning. As I watched him, I realized for the first time that although I had given money to help, I had given little of myself, and how smugly I had taken wealth for granted.' "

Armstrong pulled his spectacles down over his eyes and looked at Prudence.

"Rod isn't fair to himself. He was the best of his team, and he sold his string of polo ponies last year that he might give more to one of the charities in which his mother had been interested. I call that darn near giving himself."

He pushed the spectacles up on his forehead and squinted at the letter.

" 'The men quieted down after a while and David explained our plan. He made a swell job of it too. He told what he thought it would mean to them, what he knew it would mean to him if it could be pulled off. Then he called for volunteers to go back with us and stick—he was emphatic on sticking—until the timber was cut.

" 'About twenty-five lined up, and their expressions as they looked at David Schuyler tied my throat up in a hard knot. If anyone questions whether his work in the Mission has paid, that bunch is the answer.

" 'Send back word by the pilot if the accommodations are ready. Make it snappy. Dave and I will come by train with the—well, we can hardly call them a crew yet, gang is a better word. We don't dare let them out of our sight. If you write O.K. we'll arrive tomorrow afternoon. Have transportation at station for all. The two new trucks I ordered for hauling lumber will do. I want to get the men in storage as soon as possible. Dave will stay with me until they settle down."

Armstrong looked up. "With your brother staying at High Ledges, no need to rush the papering. Here's a message for you:

" 'Tell Prue, if you see her,—that "if" is my little joke—that her special boy friends, Terry McGowan and Shance O'Shea, are in our personally conducted party. Love to the Kurious Kid.

" 'Hope that Patch and his missis are giving you enough to eat. The cook we've hired for the bunkhouse looks like one of Wyeth's pirates. I'm sending the first lot of provisions from the city.

Yours,
Rod' "

Armstrong folded the letter. "The bunks in the cattle barn will be finished tonight; the wood stoves are in. The pilot left an hour ago with my letter telling Rod to come on with the gang. I'll be at the station with Puffer and the trucks to meet them. Calloway is too keen not to know of the work going on at High Ledges, he must suspect Rod's plan, but, just the same, I wish he might be providentially called out of town an hour or so before that train arrives."

Prudence shook her head. "Perhaps you'll think I have a four cylinder mind when it comes to experimenting—but—I'm afraid Rodney Gerard will be frightfully disappointed when he tries to make those men work."

"I'm not. Rod has—better say had—a lazy manner, but he has developed into a hard-hitting, daring business man. He's a dynamo when he gets his mind made up."

A picture flashed on the screen of Prue's mind: Rodney Gerard standing in the sunshine before the big barn; she could smell the scent of the hay, see his eyes deepen to indigo, hear his voice, low, controlled, declare:

"I'm not in that class you detest. I'll make you take back what you said about my being of that type. I'll make you! It will be a no-quarter battle. Get me?"

She had been on the verge of taking it back when Milly Gooch had—

"Why don't you like Uncle Rod, Miss Prue? Your voice prickles when you say his name." Jean's query came as a head-on collision and derailed Prue's train of thought. She accused gaily:

"There you go! Merry-pranks in your imagination again. Would Jean and I complicate matters, Jim, if from a discreet distance we watched the arrival of David and his followers?"

"Not if you keep out of sight. I'll drop in this evening to report. Take it easy Prue. Don't rush to finish that room."

"Gee, Mr. Jim, but this is our busy day! On top of everything else we've got to wash the cow's tails."

Armstrong halted on the threshold. "Wash what, Jean?"

"The cow's tails. We put peroxide and a little blueing in the water and scrub them. When they dry, the ends fluff like the cutey circus rider's skirts."

"Great Scott, Prue, where did you get that idea?"

"Look out, or you'll choke with laughter, Jim, and we can't spare you at this stage of the lumber game," Prue warned. "What is so funny about it? I got the idea from a friend who exhibits blooded stock."

"I'll bet that friend is a woman."

"She is. Now I'll bet one. A man wouldn't do it. Mr. Si almost gave notice when I asked him to."

"I can visualize his face when you suggested it. Next thing you'll be planting electric wires under the vegetable garden to warm the soil more quickly than the sun will. Well, as I said before, don't try to do too much. You might cut out the Beauty Shop act for those cows."

They heard him chuckling until the front door closed with a bang. Jean perched on the end of the bench and sniffed.

"Aren't men the limit!"

Prudence laid her face against the crimson beauty of the roses and drew a long breath of their fragrance. Lovely things! It wasn't their fault that a man whom she disliked and distrusted had sent them. Jim Armstrong didn't know that "saying it with flowers" was a habit with Rodney Gerard.

"What will you do first, Miss Prue?"

Jean's question brought Prue's attention back to the present. With long pincers she began to poke among the colorful tourmalines.

"As there is no need to hurry about getting the living room in order, I'll put in an hour at my bench. Change of work will rest me. I haven't even looked at my tools for days and days. We'll let the cows' grooming go until tomorrow. Bring me the stones from the safe, will you, Jean?"

"Goody, I love to look at them. May I spread them out?"

"Yes. You must know every one I own by this time. I get a thrill from their color myself. I'll clear this end of the bench. Spread them there."

"Miss Prue!" Jane Mack appeared in the doorway. She frowned at Jean, whose hands were full of white packets, as she entered the room.

"Miss Prue, the market man phoned. He wants eggs and wants them quick. He has a rush order, and he says, can you bring them right down to the village."

Prudence dropped the pincers and pulled off the painty smock. "Of course we can, Macky. Thank heaven, our egg production curve is on the up and up. Come on, Jean, we'll gather the eggs. Mr. Si is bossing the carpenters at the cattle barn. Put the packets of stones in the safe, will you, Macky? Don't lock it. Leave the tourmalines on the bench. I may have time to select the colors when I return. Being a farmer is thrilling, isn't it, Jean? Thrilling when one is selling eggs, not when one is paying grain bills," she amended practically.

It was somewhat difficult to make a domestic career and an artistic career jibe, Prudence decided an hour later in her shop, as again she slipped into her smock. She had brought the paper hanger from the village. David might decide to come to the red brick house instead of going to High Ledges, she had reasoned, and it would be better to have the living room in order. She picked up the pincers and commenced to experiment with the tourmalines on a pencilled design.

"This sketch isn't right. Bring my portfolio from the bookcase, will you, Jean?"

Jean, who was making life miserable for Happy stretched on the hearth rug, jumped up.

"All-righty."

Prudence poked and fitted. No combination of stones suited her. She called over her shoulder:

"Can't you find it? It ought to be on the bottom shelf."

"Where did you get this?"

"Get what?" Prudence turned. Jean was staring at the newspaper picture of Rodney Gerard and Milly Gooch.

"This. It's a picture of the same cutey circus rider I found in Uncle Rod's desk in the gun room at High Ledges. She'd written—I suppose she wrote them—some slushy words on the back. Stopped with just l o. Why didn't she finish it?"

A laugh, a hateful laugh, cut into her excited question. Jean stared at her father in the doorway; the clipping fluttered to his feet. He fingered the white carnation in the lapel of his blue serge coat as he glowered down at it.

"So you found a picture in your uncle's desk? Prying again, my darling daughter?" He mimicked his wife's tone. "What happened to the photograph with the word love unfinished?"

Jean gulped. Her eyes appealed to Prudence who put her arm about the thin shoulders.

"Answer your father, dear."

"I—I think Mr. Calloway took it."

"Calloway! Can't you talk without gulping? Calloway has it? Jean, there are times when I'm tempted to—" He took a step toward her. As his daughter crushed her face against Prue's shoulder, he laughed.

"Don't be afraid. For a minute I saw red. I hate that man Calloway like the devil. He doesn't love your Uncle Rodney, and with that picture in his possession he can make trouble for him." He paused that the implication might sink in, before he added: "Always have a brain storm when Len Calloway's name is mentioned."

His shifting eyes rested for an instant on the tourmalines shooting rays of color as the sunlight touched them. He whistled, a long low whistle.

"Where did those come from? Did a traveling jeweler drop from the everywhere?"

Prudence, relieved that his attention had been diverted from his daughter, held a green stone to the light.

"Nice color, isn't it? A State of Maine product."

He took the pincers from her hand and held up the stone. "Nice! It's a corker. Notice that hint of pink in the very middle of the green? Interesting work you're doing. Do you use precious stones as well? I did a little merchandising in those for a while."

Prudence nodded toward the safe. "Yes. In there I have a flawless emerald, a pigeon blood ruby, and a star sapphire with a number of diamonds. All of them, except the emerald, I bought at a bargain before the Schuyler income went down for the third time. I have more money tied up in gems than I can afford." Silly of her to confide her financial problems to Walter Gerard even to sidetrack his attention from his daughter.

"Do you keep the jewels in this house?"

"Why not?"

He laid the tourmaline back on the white paper. "Why not, is right. I forgot when I asked the question that for years the residents of this village haven't locked their doors at night. Have you heard when Rod is coming back? He doesn't know that I am at High Ledges, so he wouldn't be likely to phone me about his plans."

"I haven't heard from your brother nor from mine, except a postcard of the Metropolitan Museum with 'Feeling fine,' scrawled on it. As a letter writer David is a total loss."

Walter Gerard's eyes between their heavy lids were glints of sardonic amusement. "I suppose you have no idea what's being done to the old cattle barn?"

"Why not ask your brother? It is his property."

"I can wait for developments, and believe me, they'll come fast. Well, I'll get going." He glanced at the safe. "Better keep that locked. There is a convict on the loose, remember. Sure you don't want to go back to High Ledges with me, Jean?" he teased, before he turned on his heel and departed.

His daughter sighed her relief. "That's that. He didn't find out about Uncle Rod's plans from us, did he, Miss Prue?"

Farming might be thrilling, but it certainly took a lot of energy and strength when one was new at it, Prudence reflected, as late in the evening she flung herself on the couch in the firelighted living room. That wasn't fair, most of her energy this afternoon and evening had been devoted to getting the living room in order. She had helped hang paper; it wasn't her first try at it. Then she and Jane Mack had uncovered the furniture, laid the rugs, put up the Fortuny brocade and the batik of moonlit hill and ebony cedars, and hung Franklin at the Court of France.

A clock ponderously told the hour. Her glance lingered on the crimson roses straight and perfect in the tall silver vase as she counted. Eleven! She punched the pillows under her head into a more comfortable arrangement. She ought to go to bed, but she was too dead to the world to move. Eleven. What were her friends in the city doing at this hour? Just coming from theater or opera, probably. Going on to dance somewhere. The girls would be in exciting wraps and adorable high-heeled slippers, the black dress clothes of the men foils for their satin and cloth of gold frocks. Scent of gardenias. Taxi doors slamming—she adored a taxi. Masculine hands lingering as they drew fur collars about bare shoulders; masculine eyes disturbingly dark and demanding across small candlelighted tables; masculine heads bent to uplifted faces as two bodies, almost one, drifted and swayed to the smooth, mellow lure of horns, the singing of strings which set blood racing and pulses throbbing.

"Old stuff, old as the world, but it still clicks," she thought. It was a great life if one did not take it seriously. She wouldn't be the same when or if she went back to it. For her, living had taken on a new importance; she had revalued problems and experiences, had dug deep under the surface for the realities. Once she had expected life to hand her the crystal ball of Happiness. Now she would consider herself lucky if she found enough shining pieces as she went along to enable her to visualize the perfect sphere. Would her friends like her new self, or would they find her boring? Did they miss her? Was the man who had sworn he wouldn't live without her swearing that to another girl?

Happy licked her face. The vision of gayety, color, luxury, and love vanished. She laughed and pushed him away. He glanced casually at her before he sprang to the couch and wriggled down behind her.

"You know that you're bad and that I'm too far gone to discipline you," she reproached him. "This room smells painty. I ought to open a window, but I'm too lazy. Why can't you do it for me, Happy?"

She smoothed his satiny black ear and snuggled deeper into the pillows. She watched the scarlet and orange tongues of flame lick at the sooty chimney back and hiss as they licked. Her eyes flew to the red roses as if drawn by a magnet. Feeling as she did about Rodney Gerard—hadn't Jean's disclosure about Milly Gooch's photograph crystallized her suspicions into unshakable conviction—she should have thrown them away. Lovely things. It wasn't their fault that— was it the paint which made her eyelids so heavy? Perhaps—

"Miss Prue! Miss Prue!"

A scream or a nightmare? Prudence stumbled to her feet. She had been dozing.

"Miss Prue!"

The dog charged. Prudence dashed after him. What looked to be a mammoth stick of pink and white striped candy shot down the bannister. Jean and Prue reached the threshold of the workroom only one lap behind Happy. A wobbling flashlight clutched in her bony hand revealed wild-eyed Jane Mack robed in a long white nightgown, buttoned close to throat and wrists. Her gray pigtails registered each shake and shiver of her tall body. She was toothless.

"She's the stuff of which nightmares are made," Prudence thought, with an hysterical urge to giggle. Aloud she said:

"Light the lamp, Jean."

Jane Mack clutched her shoulder. "No! No! The convict might see and s-s-shoot. I know folks."

"Pull yourself together. Wait till I've drawn the hangings, Jean."

"Don't go near those windows, Miss Prue."

"Nonsense, Macky. All right, Jean. Light the lamp." Spooky shadows cast by the wavering flashlight skulked into corners as a soft glow suffused the room. It brought out the colors of the blossoms in the bay window, transformed the gaunt woman from a grotesque wraith to a living, breathing human, set little lights of laughter dancing in Jean's eyes, turned the silver bracelet on the sleeve of Prue's hyacinth blue frock to gold.

"That's better. The light will send your bad dream hustling, Macky."

Indignation stiffened Jane Mack.

"A dream? Look at the dog, Miss Prue. He knows someone's been here. He's whining round that window. Look! He's snuffling into the dining room! The man went that way." Her toothless gums quivered.

Prudence pushed her gently into a rocking-chair.

"Sit down and tell us what happened."

Jane Mack twisted her bony hands. Jean, in her candy-striped pajamas, put her arm about Prue's waist. The woman sniffed.

"You two girls think I've had a dream, don't you? Well, I haven't. I was just getting into bed—I thought

I heard a door creak down here." Her long-drawn breath was a cross between sob and shudder. "I thought you were in your room, Miss Prue, so I stole down quietly. I didn't want to scare you. I tip-t-toed to this door. A man was flashing a l-light over that!" She pointed a blanched finger toward the safe. "You'd left it unlocked.

"I knew in a minute 'twas the escaped prisoner I'd been expecting. I guess I gurgled. He pulled his hat lower over his eyes. Pointed his light straight at my face, so I couldn't see anything.

" 'Got you covered. Make a s-s-sound, woman, an' I'll s-s-shoot!' he hissed."

Prudence's eyes widened with incredulity. Could this vibrant, dramatic woman be the taciturn, dour spinster who cooked and scrubbed for her every day?

Jane Mack swallowed hard. "All I could think of was the money you had tied up in those jewels, Miss Prue, an' what 'twould mean if you lost them. What was this old body of mine good for, anyway? So I yelled."

"I'll say you yelled. Then what did the man do?" Jean demanded. "Did he shoot?"

"If he did, I didn't know it."

"Perhaps he sneaked in to look around because he was born here or his father died here; we haven't had one of those old-timers drop in on us for a week. Then when you surprised him—"

Jane Mack sniffed. With a return of her usual grim practicality, she reminded:

"Better look and see if the 'old-timer' got any of your jewels."

"Never mind the jewels, Macky. I deserve to lose them for forgetting to close the safe. Sure you are not hurt?"

"Sure, Miss Prue."

Jean was on her knees before the safe frantically examining the white packets when Prudence reached it. She looked up with frightened eyes.

"Gone!" she whispered.

"What's gone?"

"The emerald and diamonds!"

XV

"You ought to set the sheriff after that convict," Jane Mack insisted for the third time the next afternoon.

At the kitchen table Prudence was snipping the stems of the Templar roses before placing them in vases of fresh water. Outside big snowflakes were half-heartedly descending. Impulsively she put an arm about Jean's shoulders and hugged her as the child drew a long, hard breath. She knew what she was thinking, knew that she was remembering the look in her father's eyes as he had asked if the jewels were kept in the house. Of course, Walter Gerard had not stolen the gems, he wouldn't fall so low as that, but—

"I'll wait until Mr. David comes, Macky. He will be here so soon that we had better consult him before we enter complaint. If the State of Maine officials are any good, a few hours won't make much difference. Take the roses to the living room, will you, Jean; then get your coat. If we are to be on time for our errand, we ought to go."

"Well, of course, if you can afford to lose that emerald and the diamonds, Miss Prue, it's up to you. The town officers won't help you much. I know folks. If you'd seen what I saw in my teacup this morning —" With a sniff Jane Mack disappeared into the pantry.

Jean paused on the threshold with a vase of crimson roses in each hand.

"Isn't she the limit! She gets my goat when she turns on the water works."

"Just the same, you like Macky, Jean. She is pure gold. Remember what she did last night when the—

the burglar told her he would shoot if she made a sound?"

"Remember! I'll never forget her yell if I live to be as old as—as Mr. Si. He's the oldest person I know. She was just like a movie star on the screen. She was good. If we don't get a move on, we won't see that train come in. I'll be back before you can say 'mumbo-jumbo.'"

Was Jean sidetracking more reference to last night's thief?

"I wouldn't miss seeing the arrival of those men for untold gold," Prudence proclaimed dramatically. "Hurry!"

Snug in fur coats, red beret and green beret making brilliant spots of color in the gray day, Prudence backed the car out of the shed. Happy bounded and barked beside it, then squatted in lop-eared desolation at a stern command to go back.

They were too early for the train. In the village they indulged lavishly in ice-cream cones, and still the minutes lagged.

"Let's drive out the pond road a little way, Jean, we have loads of time. Want to take the wheel? It's a grand chance for you to practice driving."

They changed places. Prudence snuggled under the robe. It was getting cold. The snow, after hours of shilly-shallying, had settled into its stride. Mr. Si had prophesied an early winter. Was the last of November early?

Eyes on Jean's hands on the steering wheel, ears alert for the sound of an oncoming automobile, Prue's thoughts wandered. Why had Dave decided to stay at High Ledges? Perhaps he wanted to be nearer his shifty men—some of them were unreliable, though his faith in their potentialities was unshakable. It would make it awkward for her. Of course, she would want to see Dave daily; equally, of course, distrusting Rodney Gerard as she did, she couldn't go to High Ledges.

Rodney! She had wondered if Calloway had forged that letter about the cheque. After Jean's revelation about the photograph she had found in her uncle's desk, how could she doubt any more? Walter Gerard had been right, the unfinished word was love, of course. "Flitting from flower to flower"! Mrs. Walt had been right, too, her brother-in-law was unreliable. He was the type of man Julie had married.

She must put the Gerards out of her mind. They were becoming an obsession. Her own affairs needed all her attention. Who had stolen the jewels? The escaped convict? She did not believe it any more than she believed that Walter Gerard was the thief. Did Jean suspect her father? She would rather have lost any gems she owned than the emerald which had been her grandmother's. She wouldn't have her splashy ring now. Suppose she never could afford to set it for herself, she could have turned it into money. Money! Money! Always she was counting what things cost. Prosperity Farm must be made to pay for itself. Uncle Austin had been shrewd. Had he not been sure that it would, would he have invested his small fortune in it? She would do her best not to touch the cash which came from the sale of lumber—if there were a sale; she hadn't much faith in the sticking qualities of the men who were being imported to cut it.

"Here comes Mr. Calloway in that snappy red car of his."

Jean's excited whisper set Prue's pulses quickstepping. Calloway on his way to the village! How soon was the train due? She pushed back her glove. Maddening. She had forgotten her wrist watch. Jim Armstrong had said:

"I wish Calloway might be providentially called out of town an hour or so before that train arrives."

Evidently Providence was busy elsewhere. Could she stop him? Was Dave's friend Opportunity stirring outside her door? Had the thought that she might help been his knock? "Success" was in line with the pasture bars from which a path—now a mere shadow under the snow—led uphill to the southerly boundary of her property, The Hundreds. That gave her an idea. She would ask him to show her the trees he wanted to cut. She wouldn't go far into the woods. Suppose she did. The man was respectable. Much as the villagers evidently disliked him, they never questioned his morality. She would be perfectly safe. It would be adventure with a capital A to lead him off the scent, and she loved adventure. She gripped Jean's arm. With difficulty she kept her voice clear of the excitement which had begun to tingle through her veins.

"Stop a minute! Drive the car home, K.K. Don't go to the village. You haven't a license; anyway, you must not go. At the crossroads take the turn to the right; that will bring you to the back of the red brick house."

"What's the idea?"

"I'll ask Len Calloway to show me where he wants to cut. If he consents, I will keep him away from the village until the new gang is at High Ledges. I am taking a chance letting you drive this car back, but, if you keep your mind on it, I know you can do it."

"Of course I can do it. Haven't I driven every day since I've been with you? He's slowing up! Better pull yourself together or he'll suspect something. Your eyes are all spangles. He—"

"Good afternoon, Mr. Calloway." Prudence acknowledged the sweep of the dark-eyed man's ten-gallon hat with gay friendliness. "This is a clear case of thought transference. You must be a psychic, to appear at the moment I was wishing I could talk with you. I suppose seeing that path to the The Hundreds brought you to my mind. I hate quarreling with my neighbors, it's so—so tenement-housey. Can't we arbitrate? Perhaps when you have time you'll tramp over the land with me and show me what to cut—but I'm detaining you. Drive on, Jean."

"Just a minute!" Calloway's near-set eyes were triumphant. Their light sent little shivers tobogganing down Prue's spine. Had she set fuse to dynamite?

"What's the matter with now, Miss Schuyler? My

business at the village can wait. What say if we take that tramp now? This snow won't amount to much."

Prudence glanced at the leaden sky. Had the storm settled down to business? What did it matter if she waded in drifts to her knees if she could prevent Calloway from witnessing the arrival of the gang? She smiled the most radiant smile in her not limited repertoire.

"I'm all for it, if you are, Mr. Calloway. I'm the original 'Do-it-now' girl."

Lucky she had put on her stout boots. She slipped out of her fur coat and flung it to the seat of the car. Her green corduroy frock and matching cardigan would be warm enough for tramping. She looked intently at Jean.

"Wait here, won't you, K.K. I—"

"Don't have the kid wait. I'll take you home, Miss Schuyler."

"That would help. Drive very carefully, Jean, and straight home, remember. Tell Miss Mack that Mr. Calloway is personally conducting me over The Hundreds. Go out to the barn and tell Mr. Si. He and I were planning to set an incubator this afternoon, but that can wait." Having posted two sentinels on the ramparts of protection, she stepped over the bars that Calloway lowered.

Part way along the path she turned to watch her car. Its driver was obeying orders, it was creeping along. She stoutly disciplined a qualm of doubt. Why worry? Jean was capable of managing the wheel.

Why didn't the man speak? He was leading the way along the snowy path. Woods stretched endlessly ahead, dense, dark, dismal. She didn't for an instant doubt Calloway's respectability, but she had a shivery sense of repressed fury smoldering under his urbanity. She wasn't crazy about this decoy act. Silly! Hadn't she boasted to herself that she was keen for adventure? If there was no risk of the plan not turning out quite as she expected, it wasn't adventure, was it? Getting out that timber was as much for her interest as for Rodney Gerard's.

Pines nodded stately tips in the spicy-scented breeze which lightly tossed snow flakes at her face. A spot of color flamed on the edge of the woods. A fox! It stood motionless for an instant before it flashed away, a red streak, into the silence of the forest.

"Here we are!" Calloway stopped to brush the snow from the top of a granite boulder. "See that B cut in the stone? It marks the southeastern corner of the tract your uncle purchased from my father. The trees round here are all virgin growth. My old man must have been wheely to have sold without consulting me."

His tone was maddening. With difficulty Prudence bit off an angry retort. Her reactions must wait. He must be kept from the village.

"Here's a trail. The snow hasn't got into the woods yet. We'll go in a little way so that you can see the quality of the timber."

"All sweetness and light again, aren't you?" Prudence mentally addressed his straight back as she followed him. He paused and turned. If his eyes were not so close-set, he would be extraordinarily goodlooking, she admitted.

"Sorry to have made trouble for you about your timber, Miss Schuyler, but when I say I'll put a thing through, I do it, no matter what the consequences may be to anyone else."

Prudence looked up at him. Wistfulness was entirely out of her line, but she did her best with voice and eyes.

"Suppose—suppose—is it too late to change my mind and let you—"

The shrill whistle of a locomotive shattered the silence; it bounded from tree-top to tree-top, grew fainter and fainter, till the last echo was cradled in the green heart of the forest.

The train had arrived! In a moment or two the gang would be on its way to High Ledges, and Calloway was here! Prudence lowered her lids. She felt as if her eyes were twinkling stars of triumph.

"What were we saying, Mr. Calloway, when that

ear-splitting whistle blew? I remember. Suppose I
agreed to let you cut my timber, would you still try to
stop Rodney Gerard?"

Calloway, who had started on again, turned.
Prudence stopped so as better to preserve the distance between them. His massive figure blocked the
trail where it divided and ran east and west. The sky
was but a glimmer above his head, and a leaden
glimmer at that. The snow had not penetrated the
forest. As far as Prudence could see, pine needles and
fallen leaves made a soft carpet beneath the trees.

"Do you mean that you'll chuck Rod Gerard and
give me the contract to cut? Do you mean that?"

His eyes burned red as he hurled the question.
Perhaps it was the shadow of his theatrical hat that
gave the effect. Whatever the cause, she didn't like it,
Prudence told herself. She would back track as soon
as she was sure the men were well away from the
village.

"Can't a girl change her mind?"

Calloway's eyes flamed. He caught her shoulder.
She shook off his hand.

"Don't!"

"Sorry. I didn't mean any harm, Miss Schuyler. Say
listen, I'm a just man, but I don't stop at anything, get
me, anything when I've been double-crossed. I'll pay
Rodney Gerard for interfering in my affairs—it goes
back long before he thought of cutting timber—if I
never do anything else in my life, but I don't want a
fight with you. Marry me, and I'll cut your logs, sell
them, and turn the money over to you. You can have
your own bank account."

"Oh, c-can I!"

Prudence hoped that amazement had not set her
mouth ajar permanently.

"You don't r-really mean it? Your romantic attack of
the subject thrills me."

She must not chuckle like that, and she had better
cut out sarcasm, she warned herself. How long since
the whistle had blown? She hated the eyes looking
down at her. He was coming nearer. Perhaps he was a

little mad. Violent-tempered people sometimes ended
that way. Should she turn back and dash across the
field to the pond road? No. Rodney might decide to
pass that way with the men, and her plan for getting
Calloway out of the picture would amount to nothing.
She would make a break into the woods. The divided
trail must lead somewhere, the blazes on the trees
were old, but it was well worn. Of course, Calloway
would follow, and somehow she would elude him.
She couldn't get lost. If she ran downhill, eventually
she would come to the shore.

"Well?"

"Really, Mr.—Len—you've surprised me so that
I'm all jittery."

Her laugh made no dent in his glowering regard.

"I'm not in the habit of snapping up an offer of a
heart and hand. You must allow me time to think."
She pushed back the sleeve of her cardigan. "My
word! Have I dropped my wrist watch? I felt something crackle under my foot as we entered the trail at
the B rock. I must go back. David gave it to me and I
wouldn't lose it for all the timber in the world. Please
help me hunt for it. Let's get out of these woods,
quick. I—I've never had a proposal before in such
gloom. I don't like it. It isn't lucky."

Her suggestion roused opposition as she had hoped
it would.

"We're going on. Looking the layout over was your
idea. Don't be a quitter. You've got to check up on
this timber sometime. I've got you here; you'll stay.
I'll go back for the watch. I can find it quicker alone.
Two of us double the chance of its being stepped on
and buried. Wait here."

Taking compliance for granted, he stalked back. As
he disappeared around a bend, Prudence darted
along the trail which turned sharply east. Silence.
Cathedral-like silence. The deeply green forest
stretched ahead like an illimitable isolation.

A big brown rabbit broke from cover and scurried
ahead of her. A squirrel left a pine cone he had been
shredding and ran up a tree. A crash! Her heart and

feet stopped. What were those great animals looking at her? A moose! Two! Did one say two moose or two mooses? She wasn't frightened, but she wasn't crazy about meeting those huge creatures who looked like an able bodied nightmare. Had she better climb a tree—always supposing that she could? They were going. Apparently she hadn't given them even a thrill.

She went on cautiously looking for the blaze on trees. No sign of human occupation. The character of the woods had changed. Thanks to Jim Armstrong's tutelage, she recognized red spruce, hemlock, birch, and giant oak. The air was spicy with the scent of balsam. There was underbrush now, a profusion of it. She vaulted the moss-green trunk of a fallen tree. A cock partridge stepped daintily into the trail, shook his mottled plumage, bobbed his head, ruffed the blue-black feathers on his neck, spread his tail into a fan, caught sight of the girl, and zoomed away.

She stopped to listen. Was Calloway following? Did he think her a quitter? She wasn't. She was, to use a favorite legal term of David's, merely "in the exercise of due care," while she diverted his attention from the village.

The trees thinned. What was that sound? A brook! She couldn't be far from home if it was the stream which crossed her lower meadow. She stumbled and breasted her way through a prickly jungle of shrubs which caught at her cardigan and pulled out green threads. She climbed a high bank, drew a long, ragged breath of relief. No danger of being lost now. She had her bearings.

Smooth, shimmering, shallow, the stream slipped seaward. She could see sombre green pools under tree roots, white eddies circling mossy rocks, dark currents chuckling through reeds, scraps of pebbly beach, faint rims of ice; could smell the scent of forest and decaying leaves; could hear mysterious rustles, the tinkle and splash and purl of water, the raucous caw of a crow as it winged high across the leaden sky.

"Hulloa! Hul-lo—o!"

Calloway shouting. A thin gray fog of doubt dimmed her satisfaction in the success of her role of Providence. Perhaps her idea hadn't been such a knockout after all. She had better get home. The trail on the other side, a little way down stream, looked familiar. She would wade to that.

Zowie, the water was icy! A brook was cold enough in summer. She should have known better than to try it at this time of year. Now that she was in, she would endure it as long as she could. That wouldn't be long. Her feet were numb already. She slipped on slimy, concealed rocks, splashed through pebbly shallows, plunged into a green pool.

"I'll bet I gave the trout the thrill of their lives," she said aloud as she pulled herself up by shrubs to the bank. A fresh blaze! She had seen Jim Armstrong slash it. She was on the home trail now! Better rest for a moment.

"Hullo—o—o!"

The call set her nerves vibrating. It didn't frighten her, but she didn't like it. It was too near. The woods seemed to be closing in on her. She hated the feeling. She couldn't be mistaken about this trail. She was sure that she had been on it before. She must get into the open. She was freezing.

She ran as swiftly as clutching bushes and treacherous tree roots permitted. Her cold, wet skirts lashed her knees; her teeth chattered; the silk blouse under the cardigan clung to her body like icy new-skin. Her breath pumped. How long could she keep this pace? Darn! What fiend had looped that root across the trail? She picked herself up. Ooch! What a lump! Lucky she had struck in the middle of her forehead, not under her eye—that is, if there were anything lucky about a fall like that. Bleeding? Wouldn't you know it!

What was that? Was she just seeing things, or was it—it was a log cabin! She had been following the freshly blazed trail to her cabin instead of one to the clearing! What difference did it make? There was a chimney. She could get warm.

She stumbled toward it. Suppose it were locked? It couldn't be. She threw herself against the door. It opened! The breaks were with her! She plunged in. Lost her balance. Someone caught her.

She stared unbelievingly. Closed her eyes. Opened them. She was awake. Every hard-drawn breath had been wasted; every step she had run, every fall had been futile. Calloway's furious, triumphant eyes blazed down at her.

XVI

Sudden, uncontrollable panic shook Prudence. In the tense silence she stared up into Calloway's inscrutable face. The light from a pile of burning brush in the rough stone fireplace streaked it with sinister shadows. She shivered. How could he have gotten here ahead of her?

"Thought you'd double-cross me, didn't you? There are several trails to this cabin."

At his harsh voice her mind and courage sprang to arms.

"My cabin, isn't it? I had no idea it was so—so luxurious."

She forced her eyes to move slowly, as if appraisingly, from the antlers over the fireplace to the water bucket on the bench by the door, on to the wood pile near the hearth with an axe leaning against it. That axe—she looked away quickly. Calloway must not suspect that it had seemed like meeting an unexpected friend.

"Rather nice. I came here the other day with Jim Armstrong, but we didn't come in. What huge logs in the walls! An artist in stone must have built that chimney. Does the opening lead into a lean-to?"

She was talking against time. Surely Jean must

have reached the red brick house by this time. Must have told someone where she was.

"Better sit down," Calloway suggested with sickening suavity. He pushed forward a wooden chair.

"Thank you. I prefer to stand here." Prudence caught hold of the great shelf of rock, which served as a mantel, with a grip which turned her nails white. She wasn't quite so cold and shivery near the fire.

"Suit yourself. When you beat it, I figured that any path you'd take would lead here. I took a short cut and started the fire. There were red coals; someone's been using the place. You'd better keep it locked—after this. Sorry I can't provide a lamp. It's getting dark outside."

If Prudence had distrusted the man back on the trail, she hated him now, hated his mocking smile to which the flickering light gave a Satanic twist. She took a step forward.

"Then we had better start home at once. I'm wet and c-cold." She shut her teeth hard into her lips to steady them.

For a man so massive Calloway had a pantherlike agility. In one move he was between her and the door.

"Hold on! Why the rush? You've been fooling me, haven't you? Been trying to make me believe that I was to cut your timber, while all the time you had your tongue in your cheek. What's the game? I was ready to play fair. I've no quarrel with you. I'm a just man. But you've tricked me. Now you'll pay for it. I'll keep you here till you sign a contract for me to cut for you."

His cool, restrained ferocity stopped Prue's heart for an instant. She seated herself in the one chair, carefully spread her skirts to the blaze, and looked at him.

"You have an instinct for the dramatic, haven't you? But somehow it doesn't quite come off. You think you will keep me here, you mean. Wake up! You are in the twentieth century. You have forgotten that three persons already know with whom I came into the

woods. I'll tell you my game, as you call it. Rodney
Gerard is bringing in a crew. I preferred that you
shouldn't see them arrive. And you didn't. Easy,
wasn't it? If you, who are doing everything in your
power to frustrate our legitimate plans to cut timber,
call yourself a just man again, I shall scream with
laughter. That's what I think of you. If I were alone
in this lumber project, I would have you jailed for
conspiracy to restrict business."

There was something technically wrong in the
wording of that last threat, Prudence suspected, but
it would serve. Her eyes felt like huge sun lamps going strong, her wet hair curled close about her neck,
a steel clapper struck out the beat of her heart. The
smoky, resinous silence throbbed with the fury held
in leash by the man glaring at her. He seized her
shoulders. With all her strength she shook off his
hands and retreated to the fireplace.

"Don't touch me again! Don't dare!"

The words shivered into a whisper. The icy cold of
the brook was stealing through her bones. Calloway
folded his arms and scowled.

"He is a little mad," she thought, as she had thought
once before.

"Dare! That's a joke. Who can stop me? Your foxy
partner is busy with his gang, isn't he? I take off my
hat to you, you put your fake friendliness across. 'Hate
quarreling with your neighbors, it's so tenement-
housey.' I believed you. I asked you to marry me!
You've been laughing at me! Now it's my turn. You're
here and here you stay. You needn't shiver. You are
safe enough. I'm no bum, I'm not a lady-snatcher like
Rod Gerard. I'm a just man! Say, what's about that
to make you giggle? I am a just man. I'm entitled to be
boss of this county and no one's going to block me. Get
that. I won't stand for interference."

Prudence forgot her predicament for an instant as
she regarded Calloway incredulously. The man was
molding his life to an obsession.

"Why are you staring at me? Don't you understand?
I won't be sidetracked. I'll begin by showing you that

I'm boss. You'll spend the night here, and then I guess—"

"Say lissen! You've got another guess comin', Buddy."

A man swayed in the entrance of the lean-to. His hunted eyes, set in dark rings, glared from his cadaverous face, as vicious a face as ever scowled behind bars. His sleazy coat and trousers were a mass of wrinkles, his torn blue shirt was fastened at the throat with a safety pin. From clawlike fingers a revolver dangled.

Prudence pressed her hand hard against her lips to keep back a cry. The convict? Perhaps he had taken the emerald and diamonds last night. Perhaps she had been horribly unjust to Walter Gerard. Calloway sprang for him. He leveled the gun. It clicked.

"Hands up! Lay off! Get me? If either you or the jane yip, I'll put a bullet through each of you, an' I wouldn't stop to choose which first, either. I ain't like you, you big noise. I am a bum."

He watched Calloway's retreat through half-closed lids. The glint between them was murderous. Prudence said as flippantly as if her heart were not shaking her body with its clamor:

"This is getting to be one of those parties, isn't it?"

"Say, you're a cool one, sister. I guess you can have the cabin after all, Buddy. There'll be folks here after this skirt you kidnapped."

"I haven't kid—"

"Keep your mouth shut! Sit down!"

Calloway sat with a suddenness which rocked the chair. The man in possession of the revolver scowled at Prudence.

"Here you! Scatter that fire! Quick! Think I want the whole pack after you following that smoke? That'll do. Drop the stick! Stand up by the chimney! Gimme those pearls!"

One instant of paralyzing fright, and then an inner strength sprang to Prue's rescue. Perhaps it was courage, perhaps it was an instinctive grip on spiritual values—which in her bitterness of late she had ignored—perhaps she needed this experience to jerk her back to a realization of her self-absorption.

"Pearls!" Her laugh was a masterpiece of its kind. "Pearls! I didn't realize that my wax beads could fool anybody."

The man edged nearer. His revolver covered Calloway, whose eyes looked like those of a trapped fox.

"Wax beads! Oh, yeah? Think I don't know the real thing when I see it? What do you s'pose I was doin' a stretch—Get going, sister. Take 'em off, quick, or I'll do it, an' I won't be too easy, neither. Lissen, get a move on!"

Was this a nightmare, Prudence wondered, as her unsteady hand fumbled with the diamond and platinum clasp at the back of her neck. It must be. What had seemed an amusing plan to divert Len Calloway couldn't develop into a possible tragedy, could it? She closed her eyes. Opened them. Apparently it could. She was awake. The fitful light from the scattered brush set gaunt hollows in the tense face of the man watching her with greedy eyes, deepened Calloway's angry color, set eerie shadows skulking in the dim corners of the cabin. The fire crumbled to bright coals. An insect hissed in the moss chinking.

The man grabbed the pearls from her fingers, weighed them in his left hand. His leer was horrible.

"Wax beads! Oh, yeah! I guess they'll get me three squares a day for a year or two. You'd cash in on 'em for about ten grand, wouldn't you, even in these rotten times? I'll bet you pay for fifteen thousand bucks insurance on 'em, don't you?"

Prue's mouth went suddenly dry. She had let the insurance lapse because she couldn't afford it. She had taken a chance on nothing happening to the necklace. Was that a faint call? She caught her throat to stifle an exclamation. The man with the revolver stiffened. He thrust the pearls into his dirty shirt. His eyes went dead. No expression in them, they were opaque dots in a face gone gray.

"Lissen, you two. Someone's coming. I'm gettin' out.

I'll keep this gat trained on you. If either of you tip 'em off I've been here, I'll shoot you on the trail. I'll know."

He backed to the door. With a quick swoop, Prudence flung brush on the coals. Smoke would give a clue to the rescuers. It caught fire and roared up chimney.

"Why you—" Dazed by her daring, the fugitive hesitated. In that instant Calloway sprang and caught him about the shoulders. The revolver clattered to the floor. Prue seized it.

"Don't waste your strength, Calloway." Why couldn't she keep her voice steady? "I've got him covered. I'm not a crack shot, but I think I can drop him at this distance."

Calloway turned and took a step forward.

"Stay where you are! Hands up! Both of you! If you move, the next s-scene in this screen thriller will be cut by the censor."

Maddening that her voice should catch in the middle of her threat. Was someone pounding, or was it the beating of her heart which shook the smoky air? Gun in hand, one hand clutching the back of the chair, Prudence covered the two men. She disciplined a wild impulse to shout with laughter. Calloway's face! His mouth hung open as if surprise had permanently dislocated his jaw. The other—she shivered— never had she seen such eyes. Trapped. Desperate. Murderous. She had not known that anything human could look like that. David had known, though. Dave! Where was he? If only—

The cabin door! Opening! Slowly! Soundlessly! Something sinister in its caution. Had the escaped convict a pal? Her blood chilled. Who had come?

"Give me that gun!"

Rodney Gerard had the revolver in his hand before Prudence realized who had dashed into the cabin. With a relieved sigh Calloway dropped his hands.

"Put 'em up again!"

"Don't be a darn fool, Gerard. I—"

"Put 'em up! There's blood on your forehead, Prue. Who hurt you?"

Prue's brain felt curiously light. Her voice seemed to trickle from a great empty space behind her eyes.

"Hurt me! No one. Believe it or not, I was about to add a colorful fact to the State of Maine war against crime, when you crashed in. They're an intriguing pair, aren't they? Reading from left to right, you have first a pearl thief, then a—just man—such a just man!"

"Steady, Prue. Don't shiver like that. I'll get your pearls."

"While you're getting those, you might make that man return the jewels he stole from my safe last night."

"Lissen, what does the jane mean, jewels? Do you think if I had anything I could turn into money I'd be hangin' round here? Say, she's crazy."

Was the man acting amazement, or hadn't he taken the emerald?

"Crazy or not, you'll come along with us. Get going!" Gerard gave the revolver a suggestive hitch. "Follow him, Calloway. Keep your hands up, both of you. Prue, come on."

She nodded. Her teeth chattered uncontrollably when she tried to speak. Nervousness or cold? Whichever it was the result was the same. Len Calloway looked as if he were burning up, his face had a purplish tinge. He spoke between clenched teeth.

"I'll get going all right. But watch out, Gerard. I'm not through with you. Miss Schuyler's all for you, isn't she? Have you told her that you've been paying Milly Gooch's bills? Have you—Hi—there—you!"

He lunged for the man in front. Caught him about the waist. Fumbling for holds, the two strained and panted. The fugitive was smaller, but fear of a return to prison gave him superhuman strength. He twisted and twined about Calloway's legs until both went down with a crash. With the agility of a cat and the cry of an enraged animal, the victor was on his feet, whirled, and grabbed the gun from Gerard's hand.

Crouching, he backed toward the fireplace. His eyes were flames. He aimed the revolver steadily.

"Beat it, you two guys—and beat it quick! I'll keep the pearls—and the girl."

XVII

Prudence retreated to the wood pile. She had thought her mind geared to surprises, but this quick turn stopped her heart. Jerk, clang! Jerk, clang! It went on again tripping up her breath with every beat. Could she ever tear her eyes from the man backing toward her? How many hours had she been watching him? Suspense and inaction. Nerve-racking twins. Couldn't she move? Couldn't she do something to help? Would she be left alone with this vicious creature? Calloway was already backing toward the door. It was getting dark outside. Suppose she made a dash for it? Would Rodney Gerard leave her?

She brushed her hand across her eyes. Was she seeing things, or had he produced a cigarette? He smiled across the flame of the lighter. That smile was a challenge to her. Neither he nor Calloway could help. It was up to her. What could she do? There must be something. She had been thinking only with the roof of her mind. Couldn't she dig into the depths and drag up some idea which would help?

She couldn't back away further; the wood pile was like a wall behind her. Hadn't David said that nine times out of ten when one was backed against an insurmountable wall, a gate would open behind if you put up the fight of your life? Dave knew. Dave never surrendered. He fought. Perhaps there was a gate in this wall—perhaps. A gate! She brought her teeth down on her lip to bite off an exclamation. Had she found the gate? Cautiously, breathlessly, she groped behind her.

The convict's clawlike fingers tightened on the revolver. He scowled hideously at Gerard. "Hey, you! Cut out that cig. stuff! Beat it, or I'll fire and—"

With all her force Prudence brought the dull side of the axe down on his arm. His sentence shattered into purple profanity. His gun clattered to the floor. Gerard seized it, thrust it against his back as he whirled on Prue.

"Hey! Cut that out!"

"Beat it, or I'll fire!" Gerard's words, if not his voice, were a perfect imitation as he prodded the cursing, shambling man toward the door.

Calloway thundered: "You're not letting him get away, Rod? Don't you know he's the escaped prisoner they're hunting ?"

"He won't make his get-away with you at his heels. It's your job to deliver him to the sheriff after you've frisked Miss Schuyler's pearls off him. Get busy, Len."

How could Rodney be so cool, so smiling, Prudence wondered frantically.

"He don't need get busy. Here they are." The captive pulled the lovely, lustrous string from under his ragged, dirty shirt. Prudence snatched it from the floor and clutched it tight against her breast.

"Come across with those jewels!" Gerard poked a reminder.

"Lissen, don't get fresh with the gat. I've coughed up the pearls, ain't I—an' I don't know nothin' about no jewels."

"Let him go! Let him go! I don't care about the jewels. Please let him go." The break in Prue's voice maddened her.

The muscles of Gerard's jaw tightened.

"On your way!" He held out the revolver. "Take it, Len. Don't let this bird stop till you have him safe behind bars."

Calloway gripped the gun. He said through clenched teeth:

"You're taking chances. How do you know I won't shoot you?"

Rodney Gerard regarded him through narrowed lids and smiled.

"Because you're such a just man, Len. Drop that axe, Prue, you won't need it again."

"Get going!" Calloway's fury was partially expended in the jab he gave the man at the other end of the revolver.

The door swung on its hinges. Through the opening came the crackling of twigs under stumbling, heavy feet, rough voices. The sounds dwindled into forest silence. The note of a bird, hauntingly sweet, broke the tension inside the cabin.

"Is it s-safe to go now?" With unsteady fingers Prue tried to clasp the pearls about her throat.

"In just a minute. Let me do that. Bend your head, Gorgeous."

The husk in Gerard's voice, his fingers against the back of her neck set Prue shivering again.

"What's the matter?" He looked down at her skirt. "Your clothes are soaked. Your lips are blue. How did you get so wet? That's a mean bruise. What happened?"

"Lost my way. Fell into the b-brook."

He pulled off his coat. "Put your arms in. Don't argue. Do as you're told. It's not a perfect thirty-six, but it will help keep you warm."

He buttoned the coat. "No wonder you won't look at me. What put the fool idea of that sight-seeing excursion into your head?"

"Dave's old pal Opportunity. He was waiting outside my door."

"Are you feverish, darling?"

He put his hand to her cheek as he asked the anxious question. She moved her head quickly.

"No! No! I'm quoting. I am foolish with relief, that's all. How did you know where I was?"

"Jean got anxious about you. Turned back and met us. I sent her home with Dave and Jim and took your car. That child has a brain. She knew you shouldn't have gone with Calloway. Why, why did you do it?"

"Jim wished he could be out of the way when the

g-gang arrived. I tried to help, and now you c-crab—"

"I'm not crabbing. Don't you know that I almost lost my mind when Jean told me where you had gone? Don't you know that I went through hell getting to you? Don't you know that it's torture for me to see you shiver and have my hands tied by that infernal promise I made? If I were to touch you—"

The caressing break in his voice, the faint tremor of his lips sent the blood burning to Prue's hair.

"Oh, come on! Let's get out of here!" He pulled a flashlight from his coat pocket.

"Let's. Hurry! Hurry! I'm frozen!"

"Go on."

He followed as she entered the trail. Every swish of her wet skirts about her knees sent a million little icy shivers coasting along her veins. How dark the woods were! She couldn't distinguish now between the rusty-red oak leaves and the shadows which were evergreens.

A crash! Underbrush! The convict? Calloway? Were they following?

"Listen!"

"Go on, Prue. They won't follow, if that's what you fear." Gerard faced her down the trail. The hand that touched her was like ice. Contrition swept her.

"You're freezing! Take your coat. I don't need it, r-really I don't."

"Stop talking. Go on! If you don't, I will carry you, and you are not a fairy, girl."

He was cold, but of course he wouldn't acknowledge it. Had he heard what Calloway had said about Milly and money—Ooch, how cold her legs and feet were—like sticks of ice! There! She had put the right one forward. Now the left—right—left—right—Had Rodney paid the circus girl's bills? Left—right. "Keep on feet!"—left—right—march time—the words were like a merry-go-round. She couldn't stop them. The clearing at last. Copper-red light on the trees. A fire? No, the sunset! A sky of rainbow splendor. The color warmed her, all except her feet. Right—left— they had frozen—

Someone caught her as she stumbled. Someone picked her up in his arms.

"How warm—how heavenly—Left—right—Please—p-lease—Jim—Jim—stop those words going round and round—"

Someone smothered something between his teeth. Someone pulled off the coat, bundled her into something woolly and soft, something that smelled of tobacco, lifted her into a car. She knew that it was her car. She hadn't known that it could go so fast. It was burning up the road. She was warmer. Those horrid words had stopped whirling. Why should she have thought for an instant that she was with Jim Armstrong? Could cold, exhaustion, and excitement muddle her thoughts like that? Her mind was quite clear. She looked at the man at the wheel.

"Thank goodness, you have put on your coat! It would be you—the man-of-the-moment," she said unsteadily.

He looked straight down into her eyes. Straight and deep.

"But all the time you thought I was Jim."

Prudence closed her lids tight. That pesky, "Left!" "Right!" started in her head again. She had better keep them open. Rodney Gerard needn't growl at her. Suppose she were to remind him of Milly Gooch and—lucky she had found that out in time! When he had taken her in his arms she had been radiantly happy. Suppose she had? When she let herself love, it would be without risk of heartbreak. Julie probably had felt like that about the playboy she had married. He had had money to give to other women—perhaps not to a circus rider, but to—

Gerard drew the robe closer about her.

"Warmer—Gorgeous?"

If he spoke to her again in that unsteady voice, she would cry her heart out on his shoulder, then where would she be?

"Warmer—but—a roaring fire and a cup of hot tea will seem like heaven. Jim will—"

"Jim! Jim! You think of him every minute. Why don't you marry him?"

Prudence shut her eyes. She had been about to say that Jim would think him lost. He had handed her a weapon of defense. She rushed to her own destruction.

"I have had that idea myself—in fact it is quite settled."

The words seemed to twang in the air long after they were spoken, to vibrate like a violin string which had been roughly struck. What a lie! What an outrageous lie! She had stripped off honor and truth in a determination to protect herself from future heartache. What would Jim Armstrong say if he knew? He mustn't know. After what seemed hours of time and miles of road, she begged in what she recognized as absurd anticlimax:

"Please don't mention what I told you to anyone—even David. We—we don't want it known—at present. I—I—well, you made me angry and—and I just flung it at you."

"It isn't the initial cost of a lie, it is the upkeep which counts so terribly," Prudence told herself miserably.

"Don't worry. I shan't broadcast the good news. You are hoarse. Still chilly?"

"I'm warmer, but my throat feels like a nutmeg grater in the wrong place. Thank heaven, we are almost home! There's the red brick house!"

"David and I had planned for you to dine at High Ledges tonight—he wanted to tell you of our experiences—but if you've taken a cold—"

"I never take cold. As soon as I get off these wet clothes I'll be all right." How could she face Jim Armstrong, she wondered, even as she asked: "What time do you dine?"

"Seven, the temperamental Mrs. Patch permitting. I've learned one thing since I have become a housekeeper, and that is that all loss of jobs can't be charged up to old Debil Depression. If I were not determined to finish the lumbering, do you think I would pay money to have that woman's cranky disposition in my house? Not a chance! Here we are, thank goodness."

"You needn't appear quite so glad to get rid of me. I won't detain you a minute if ever I can get unmuffled."

"You like playing with explosives, don't you? Wait! Don't be in such a rush!" He lifted her out of the roadster and pulled off the robe. "You're shivering. There isn't a light in the house. Where is Jane Mack?"

"Having t-tea with Mrs. S-Si, probably." Prudence frowned at the red brick house whose snowy ledges and roof glistened in the afterglow like an old-time frosted Christmas card. The windows looked like dead eyes staring back at her. Dead eyes! The convict's eyes had gone dead when he had seized the gun. Did the windows know how she despised herself for her cowardly lie? Was that why they stared?

"You're shivering again. Come on! I'm going in with you!"

"No! No! Go home! I don't need anyone."

"Sez you! Come on!" He laid a compelling arm about her shoulders and drew her along the path. The knob of the front door turned under his hand. He followed her into the living room which was faintly lighted by blinking coals on the hearth.

"Sit in that wing chair. Don't try to talk."

He flung pine cones from the big copper kettle beside the fireplace on the embers. They blazed. Carefully he laid birch kindling; when that caught he piled on large logs. As the yellow walls turned to red gold, he crossed to the table and lighted the lamp.

Prudence protested hoarsely: "Please don't do anything more. I can take care of myself."

"Got a heater in the house?"

"Of course—central heating—a one-pipe furnace."

"Glad you can take this as a joke, even if your laugh was a croak. Is your room warm?"

"My own room upstairs? Only when I have a fire in the stove."

"Then I'll get your dry clothes, you can't stay in those wet things, and you are not going up to that cold room to change. Stick out your foot."

He dropped to one knee and unlaced the boot she automatically held out. For an instant she was dumb from surprise, but only for an instant.

"Rodney Gerard, don't dare go to my room."

"Did you say 'dare'? I'm going under the Trading with the Enemy Act. It's being used this year."

He carefully removed the other boot, placed the pair side by side on the hearth, and crossed the room. She started after him, stopped in the hall. Ooch! It seemed bitterly cold after being near the hot fire. Macky must have forgotten to stoke the furnace. She would shiver to pieces before she reached the top of those steep stairs. Better go back where it was warm. She could refuse to put on the clothes he brought down.

Huddled in the wing chair, she regarded him as he returned to the room. Green crêpe pajamas hung over one arm, her flannel house coat striped in blue and green over the other. How had he known what to bring?

"Here you are! Get out of those wet things and into these."

He drew a chair in front of the fire and laid the garments over its back. He pulled a pair of sequined sandals from his pocket.

"These look a trifle ritzy for the rest of the outfit, but they were the first pair I picked up. Couldn't find your stockings; didn't want to mess up things hunting for them. I'll bundle your feet in the afghan when you have changed."

Prudence regarded him with a superior smile, as superior as a smile could be with chattering teeth behind it.

"Just naturally helpful, aren't you? I haven't the slightest intention of ch-changing. I'll stay here until M-Macky gets back."

"You have another guess coming to you. You'll change to dry clothes while I'm in the kitchen making a cup of hot tea. Now get this. If you haven't when I come back, I'll peel off those wet things myself." He paused on the threshold. "Make it snappy. It doesn't take long to boil water."

Prudence wrinkled her nose at his back. The act of defiance precipitated a body-wrenching sneeze. She sniffed and shivered and searched for a wet sop of handkerchief. Let him try to make her change. Just let him try.

She glanced furtively at the pajamas and coat over the chair. They looked blissfully warm, and she was frozen. Why not put them on? Why freeze for the pleasure of defying Rodney Gerard?

What was that sound? Was he coming already? With shaking hands she pulled off the green cardigan—lucky she had kept her shoulders above water, the color might have come off on her pearls.

Of course, the lordly male would think he had frightened her into obedience. She knotted the cord of the green and blue housecoat. He hadn't. It wasn't that she was too proud to fight—was her reaction to that thought a chuckle or a shiver—she was too c-cold to f-fight. Silly not to have put these toasty warm things on at once.

He was coming! She caught up the wet clothing and jammed it into the wood box. Back in the wing chair she thrust her bare toes, still white from cold, into the glittering sandals and sat on them.

When Gerard entered he glanced quickly at the chair in front of the fire. He drew forward a Chinese teapot and set down the tray in his hand.

"There you are!"

Prue bit her lips to discipline a smile—he mustn't think that she had forgiven his high-handedness. Where had he found such a battered collection? She hadn't known the things were in the house. The spout of the teapot was chipped to a saw-edge; the cover could never have been even a collateral of the sugar bowl; the cream was in a handleless pitcher; a small teakettle of hot water, and a cup and saucer of a thickness warranted to withstand the wear and tear of time, on a battered tin tray completed the equipment. He had found a silver teaspoon.

He poured tea, strong enough to curl the straightest lashes up tight, and passed her the cup.

"Sugar? Cream? I had some difficulty in finding things, but I'll say I did noble. Drink it. Drink it while it's hot."

Her scornful manner was slightly denatured by a sneeze.

"I suppose the sooner I get it down the s-sooner you'll go home and s-stop trying to order my life." She took a hasty swallow.

"It's boiling! You—haven't a c-copper-lined mouth up your sleeve, have you? You're such an efficient p-person."

"Did it burn?"

"Oh no, it froze and frosted all the way down."

He pulled the chair away from the fire, sat astride, and folded his arms on the back.

"Don't try to be funny. Drink it. At least, you're not shivering now. What the dickens have you done to this room?"

Prudence knew that even as he looked about he was aware of every swallow of the hot tea she drank. It was warming. She had stopped shaking and her spirits were mounting.

"Paper and paint. I wanted it fresh for David when he returned." She started to her glittering feet. "Dave! How could I have forgotten. He must be wild with anxiety about me."

"Sit down! Finish that tea! I phoned him from upstairs. Told him that you were okay and that you would be at High Ledges for dinner. I—" A door banged. "Who's that? Sit still!"

Before he could reach the hall, Jane Mack appeared on the threshold. A black scarf over her thin gray hair was knotted under her sharp chin. A man's topcoat hung loosely from her spare shoulders. The tops of black overshoes flopped at every step. Her cheeks were as red as stop lights, her usually pale eyes snapped like a terrier's.

"Miss Prue! Miss Prue! They've caught the escaped prisoner! Now perhaps you'll get your jewels." She took a step into the room and pulled down her spectacles. "What's the matter, child? What's happened to her, Mr. Rodney?"

Gerard moved to the mantel and looked down at the fire. Was he waiting for her to explain, Prue wondered. She reassured quickly:

"Nothing happened, Macky, except that I went to look at my timber and got wet. Mr. Gerard made some tea and—here we are."

Jane Mack frowned down at the tray. "My soul and body, it takes a man to get hold of things tucked away, don't it? No woman could ever have got that crazy lot of things together." She put her hand against Prue's cheek. "You look feverish. Sure you haven't taken cold?"

"Of course not. I never have a cold. What did you hear about the convict, Macky? Tell us, quick."

Jane Mack untied the scarf. Gerard lifted the heavy coat from her thin shoulders—Prue wondered if that attention ever had been shown her before—and drew forward a chair.

"Sit here, Miss Mack. How did you hear about the capture?"

She looked up at him as he backed toward the fire. "Macky has forgotten that I'm here," Prue told herself as she watched her, "she adores Rodney Gerard."

The woman sat stiffly erect on the edge of the chair. "The news broadcast about ten minutes ago. The convict was brought to the county jail by a leading citizen—didn't tell his name over the radio—who caught him in the woods, dared death from the desperado's revolver, and captured him single-handed."

Jane Mack's theatrical "dared death" unleashed Prue's shivers.

"Single-handed!" she echoed.

The leading citizen was Calloway, of course. Evidently he had forgotten to mention Rodney Gerard's

timely entrance at the cabin, had forgotten her mas-
terly stroke with the axe.

"Single-handed!" she repeated, and looked at Rodney Gerard. He shook his head as his eyes met hers.
She turned to Jane Mack.

"So the leading citizen caught him single-handed.
Ain't human nature grand!"

XVIII

Perched on a stump among others which reminded
her of Henry Hudson's goblin crew in the forest set
of Rip Van Winkle, Prudence listened to the warning call "Timber!" before the crash of a tree; to the
clop of axes, the rasp of saws that shattered the
brooding silence of the woods. As had been predict-
ed, winter had come early. Sheets of snow dappled
with sunlight in the clearings dazzled her eyes; mats
of snow lay on the blue-green needles of the white
pine; snow drifted down when a breeze tinkled dark
crystal-tipped twigs; snow was pocketed in pine
cones. The sharp, resinous air was heady when she
drew it deep into her lungs.

Her thoughts wandered from the brilliant bluejay
on which her eyes rested. Was it only two weeks
since Rodney Gerard and David had personally conducted their crew from New York? Probably it
seemed months to the men, who, unused to hard
work, had been instructed gradually in the art of
handling and grinding axes, twisting peaveys, and
pulling on cross-saws.

She dug the heel of her overshoe into the soft
snow. If it didn't seem long to them, it seemed an
aeon or two to her since that cabin adventure of
recent and thrilling memory. The convict was safe
behind bars, but hadn't a man quite as dangerous to
the Schuyler and Gerard interests been left at large?

Had Calloway given up the fight to stop them from cutting the timber? She couldn't believe it, even though Dave reported that work in the woods was progressing satisfactorily considering the greenness of the crew.

Two weeks since they had arrived, and this was the first time she had seen them at work. She had not dined at High Ledges the evening of their arrival. David apparently had burned up the road getting to the red brick house after Rodney Gerard had phoned him. She was in an advanced state of shivers by that time—at the memory she drew the collar of her fur coat tighter—and he had ordered her to bed. She had protested—it was maddening to be treated like a fragile flower when she never had been ill a day in her life, she had croaked.

The croak had settled the matter. Before she had finished the sentence, Rodney Gerard had her in his arms. She had stopped shivering long before he had set her on her feet in her own room; she was burning with righteous indignation. He had said to Jane Mack who had followed them:

"If Miss Prue doesn't do as she's told, call me. I'm the world's best disciplinarian."

Such a fuss over nothing. Except for a slight hoarseness she had been perfectly fit the next day; but until now she had kept away from the centre of logging activities. What time she hadn't spent on the poultry and at her bench completing Christmas orders had been devoted to teaching Jean to ski. Although the child was supposed to be living at High Ledges, she spent every hour possible at the red brick house. She brought news of the logging activities. Her reportorial flair was curbed only by time and breath. The newsreel slogan, "Sees all. Hears all," might have been invented for her.

Absorption in work and sports was not the only reason that had kept her from the logging belt, Prue acknowledged to herself with heightened color, she didn't care to meet Rodney Gerard, and she couldn't face Jim Armstrong. Of course, he didn't know of her absurd statement that she was engaged to him, but until she felt less ashamed of herself she would keep out of his way. She must have been dazed with cold and excitement that day to have fabricated such a story. She had come today because David had cross-examined her this morning as to her lack of interest in a business enterprise which was half hers, had seemed hurt that she had not cared to see his protégés at work.

She shook off the past, filled her lungs with the sparkling air and her eyes with the present. They glowed with laughter as she watched the men she could see. They were a motley lot, in shirts of a hectic plaid and baggy corduroy trousers. They were bare of arm and throat. They had lost the unemployed slouch, were clear-eyed and hard of muscle. They seemed happy and clean. David had told her that Gerard had had a couple of showers installed in the cattle barn—the building had an abundant water supply—and had insisted that each man take a bath before supper. He had related his bit of news, and had added:

"Imagine the result at the Rescue Mission if we had insisted upon that every day. We would have had a riot on our hands. They will stand even the torture of cold water on their skin from Gerard; they call him the Big Boss. They like him and they like the food he serves."

She blinked away sudden tears of gratitude as her brother appeared between the snowy trees. It seemed incredible that the erect, vigorous man in army breeches, high boots, and heavy sweater was the same person whom she and Gerard had tenderly assisted from the black roadster not so many weeks ago.

" 'Lengthening roads that wind through dust and heat to hilltops clear,' " she repeated softly.

Eyes on the men, her thoughts trooped on. She might have known that David wouldn't keep plod-ding in the dust and heat of despair and depression if there were a hilltop in sight for him to travel toward. Weren't there always hilltops clear if one had the

vision and the will to see them? There could be no
doubt that the back-to-the-land move had saved his
life—that and his determination to grapple with
heartbreak and ill-health instead of surrendering to
them. His vital concern that his "boys" should make
good had completed the cure. After all, was there
anything equal to an absorbing interest for keeping
one well and happy and efficient?

The men from the Mission were making good,
Prudence approved, as she watched them. Gerard,
Armstrong, and Si Puffer were each directing a crew.
They had been stationed far apart at first to avoid
accidents, but as they gained in experience they had
been moved nearer together. Twenty of the original
importation of twenty-five had stuck. Three had
sneaked away after their first day at hard labor; two
had deserted to Calloway.

Calloway! The repetition of the name brought
Prue's doubts of the man's acceptance of the present
situation crowding back into her mind. Had he given
up the fight? She couldn't believe it. He was too
resourceful, too relentless. Elbow on her knee, chin in
her mittened palm, her thoughts raced on to the
accompaniment of the ring and thud of axes, warning
yells before the slow splitting, tearing fall of a tree,
the rasping groan of the cross-cut saw, the lighter,
quicker stroke of the limbers as they cleared the
branches from a Titan of the forest. If only she could
think of the devastating things to say when she faced
him that were thronging on the tip of her tongue
now.

"Warm enough, Prue?"

Her brother's voice startled her back from an imagi-
nary verbal battle with Calloway.

"Warm! I'm fairly wadded. You would have
thought I was embarking on an expedition to the
South Pole. What Macky didn't suggest as a cold-
protector, Mrs. Si did. This air is balmy and so deliciously spicy. How are the men getting on?"

"Great. I knew they would make good. They are
not fools. Never in their lives have they had such

good food nor such consideration. Probably mere material comfort will pall after a while, but, if they do go back to old haunts and associations, I'll bet the memory of this experience will yank them away. As a financial proposition this experiment of Gerard's is likely to prove costly; as an experiment in human values I believe that it will pay a dividend."

"They look happy and fat in spite of their hard work."

Two little lines cut deep between David Schuyler's brows as he perched on a nearby stump.

"Fat! You said something then. They eat enormously, and they sleep like logs on the balsam boughs under their blankets. Even the hard work won't take care of the energy they are storing up. All their noise and guying is good-natured now; but let one of them get ugly or just one drink, and victors jubilating about goal posts would be a Sleepy Hollow compared to the inside of that cattle barn."

"Can they get a drink, Dave?"

"Not unless they walk miles for it, and by the time they have tramped back to the bunk-house at the end of their work day they've had all the walking they care for. Armstrong, who is the woods boss, has moved from the big house to a cabin near them so that he can keep an eye on things. They are happy enough now, with a radio and one of those small moving picture machines—but, in spite of that, I can't explain it, I feel a pricking in my thumbs."

"It isn't like you to worry, David. Are the men slacking on their job?"

"No."

"Have you heard from the two whom Calloway subtracted?"

"Not since the night they appeared at the bunk-house to make a neighborly call. On that occasion they were greeted with such a storm of abuse and such a fusillade of missiles that the place looked as if it had been the storm center of a five-and-ten store explosion. They won't try that again. Here comes Rod. He works like a beaver driving his crew."

Rodney Gerard leaned against a small tree and regarded Prudence with smiling aloofness. He was as unbending as a steel robot and about as warming, she told herself derisively.

"We have with us today—Prue of Prosperity Farm. What do you think of our logging enterprise, partner?"

She gripped the stump with both gloved hands. A small cold tremor of fear quivered through her. He hadn't moved, yet she felt as if irresistibly she were being drawn into his arms. Why, why did it have to be he who set her heart thumping, whose eyes seemed to stop her breath? How could he in a few weeks have so possessed her? Magic? Black art? Almost she began to believe in them. Why couldn't it have been Jim Armstrong, who all his life had had to work for what he wanted, who had had neither time nor money to finance circus riders? Jim, who gave such a sense of peace and security, not much like the effect Rodney Gerard had on her. Tumult was the word for that.

"How about it? This is Prue of Prosperity Farm, isn't it?"

Had she been staring at him dumbly? She said with an attempt at lightness:

"It is. The silent partner of Schuyler and Gerard in person."

She kept her eyes on her brother as hands deep in the pockets of his heavy sweater he walked away. She said unevenly:

"David is unbelievably better, isn't he?"

Gerard perched on the stump Schuyler had vacated and clasped heavily gloved hands about his knee.

"Better! He's pretty nearly okay. When we were in New York, I persuaded him to see a specialist I know. He said that if your brother would keep out of blankety-blank—I am giving you a carefully expurgated version of his opinion—places full of dead air and live in the country for a time, that nature, who is the greatest repair specialist in creation, would have him on his feet in—"

"Timber!"

Gerard jumped to his feet at the warning call. Prue's eyes followed his. The men had taken to the cover of big trees. All except one. Why—why didn't the stupid creature—

"Hi! O'Shea! Look out!"

Gerard yelled the warning as he dashed toward the red-headed giant. Prudence clutched her hands over her heart. Would he be in time? Couldn't Shance see that he was in line with that crashing tree? Didn't Rodney realize his own danger when he hurled himself at the man? The tree was down! So were the two men! Crushed? The crew dropped their axes and rushed forward.

She shut her eyes for an instant. When she opened them, Gerard was on his feet with his hand on O'Shea's shoulder. His voice rang through the keen air.

"Sorry to treat you rough, Shance. You had to take the chance of being knocked out by the tree or by me."

The dazed man on the snowy ground blinked small red eyes at the prostrate forest monster—harmless now—which had cleared him by an inch. His red beard bristled, his redder hair stood on end, his gorilla-like hands and arms waved wildly. He spat with exceeding care.

"Sure, an' ye're sayin' little about the chance ye took," he growled.

"Three cheers for the Big Boss!" someone shouted.

In the midst of the deafening response Prue started down the trail to her car parked on the road. Body and mind were in a tumult. When Rodney Gerard had flung himself under that falling tree, the world had stopped for her. Nothing, nothing mattered if he were safe, she had vowed passionately.

As she drove home she thought of her sister's brief unhappy marriage, of the note from Milly Gooch to Rodney Gerard which Calloway had read to her. She had tried to question Mrs. Puffer about the girl, but she had evaded answering. Through loyalty to Rodney Gerard? Would she have been so evasive had there been no truth in Calloway's charges? After all, what difference did it make—what difference could it make to Prudence Schuyler what he felt or did for the circus rider?

In her angry absorption she almost ran Success through the back of the shed when she reached home. As she stepped from the car, Jean flung herself upon her.

"Oh, Miss Prue! Miss Prue! I'm so glad you've come!" Her breath caught in a sob. "I've got something cagey to tell you!"

Prue's thoughts flashed back to the woods. Jean couldn't mean that anything had happened to David or Rodney, they had been laughing when she had stolen away. She laid an arm across the fur-covered shoulders.

"Don't get jittery, dear. Come into the house and tell me about it."

Had the child been prying again, she wondered, as she broke up the cannel coal in the grate in her shop. She pulled off her green beret and her swagger coat. Jean flung hers into a chair, then carefully closed both doors. She stood in the middle of the room in the patch of sunlight which filtered through the plant-filled bay window.

"Can anyone hear?"

Her hoarse whisper sent little chills bounding from vertebra to vertebra of Prue's spinal column, it froze her voice. Impatient at her temperamental response to Jean's histrionics, she shook her head vigorously.

"All righty. Come over by the mantel."

Standing close, she whispered:

"Len Calloway's got something up his sleeve."

The information coincided so exactly with what Prudence had been suspecting that her response was immediate.

"I thought so. What have you found out? Quick! Tell me!"

Jean tiptoed to the hall door, opened it and peered out. Repeated the business with the door to the dining room, looked from the bay window. Came back to the fire.

"About an hour ago I was looking round the gun room at home—I had a hunch that I might find your jewels there—I thought—well, I thought perhaps I might—I might have walked in my sleep when I was visiting you—you know I was nuts about them—and have taken them—not knowing it—understand?"

Prudence nodded. She understood perfectly. Loyal little soul. Jean drew a long, relieved sigh.

"You would. I was poking round when I heard someone coming. I was scared! My father uses that room. I knew he'd be mad if he found me there, so I slipped behind one of the long hangings. He opened the door swiftly. Said to someone:

" 'Come in!'

"My heart was pounding as if its engine was running on high. Two people! I thought, 'I'll never get out.' My father growled:

" 'Come across, Calloway. What's on your mind now?'

" 'Sure your brother isn't around?' It took me a minute to realize that Mr. Calloway meant Uncle Rod. I never think of Father and he being related."

"Never mind that. What did Calloway want?"

"I don't know. I remembered that I'd promised you, cut-my-throat-an'-hope-to-die, that I wouldn't pry, so I stuck my fingers in my ears hard."

If only the child hadn't taken that vital moment to keep her promise, Prudence wished fervently.

"Go on, Jean. You must have heard something."

"Sure, I heard something. After I'd kept my fingers in my ears for—it seemed hours, I pulled them out. I heard Mr. Calloway say:

" 'I'm going.'

"I almost dropped dead from fright. Suppose he left by the French window the way he did the last time he caught me in that room!"

"He didn't see you, did he?"

"Gee, you're pinching!" Jean rubbed her shoulder as Prudence quickly removed her hand. "Guess you're as excited as I am. Mr. Calloway didn't come to the window. His voice sounded as if he was at the door, for he said quite loud:

" 'Tonight at the old smithy. Eight. Report there. Safer than here. Too many doors and windows in this house.'

"When he said that I almost died, but I was live enough to hear my father say:

" 'It's a payment on delivery proposition, Len? Sure?'

" 'Sure. Ever know me to break my word? I may be a hard man, but I'm just. Milly Gooch is at the Puffers. I suppose she's come to see Rod.'

" 'Milly—'

"That was all I heard Father say for the door closed. I waited till I was sure they were gone. Then I sneaked out and made Patch drive me over here. His wife had a terrible grouch on when I asked him, but he didn't dare not bring me. Uncle Rod had told him to take me out whenever I wanted to go. It's awfully slow living at High Ledges after staying at the red brick house. I never feel tempted to pry here or get mad, everything's so kind of happy and peaceful. Uncle Rod and Mr. Jim are too all in after dinner to do anything but stare at the fire and smoke as fast as the women in Mother's card club. Uncle Rod hardly speaks to Mr. Jim and looks as if he were going to bite, and I know he hates having Father around. It's about as lively as what I think a funeral is like."

Prudence crossed to the window. The sun, like a glossless copper plaque hung low in the sky, slid suddenly below the horizon. So—Milly Gooch had arrived on the scene. Now what would happen? She thrust the thought of the circus rider into the back of her mind and said without turning:

"Repeat what Calloway said about meeting your father, Jean."

"Tonight at the old smithy. Eight.' "

"Eight o'clock? Are you sure?"

"Yep."

"Where's the smithy?"

"He meant the old blacksmith shop. Gee, how your eyes shine! You know that steep hill we tried to ski down the other day? The smithy is at the foot of that near the pond road, the same road that leads up to the cattle barns. When Grandfather ran a big farm he had the horses shod there. Uncle Rod keeps it in repair because he thinks it's interesting." A worried pucker came between her eyes. "What do you suppose they were talking about? The—the—emerald and diamonds?"

"Forget those jewels, Jean. Perhaps Mr. Calloway has engaged your father to boss a lumber crew for him."

"Payment on delivery doesn't sound like that kind of a job. Father boss a crew? Don't be dumb! It's something else. You don't think it is anything that will hurt Uncle Rod, do you, Miss Prue?"

"Of course not. Perhaps they are planning a party for—for Milly Gooch. That's just what it is. Weren't we foolish not to think of it before? By the way, Jean, tell me again where to find that blacksmith shop."

Jean gripped her arm. "Miss Prue, Miss Prue, you're not planning to go there too, are you?"

"Silly! Merry-pranks in your imagination again. Didn't I tell you the other day that I'd give my best baroque pearl for a man-sized bellows for enamelling and soldering big things? Perhaps I will find one in the smithy."

"That's grand." Jean's brows puckered above eyes which gazed into space. Evidently her mind was back in the gun room at High Ledges. She whispered:

"What's their racket? That's what I want to know. What's their racket?"

XIX

"You are a hang-over from the days when I had leisure and money," Prudence reflected before the mirror in her room, as she zippered the jacket of her ski-suit over the orange shirt. She pulled on warm oversocks, fastened heavy boots, while her thoughts ran on:

"What luck that Dave phoned he was dining at High Ledges—important business to discuss, he said. He would go into the air if he knew what I am about to do. What he doesn't know won't hurt him. I suggested that Macky go to the early movie with the Puffers, and presto, the way was cleared for my personally conducted expedition to the smithy to find out what the rendezvous of Calloway and Walter Gerard means. It is a safe enough safari. I'll follow the old wood road to the ledge, then down the other side. I can't get lost. The snow is marked with ski-tracks. No danger of meeting anyone. Didn't Dave say that his boys were too tired to leave the bunk-house after the day's work? I am friendly with every man and boy in the village. I've given the plan a thorough look-before-you-leap once over. I can see no danger in it, even if I was too excited to eat supper. Believe it or not, I won't get panicky as I did when I looked up and saw Calloway in the cabin. Ooch! That was a moment! The mouse-in-the-wall act rocketed to the surface of my mind when Jean told me what she had overheard. Eight o'clock is zero hour. How soon should I start for the blacksmith shop? I ought to be parked there long before the conspirators arrive."

She counted the strokes of the old clock in the hall. Seven. Better get going. She wound a gay scarf about her throat, caught up an orange and blue cap and a pair of torrid mittens. She thrust a flashlight into the pocket of her trousers. At the hall window she stopped. Perfect night! She listened to the ghostly drill of a woodpecker boring for a late supper, watched cold, keen sparks prick through the heavens. The horizon was a haze spun of amethyst and silver tissues. Woods, carpeted with snow, rose from road to sky line. Snuggled in the valley on the other side of that rise was the blacksmith shop.

"Perfect night," she approved again, drew the cap over her ears, and ran down the steep stairs. The setter bounded out of the living room, capered and whined and yelped deafeningly at the prospect of an outing.

"Down! Down! Happy!"

Why was she whispering? Prudence said aloud:

"You can't go, old dear. Stay here and keep house."

The dog slumped in dejection. She looked back, waved to him, and closed the door between them. Lucky he had appeared before she started; she couldn't have shaken him out of doors.

In the back hall she frowned appraisingly at the collection of impedimenta hanging and leaning against the walls. When she and Jean had gone sportsminded, they had experimented with everything that slid, from sleds to skates.

"Skis or snowshoes?" She visualized the steep declivity from the highest ledge to the pond. "The skis have it," she decided, and shouldered a pair. Poles in hand, she stole around the house to the road.

Why the dickens did Happy feel called upon to bark furiously? Didn't he recognize her step? He had stopped, thank heaven!

With frequent pauses to listen, she entered the old lumber road that wound up to the sky line. She looked back. Light from the windows of the red brick house patterned the snow with gold. The roof glistened. Pale violet smoke wreaths spiralled from the two chimneys. What was that? A shadow across a patch of light! She waited. Held her breath. Would it come again? No. Must have been a vine swaying.

Resolutely she turned her back on warmth and

security and slipped and stumbled over the rough road whose hidden pitfalls were tricked out with spotless snow. The skis caught in branches, seemed to increase unbearably in weight. Was she doing a crazy thing to try to find out what Walter Gerard and Calloway were scheming about? She was not. In spite of her reassurance to Jean, she was convinced that they were conniving against the lumber firm of Schuyler and Gerard. That being the case, it was her job to find out what it was all about, wasn't it? Of course, she could have told Dave—no, hadn't Jim Armstrong exclaimed, when she had told him that only four knew about the jewels in her safe:

"Four! It's four too many! There's bound to be one broadcaster in the bunch."

Jean and she were the only outlanders who knew this secret; it was safe.

A hole in the road shattered her reflections. "Serves you right!" she scolded herself, as once more erect she brushed snow from her clothing. "Better keep your mind on your feet."

She adjusted her skis, picked up her poles, and slid on between serried phalanxes of evergreens. Mysterious alleys rustled with whispers; frost in the branches snapped sharp and clear like pop-guns; gray tips of boulders poked through snow. She glanced furtively from the corners of her eyes. She had a prickling sense that she was not alone in the woods. Had a shadow slipped behind that large pine, or was it a ghostly illusion?

"Don't be foolish," she scolded herself. "Everyone you know is too busy with his own affairs to be stalking you."

It seemed hours before she reached the top of the ledge from which she could see the pond glimmering between strips of ice. She rested on her poles and drew a long breath. Glorious moon! Half way to the zenith. Full, luminous, like a lump of bluish silver hammered flat against an indigo velvet sky. Already its light had put out the lesser stars, but Mars and Jupiter retained their brilliancy.

This was the very spot from which she and Jean had started yesterday. The tracks of their skis twisted and turned like dark ribbons flung on diamond dust. The patterns proclaimed Jean's inexperience and her own lack of practice. She had been proficient once. She could see no sign of a building. Probably the trees at the foot of the slope hid it.

She proceeded cautiously. The snow was deceptive, as she had discovered yesterday. In some places it slid in little avalanches from under her feet. The clamp of a ski snapped open, the leather binding slipped from her heel.

"Darn!" she muttered, and readjusted the ski. Upright, she rested on her poles until she could collect her breath. What a night! She might have missed this beauty had she remained at home warm and snug and—she hustled the word "safe" into the back of her mind. The air sparkled. The world was flooded with cold blue light. Evergreens and stark trees were blotched and silhouetted in royal purple against a translucent silver mist. Clear and aloof, Orion and the Great Bear shone brilliantly.

How still and solemn! Almost she could hear the faint swish of the robes of Father Time as he swept on. It was getting colder. Her scarf was coated with hoar frost where her breath had frozen.

Why was she standing still? A little afraid? What was there to fear now that the convict was behind bars? Didn't every minute count? She looked over her shoulder. She had shaken off that skulking shadow. Of course, it had been but a creature of her always super-active imagination. Just the same, she was glad to have left it behind.

She started on. The trees were thicker now. She couldn't lose her way. The old ski tracks were like sign posts to inform her that she was still in known territory. A white furry shape leaped into the foreground. She stopped. Held her breath. A rabbit! An adorable rabbit. For the fraction of a moment it squatted on its hind quarters, stiffened its long ears, glanced warily from its bulging eyes, wrinkled its sensitive nostrils.

A twig snapped. It stretched its long body and hopped away, leaving a trail of little footprints. A dark, noiseless shadow flitted overhead, obscurely threatening, sinister in its passing. An owl! An owl in pursuit of that darling rabbit. Its wings made no sound, though they seemed to flap as well as glide. A forest tragedy. Could she avert it? She pulled off her mittens, clapped her hands.

A screech! A hideous screech. It rose to an incredibly high note, dropped to a snore, slithered into a sinister hiss-s-s. The world seemed weirdly quiet after it. Had one owl made that fiendish noise? From now on she would swear to the truth of hair standing on end; she had felt hers rise.

She stemmed and slid on. Enchanting night! The moon rode in cloudless splendor. She had a curious feeling of being someone else, not herself. Perhaps the girl who had set out on this quest wasn't the usual Prudence Schuyler, but was one of those potential personalities psychologists claim lurk behind one's every-day self. That was a thought.

She stopped on a little shelf of level land on the hillside. Below, through the transparent vapor of a valley, wound a dark ribbon. A road! Rough, rutted, winding as a forest stream, but a road. Beyond the road the pond glimmered like polished steel. Was that shadowy blotch near it the blacksmith shop?

Her heart caught and raced on. Was she becoming infected with fright? She wouldn't turn back now. Time was flying. Calloway and Walter Gerard might reach the smithy first. Then where would she be? She couldn't see herself listening at cracks and windows. She must get inside before they came.

She frowned at the slope which, until it neared the road, was almost clear of trees. It was smooth as the icing of a mammoth cake, unbroken as an Artic snow field. White. Hard. Dry. A jump would save time. Dare she try it? She had been good once. Why not? It was a short jump. Suppose she flopped? What was one flop in the day's work?

She dropped her poles, skiied back on the level, rounded up all the instructions she could remember.

"Slide. Don't walk on your skis. Bend your knees. Knock 'em. Remember nothing will jump into your way after you light. Go!"

She turned. Raced forward. She was in the air! Breath-snatching. Exhilarating. The rush of cold nipped her nose, slashed her chin. She landed. Was she going over? No. She clasped her hands behind her. Not too bad when she had been so long without practice. Steady on her skis again. They barely etched the hard surface. She was going like a thousand race horses merged in one.

The smithy! Not so far away as she had thought. Straight ahead. She would crash into it! That wouldn't be the only crash. If the two men were already there, she never would find out their plan. She must stop! How did one stop? She had forgotten. She would drop.

Stars rained in a golden shower. The Leonids pelting down at her? The world rocked. She opened her eyes. That crash ought to have broken every bone in her body, she reflected, as she rolled over on her side. She pulled herself to one knee, floundered upright on her skis.

The blacksmith shop was barely two feet away. Its one window stared at her like a lidless eye. Its roof was fringed with icicles. It looked frightfully cold. No light! That meant that she was the first arrival at the conference—it was a Conference year—only hers would not begin with a capital C.

In a pool of purple shadow at the foot of a giant spruce, she removed her skis cautiously and rested them against the tree. A cold, spicy breeze had sprung up. It splintered into a thousand icy tinkles as it swept through the boughs above her head.

Crunch! Crunch! Did her feet have to go down so hard? Anyone near to hear? She stood motionless. No sound but the whispers among the dark green boughs and the chime of fairy ice bells. No shadow could stalk her down that slide. She had better get under cover.

Crunch! Crunch! She tiptoed to the shop.

Soundlessly she pressed her fingers against the door. Noiselessly it swung in. Too easy. She could hear her heart thumping in the ominous silence. She peered into the dim interior. Swallowed the lump in her throat.

"Anyone h-here?" she inquired softly.

Quiet as a tomb and cold as death. Cheery comparison! She stepped over the threshold and closed the door. Moonlight on the snow outside provided a pale light which added to the sombre air of mystery. She could make out the great forge of brick, red leathern bellows, a tie rail of nibbled gnarled oak, iron rims for cart wheels, and horseshoes of all sizes. There was a laden tool-bench with a worn stool before it. On the side which she assumed faced the road were great double doors, closed and padlocked. She crossed the floor, which broadcast a creak with every cautious step, and appraised the narrow space between forge and wall. Should she slip in there? No. Too near the conspirators. Did the opening at the left lead into a shed?

The glow of her flashlight illumined the corners of a lean-to. She hesitated. She wasn't crazy about this part of her adventure. Too much like poking one's head into a bag, but she couldn't back out now. The place seemed fairly clean; there were no signs of four-footed occupation. That high pile of firewood would serve as a screen if either of the conspirators felt moved to investigate. She pulled off her mittens, glanced at the illuminated dial of her wrist watch. Five minutes before eight.

She leaned against the door frame. How the place rustled! Must be something alive in that wood pile. Someone outside! Only an icicle dropping. Why didn't the men come? How would they come? By automobile along the road, or by snowshoes? It must be long after eight. Jean might have been mistaken in

time and place. Perhaps the mystery of their voices
had been fabricated by her vivid imagination. Perhaps because she herself had been looking for trouble
she had dramatized a few commonplace remarks.
Walter Gerard might be working for Calloway and
not want his brother to know it. How long should she
wait? It would take longer to go back than it had to
come. If she weren't at home by nine-thirty, when the
movies were out, David would be wild with anxiety.

Only three minutes before eight! She held her
watch to her ear. It hadn't stopped. It was ticking
with the regularity of Happy's breathing when he
snoozed on the hearth rug. Good old Happy! What a
break that she had seen him before he had a chance
to sneak after her. He would have thrown sand in the
gears of her plan. He—

Crunch! Crunch!

Someone coming! This time her heart refused to be
swallowed; it parked in her throat and thumped
deafeningly. Calloway or Walter Gerard? As a com-
panion in a lonely shack there wasn't much choice
between them. Of course, the fiery Len was a "just
man."

She must not chuckle like that again. A sense of
humor was all right in its place, but its place wasn't in
the lean-to of an old smithy at zero hour.

A light! It flickered. She crouched behind the wood
pile. A door closing? The pad-pad of moccasins. One
man had come on snowshoes; he must have shed
them outside. The sound as of a lantern set down.
The lean-to doorway framed a soft glow. The door
again!

"I beat you to it, Calloway."

That was Walter Gerard's silky, assured voice.

"Come across with the money, Len."

"How do I know you've done the trick, Walt?"

"If you don't believe me, go and look at the truck.
It laid down and died almost at the door of the cattle
barn. That will spike the wheels of the great Schuyler
and Gerard combination. Neatest trick of the week."

"What time did it crack-up?"

"Didn't you set the time? Just as the crew had finished supper. They got the full effect of the crash. Men tumbled out of the doorway, some of them still gripping their tin mugs of coffee. I hung around for a few minutes to make sure they were on; then I beat it. No chance of a flop now, the cart's backed up, you win. Don't stall, Calloway, come across with the money you promised when you wrote asking me to come to High Ledges to do a little work for you. The letter arrived just as I lost my job. Rod had refused to clean up a few debts for me, so I snapped up your proposition. Cash on delivery, remember—but, of course, you won't stall, you're such an honest man."

There was sardonic mirth in Walter Gerard's voice and a hint of hatred.

"Oh, all right. I'll pay. Here's your money."

Prudence crept on hands and knees to the doorway. She must watch the passing of that money. Someone would pay for the destruction of the truck belonging to the firm of Schuyler and Gerard, and it wouldn't be either of the partners. Had it been loaded with lumber? But what would these men gain if a truck "lay down and died" near the cattle barn? It would block the road, of course. Whatever the explanation, nothing would please her more than to appear on the witness stand and testify as to what she knew about the cause of that spilled lumber. Her bubble of triumph burst. Of course Rodney Gerard would not allow his step-brother to be prosecuted.

Crouched in the dusk, she watched the two men standing within the radius of light from an oil lantern on the forge. A knitted cap was pulled low over Calloway's ears, his bold dark eyes glittered in a face the color of old wax, his white teeth gleamed between red lips. Facing him, Walter Gerard counted the bills in his hand.

"Okay. Now I'll light out. I'm not going back to the house. I'll catch a ride—"

A tap on the window! Another tap!

"Put out that light!"

The harsh whisper was Walter Gerard's. The shop

went dark. Prudence tiptoed to the wood pile. She misjudged the distance, struck it. With sickening moderation and rumble the sticks began to slide.

She held her breath. Now what would happen? Someone was breathing hard at the lean-to opening.

"Find out who's at that window, Walt." It was Calloway's hoarse low voice; she couldn't mistake it. "I'll take care of the snooper hiding in here."

XX

Dusk in the living room at High Ledges. A glowing fire on the hearth. A vague sense of tension in the air. A coffee table with empty Sevres cups. Jean in a gay little frock behind it. The black kitten curled close to her feet. A silver vase of long-stemmed Talisman roses on the piano. A pile of untouched newspapers on the large table. Soft-toned hangings drawn over long windows. Jim Armstrong sprawled in a big chair. David Schuyler, chin in cupped hands, frowning at space. Two black field spaniels prone on the rug. Rodney Gerard, arm on the mantel, staring at the licking flames. Richness and splendor in the voice singing:

> "On the road to Mandalay,
> Where the flyin'-fishes play,
> An' the dawn comes up like thunder outer China
>   'crost the—"

"For Pete's sake, shut that off, K.K.!"

Jean flew to the radio. The musical voice was cut off in the middle of a word. David Schuyler leaned back in his chair.

"I never can get over the feeling that I've been unconsciously rude to the performer when I shut him off like that."

Rodney Gerard thrust his hands hard into the pockets of his tweed coat.

"That poetic Mandalay stuff was getting my goat when I know as well as I know that I'm standing here that someone is working on the crew. That's why I persuaded you to stay for dinner, Dave. Wanted to talk it over. Two of my men slacked today. They were surly when I asked why. Said they had a pain. 'Something they'd et, they guessed.' Switch on the light, K.K."

The lamps glowed like enormous cloudy jewels.

"That's better. Light is the champion reducer of problems. Have either of you noticed anything to make you uneasy, or am I having a bad case of the jitters?"

"A little reason but mostly jitters, I should say, Rodney. The boys were full of rowdy enthusiasm over your rescue of Shance O'Shea."

"Yes, Dave, but it wore off quick enough. What do you think, Jim?"

Armstrong rose precipitately to knock his pipe against an andiron. "I agree with you, Rod. Something is working on the crew. Via the grapevine route. In fact I'm so uneasy that I'm going back to my cabin now."

Rodney Gerard threw his cigarette into the fire. "I'm going with you."

David Schuyler rose. "I haven't seen the inside of the cattle barn since it was made into a bunk-house. I'll drop in on my boys."

Armstrong stopped on his way to the door. "Better not tonight. I may be having the heebe-jeebes, but I have a hunch we'll find things in a mess."

"All the more reason I should go. I—"

"What's the matter, K.K.?"

Rodney Gerard's sharp question focussed attention on Jean, who was standing in the geographical center of the room twisting the gayly printed crêpe of her skirt between nervous fingers. Her brow was as furrowed as a thirteen-year-old brow may be. Her eyes seemed enormous as she looked at Gerard.

"I—I—was wondering if what I heard—"

"What did you hear?"

The three questions were perfectly synchronized as the men closed in. Jean's lips quivered nervously. Rodney Gerard put his arm around her shoulders. He struggled to keep his voice casual as he reassured:

"We didn't mean to pounce, K.K. We were startled, that's all. What did you hear?"

"I really didn't go to the gun room to listen, Uncle Rod, and I kept my fingers in my ears a long time, honest. I went there to—"

"Never mind what you went there for. What did you hear?"

With anxious eyes roving from one face to the other, Jean told of the conversation between Walter Gerard and Len Calloway. The men listened without interruption until she said:

"I heard my father say,

" 'It's a payment on delivery proposition, Len? Sure?' "

"Tell me again, what time were they to meet?"

"At eight, Uncle Rod."

Gerard glanced at the clock. "We can make the smithy before that time easy in my roadster, Jim."

"Better pass the cattle barn first. We will leave Dave there to make his friendly call, then we'll go on and catch the conspirators red-handed."

Jean caught her uncle's arm. Her eyes were frightened.

"You won't hurt Father, will you? Perhaps I shouldn't have told—but—I was afraid he might be making trouble for you and—and Mr. David,"—a big tear rolled down her cheek, her breath caught in a sob—"but Miss Prue said—"

"Prue! Did you tell her this same story?"

Surprise dried Jean's tears. "Of course, Uncle Rod. I tell her everything. What makes you so white?"

Gerard rubbed his hand hard over his face till the blood burned under his skin.

"What did she say, K.K. Quick, tell us everything."

"Everything!" echoed Schuyler and Armstrong tensely.

"First she guessed Mr. Calloway had hired Father to boss a lumber crew—then she said perhaps they were planning a party for Milly Gooch—"

"Cut that. What else did Prue say? Hurry! Can't you hear the minutes ticking away?"

"She didn't say much more, except to ask me where the blacksmith shop was. What did you say, Uncle Rod?"

"Nothing fit for publication." Gerard crossed the room to the telephone.

"Why did she want to know? Why?"

Jean patted the hand which gripped her arm. "I guess you've got merry-pranks in your imagination too, Mr. David. She was only tickled to pieces to think perhaps she'd found a bellows for enamelling and soldering big things. You know she has a lot of Christmas orders for boxes. I've been helping her. She was all twinkly about it."

"She would be. Can't you get the red brick house, Rodney?"

Gerard replaced the telephone. "No answer." He cleared his voice of huskiness. "This is movie night—she may have gone—that's a thought."

He picked up the phone again and gave the Puffers' number. Impulsive as she was, Prue couldn't have done such a mad thing as to go to the old blacksmith shop, he told himself. But suppose she had? Suppose that yarn about enamelling and soldering big things was merely a camouflage?

"Keep on ringing, operator. Important."

"I'm making a break for the cattle barn, Rod."

Gerard nodded response to Armstrong's husky voice. Boy! How white he was! White. If he was so anxious about the girl to whom he was engaged, why waste a minute on that infernal crew? Why not make a break for the smithy?

"Pull yourself together!" he gritted his teeth. "It's just your crazy idea that Prue has gone to the shop.

Probably Jim knows her too well to think she'd do such a fool thing."

He laid down the phone. "No answer, Dave."

Color stole back into Schuyler's face. He drew a long breath.

"She has gone to the movies with the Puffers and Jane Mack of course. Let's get going, Rodney. If you mean to make the blacksmith shop before eight, we will have to hustle."

"We'll hustle, all right. Good-night, K.K. Go to bed and to sleep."

"You—you—won't be too hard on Father, Uncle Rod?"

Gerard managed a smile. "Of course not. Why should I be? Miss Prue is right; probably Calloway has given him a job to boss a lumber crew. Be a good child. Don't worry."

As he hurried along the hall beside David Schuyler, he speculated aloud:

"I wonder what mess Walt is in now? Whatever it is, I'm through mopping up for him."

"There is always Jean to consider," David Schuyler reminded. "You can't let her down."

"Of course I can't and he knows it. He has been hiding behind skirts all his life. He tried it with Milly—oh, for Pete's sake, let's get going, Dave!"

Neither man spoke as the black roadster raced along trailing a cloud of snow like the wake of a vessel. The stillness of the woods on each side of the road was like the consecrated silence of a church. The tumult in Gerard's mind quieted. He certainly had had a brain-storm back in the living room. Of course Prue wouldn't go to the smithy. What did she really care about the firm of Schuyler and Gerard? Not a hang. Jim Armstrong was her—

"I feel as if I ought to apologize to Prue,"—he cut in on his own conclusions—"for even thinking she would do such a dumb thing as to try to get to that shop."

"Do you? I don't. She would do that if she thought she could help. Great night. How low the stars seem!"

"We could almost reach up and pick a few. What's all the shouting for? Hear it? Must be the crew at the cattle barn—I still think of it as a barn, though it is really a bunk-house."

"Hear it! It would rouse the Seven Sleepers. They are yelling now. Sounds to me like an able-bodied riot with a fight or two thrown in for good measure. Step on the gas, Rodney. I haven't helped much in the woods, but I can stop that."

The roadster sped on. The uproar increased. Gerard peered through the windshield. Thank heaven, the headlights were powerful. Something might be in the road—might be!

He ground on the emergency brake with a suddenness which flung them both against the unshatterable windshield.

"What—"

Rodney Gerard was out of the roadster before David Schuyler could finish the sentence jerked out of him by the shock. He stared at the bulk sprawled across the road. A truck. The lights from the windows of the bunk-house patched the snow beyond it with oblongs of gold. The accident must have happened sometime ago or the men would be swarming about it. Not one of his trucks. Where had it come from to be on the pond road at this time of night?

"What the dickens is it, Rodney?" David Schuyler peered over his shoulder.

"A truck. Gone blooey. Not one of ours. That smash didn't just happen in this spot. I'll bet it's a plant. Calloway and Walt conspiring! What's the big idea? If it were our truck, the answer would be easy—holding up our shipment; but a strange—" He sniffed. "Oh, my gosh! Smell it!"

David Schuyler, who had been bending over the wreck, straightened.

"Smell it! I'll say I smell it. What master-mind conceived the scheme of wrecking that load of liquor in front of the bunk-house? We must keep my boys from finding this."

"Judging from the sounds of whoopee ahead, I'd

say we were several hours too late. What a dirty trick! What a damnably dirty trick! Who's coming? Whoever it is won't get any more."

He picked up a bottle which had escaped breakage. "Clever guys. They didn't have the stuff cased. Just handed it to our crew all ready to drink." He swung his arm experimentally. "I haven't done much at head-cracking lately, but I'll do my darndest with this."

David Schuyler seized a bottle. "Wait till you see the whites of his eyes, Rodney."

The light touch eased the tension. Dave certainly knew how to play the notes of human nature, Gerard admitted, as he tried to recognize the dusky shape dodging forward among the trees. He had been so angry that he wouldn't have cared where or how he hit; now his mouth was stretched in a grin. His muscles tightened. Who was coming?

"Rod! Rod!"

The sharp call was barely audible above the din in the bunk-house. Jim Armstrong! Of course! Gerard dropped the bottle. It cracked like a pistol shot.

"Rod! Rod! It's Jim! Put up your gun!"

Gerard laughed as Armstrong's face shone weirdly white in the glare of the roadster's headlights. Thank goodness his sense of humor had not been caught in the maelstrom of anxiety which was giving him a whirl.

"Haven't a gun. No such luck. That crack was a bottle passing out. Come on, Dave. Let's get round this messs so we can talk to Jim without yelling our heads off."

They stepped cautiously to avoid barbed spikes of glass which glittered in the trodden, sodden snow about the wreckage. When they reached Armstrong, he shouted to make his voice carry above the din in the bunk-house.

"I beat it across lots on the short-cut trail. The men were raising the roof when I reached the bunk-house. I snapped in on their wild party. Had just time to see that they'd pulled blankets off the bunks, had scattered balsam boughs which served for mattresses all over the place, when a shower of tin cups deluged me—hadn't supposed there were that many in the world. The crowd roared as I backed out. I know when I'm in a hopeless minority. They've been fairly good-natured. Perhaps they will get sleepy and quiet down."

Gerard glanced at his wrist watch. "I'll give them two minutes; then I am going in. Think I will stand outside while my property is being destroyed? Suppose they kick over a stove? Drop a match? Those balsam boughs would flame like tinder."

"Right. I'm with you, Rod."

"I'm with you and Jim, Rodney."

"Keep out of this, Dave. I—" The door of the bunk-house banged open. Men crowded and pushed their way through the opening. "Here they come! After more booze! Back into the shadow. Quick."

The crew swaggered and staggered toward the truck which sprawled like a wounded monster across the road. They stopped and blinked in the glare of the roadster headlights.

Gerard seized their moment of indecision. He started toward them, shook off Armstrong's grip on his sleeve, and with his hands in his pockets faced them in the light.

"Party's all over, boys. There isn't any more."

"Who says so!"

Gerard recognized the burly brute who lurched forward as one of the two men who had deserted to Calloway. Had he driven and dumped the truck?

"Always merry and bright, aren't you, Kusciko? Keep back! You're not in this! I'll talk with my own men."

"Sez he! He's givin' you the razzberry. You guys back there goin' to be told what you can do when you're not on the job?"

The men surged forward. Their muttering was an angry undertone to the bedlam in the bunk-house. Gerard counted. Eleven of them against three. Armstrong and Schuyler had closed in behind him.

Why didn't they stay out of it? This was his fight. His and Calloway's. That last name steeled his muscles. Somewhere Len was gloating over the situation, might even now be looking on. He stepped forward. The shouting and singing inside the bunk-house ceased suddenly. The world was weirdly quiet; he could hear the hiss of a meteor overhead.

"Quit this fool business and go back, men. If you don't you'll lose your jobs tomorrow."

"Yeah! Listen, you guys!" Kusciko swayed forward and leered into Gerard's face. "Who'll this fella you call the Big Boss get to finish the job if he gives you your time? Let's teach this white-collar gent to keep out of other guys' business when the day's work is done. What's he here for—"

Gerard caught the braggart by the collar of his plaid shirt, dragged him from his feet, and with stupendous effort flung him among the men.

"That's what I'm here for!" The words gritted between clamped teeth. "Anyone else want to know?"

For an instant the crowd hesitated, then with a concerted growl it lunged forward. Gerard's blood chilled. Ugly faces. Cruel faces. What would it feel like to be torn to pieces. A man died but once. He wasn't a man if he let a lot of dirty drunks tell him where to get off. His eyes narrowed. Which head would he punch first? He doubled his fist. He'd begin on that chinless mug and make it noseless.

Boy! What a crack! He got his man. Northwest mounted stuff. Why didn't Jim keep out of this?

"Look out!"

Someone yanked him aside, someone struck something that glittered out of Kusciko's hand. It lay, long and keen and cruel, on the trampled snow.

"Keep out of this, Rodney." David Schuyler pulled him back. "Quit pounding that man, Jim. This is my job now."

He walked toward the silent men who, jaws dropped, stared at him with bleared eyes.

"Your little joke has gone far enough, boys." He clamped his foot down on the glittering knife. His voice was steel in a velvet sheath. "Nothing doing, Kuscikol"

The man, who had crawled forward, glared at him from his knees and snatched back his dirty hand.

"Spiritual force against brute force. I seem to remember that as a noble experiment in a far-off country," panted Jim Armstrong at Gerard's shoulder.

Rodney nodded without moving his eyes from the group ahead. Every muscle was tense, he was ready to spring if a hand were laid on David Schuyler. The cool voice went on.

"McGowan, roll Kusciko in the snow. Cool him off. Better all of you play Polar Bear. You—"

"Hi there!" yelled a man on the steps of the bunk-house. "Bring along that—"

Shouts behind him drowned his words. The sounds of scuffling followed, then a crash. Ominous silence for a second. Then yells of fright. One voice pierced the tumult:

"Look out! The stove! Fire! Fire!"

XXI

"I'll take care of the snooper hiding in here!"

At Calloway's harsh threat Prudence flung herself flat on the dirty floor behind the wood pile.

"Smiling—the girl fell dead." She paraphrased a line she had seen recommended as a snappy story ending. That was funny. She buried her head in her arms to stifle nervous laughter. She was nearer hysterics now than she had been the day of the beet crash; then she had been near enough.

A light on the wall! How soon would Calloway grab her? It was coming her way! Had she better crawl out and appear nonchalant? Nearer! Nearer—a door banging!

The lean-to went pitch-black.

"Tried to walk out on me, have you, Walt? You—Milly!"

With utter disregard of the broadcasting quality of the wood pile, Prudence stood up. Milly Gooch! What was she doing here? She waited motionless for a sound in the smithy. Had surprise turned the occupants to stone, or had they gone?

"What are you doing here, Milly?" It was Calloway's voice, shaken, ugly.

"You tell me."

"You'll tell me. Where's Walt Gerard?"

In his surprise the snooper in the lean-to had been forgotten. Prudence tiptoed to the door. It was like looking at a scene in a play. Calloway held the lantern high; the motion of his unsteady hand sent a little whirl of drab smoke against the glass chimney. His black eyes glittered in the wavering light as he scowled at Milly Gooch perched on the forge. Her dark hair, curling from under a gay kerchief, framed her face. A cougar coat almost covered a rose-color wool skirt. Her swinging feet, encased in shapely overshoes, cast long, darting shadows on the rough floor. She pulled a bunch of cigarettes from her pocket, tapped one on her Chinese-red thumb nail, snapped a lighter.

"Gosh, I'm tired from that tramp here. Don't walk much. My feet ache like a tooth gone nervy. I've spent every minute since Sassoon's Smashing Show closed working up new acts for the movies. The people who think circus riders spend their spare time with wine, gents, and song should watch me slave, Len."

"Why did you come? Has Walt Gerard double-crossed me? You'll tell me, and you'll tell me quick."

Milly Gooch glanced at him from between half closed lids. She flicked ashes from her cigarette.

"Cut the act. Too much of that snapping-the-whip stuff is bad for the little mind. So you and Walt Gerard are pals? It's a mean break I didn't know that when I saw him skulking away. What have you two bozos up your sleeves?"

Calloway set the lantern on the forge beside her. "Now look here, Milly,"—his tone was propitiatory— "I'm a just man—"

"Nothing else but—"

She slipped to her feet. With incredible swiftness she reached the door and bolted it. Backed against it she thrust her hands into the pockets of her cougar coat. Her eyes looked enormous as she defied him.

"You're so just, Len, that of course you won't mind staying right here till you've told me what dirty deal you and Walt Gerard are putting across."

Calloway's glance flashed to the double doors. Prudence's blood tingled. He was planning escape that way, was he? To her surprise, instead of turning purple with anger and blustering, he shrugged and put one foot up on the stool. Elbow on his knee, he swung the lantern in his free hand as he faced Milly Gooch.

"I'm not kicking—with you to look at."

"Quick on the uptake, aren't you? What's the racket?"

"Now that my job is finished and the cart's backed up, I don't mind telling you."

"What do you mean, your job? What cart? Have you two been making trouble for Rod-dy?"

Her voice caught in the middle of the name. Prue's nails cut into her hands. It didn't take much perception to realize that Milly Gooch loved Rodney Gerard.

"Trouble for Roddy! Trouble for— Just a little, just a little."

Calloway's repetition was ugly. He kicked away the stool and approached Milly Gooch. The skin at the back of his neck was dark red. He was angry and he was cornered. A menace to the person who crossed him. Prudence squeezed herself between the forge and the wall. She couldn't let that other girl fight alone. Had she been heard? Had she been seen? She held her breath. No. They were too absorbed in each other.

"I told you when you threw me over for him that I would make him pay, didn't I? First he stole my girl—"

"Meaning me? I never was your girl!"

"Engaged to me, weren't you? What do you call that?"

"Guess you mesmerized me. I jumped through the wrong hoop, that's all. Gosh, I don't know why. Suppose Roddy—suppose I did like Roddy better, are you going round making trouble for every man a girl likes better than you? You'd better move to the desert."

"That isn't all Rodney Gerard has done!"

In spite of her defiance, Milly's face was slightly drawn with fear. Had the man's eyes gone red? Prudence cautiously edged along the wall till she reached the double doors.

Calloway jerked at his collar. "He has come between me and business. He is cutting timber that it's my right to cut. I would have winked at that if he hadn't already taken you away from me."

"Don't cry, Len," Milly Gooch tormented.

He caught her shoulder. "Now he's set Prudence Schuyler against me."

"Another girl friend! Listen, you're the original great lover, aren't you?"

She was mad to taunt him. Couldn't she see that he was working toward frenzy? Prudence looked at the bolts on the door behind her. Suppose Calloway turned the tables and kept Milly and herself prisoners here? That was a thought. It sent icy prickles soloing up her spine. She glanced at the window opposite. Through the dusty pane she could see snow silvered by moonlight, patched with the purple shadow of a spruce, icicles glittering like diamonds. Glorious world, and God in His Heaven. With the thought came the sense of the grip of a steadying hand. Why be afraid?

"Let me go, Len! Make it snappy!" Milly's voice was strained.

"And suppose I don't?"

"You will. You are such a just man," Prudence reminded sweetly.

Calloway wheeled and scowled at her backed against the double door. Milly shrugged, pulled a vanity case from her pocket and applied a lipstick.

"Took you a long time to put on your act, didn't it?"

"What do you mean?" Prudence resisted the impulse to dash toward her. She must guard the door.

"I saw you stealing away from the red brick house. I went there to ask if I might see the rooms; I lived there once. You sneaked across the road. I knew—I knew Roddy liked you. So I followed to see what you were up to. Don't kid yourself. I found out. You came to meet that rotten Walt Gerard!"

Had the roof collapsed on her? She, Prudence Schuyler, was being accused of a rendezvous with that sneaky man!

"Don't be foolish!" She tried to keep her voice condescendingly amused; she succeeded only in producing words which shook with anger. "If you are interested to know, I came because Calloway and Walter Gerard are conspiring to hurt Rodney."

"Hurt him! What do you mean, hurt him?"

"Ask him."

Milly caught the arm of the man who stood scowling from one girl to the other.

"Have you hurt Roddy, Len? If you have—"

Her small pointed white teeth set in her under lip like those of an angry cat.

The veins in Calloway's temples stood out like cords. "Didn't I tell you when you threw me down for him, Milly, that I would run Rodney Gerard off the earth? Well, I'm doing it, off this part of the earth. He'll think twice before he cuts in on my girl or my business again."

Milly shook him. "You great sap! You—you flat tire!" Her voice rose in shrill invective. "Rodney

Gerard had nothing to do with my throwing you over. It was Walt! Your present pal! Walt!"

"Walt! Don't try to be funny. Did Walt have your picture with, 'From calico and Calloway to liberty and love,' written on the back of it? Did he keep it in the room Rod uses for his office at High Ledges?

'Walt!' Try another alibi, Milly, try another."

She shook him again with as much effect as a mouse attempting to pull down a stone lion.

"Have you gone haywire? I never sent a photo to Roddy—the one you saw belonged to Walt. I suppose he could use a desk at High Ledges, couldn't he? You make me sick with your suspicions of Roddy. What have you two—racketeers done to him?"

Calloway's face was as colorless as white chalk. "Say that again about Walt Gerard having that picture, Milly."

"I'll say it again. Shall I tell all? It isn't a bedtime story. It might have been more snappy if it hadn't been for Rodney Gerard. I was dead sick of working and one-night stands and shabby clothes and Grandpop sick and out of a job most of the time. Walt came along and offered to make life's walk easy—for a consideration. And can he hand out a line, I'm telling you!" Her eyes and voice tormented. "Before I closed with his offer, Roddy found it out and—and he made it easy for no consideration. Get that, Len?"

"Is that right?"

"Sure, a hundred per cent right. I'm telling the truth. Rodney Gerard doesn't know I'm on earth—except when it's time to send me a check or bring me one. I've kept on taking the money so I would see him sometimes. What have you done to him, Len Calloway?"

He glared at her unseeingly. "So-o I've been hunting the wrong man, have I? Walt was back of your break with me! I knew that he had hung around you—but he was married. Rod Gerard has been shielding his no-account brother. And I thought I was such a just man! I—"

His face worked horribly. Prudence felt as if a

stripped soul had been laid bare. She looked across the smithy. Was she living in a nightmare, or had the glistening world outside turned crimson?

A wail like the warning of a giant banshee swelled to a deafening screech, dwindled, rose again to ear-splitting proportions, died down.

"What's that?"

"Shut up, Milly! Listen! Count!" Calloway's voice was hoarse.

Prudence clenched her hands. The fire siren! Suppose it were the red brick house. Would Macky think to rescue the Paul Lamerie kettle?

Once more the wail shattered the forest quiet. No one moved in the stillness which followed.

Calloway pulled Milly away from the door. She gripped his arm.

"What is it, Len?"

"Fire! Gerard place! I—I—did it! I didn't mean that—I only wanted to keep the men from work!"

He jammed back the bolt and plunged into the snow. Prudence dashed after him. She stopped for a breathless instant. Sky and snow and glistening icicles were rose-color. The fire must be near. The cattle barn! Walter Gerard and Calloway! "The cart's backed up." Had that "cart" been loaded with explosives?

The headlights of a car flashed. Calloway's! A tail-light swept away like a meteor pursued by furies.

"That red roadster weaves in and out of my life like a theme in an opera," Prudence thought, as she stumbled and slid and ran along the road made smooth and treacherous by the passing of many trucks. She couldn't go back for her skis.

"Wait! Wait! What's burning?" Milly Gooch shrieked.

Prudence stopped long enough to call over her shoulder:

"The barn—where—the crew—is living—I think!"

She couldn't say more. She must save her breath. Neither would she wait. Of course, Rodney would be in the midst of danger. She must tell him that she was sorry for her suspicion. Sorry! Lot he'd be interested now. She had had to be shown by Milly Gooch. She had taken Calloway's word against his. She might have trusted him.

Shouts ahead. Crashes. Timbers falling? A curious sky. Red. Sullen. Shot with flame. The light had put out the stars. She coughed and tried to get her breath. Smoke. Not much like the clear, sparkling air as she had taken the jump down the hill. That jump seemed a million light years away.

She skidded on a sharp turn. Caught at a giant pine. That was a break. She shut her teeth hard in her lips to keep back a cry of horror—not that one more sound in the pandemonium of shouts and yells would have counted. Ahead the cattle barn loomed darkly against the sinister glow. Its windows were like demoniac eyes burning with scarlet and orange and crimson flames; spurts of fire leaped from the roof like snaky hairs on the head of a giant. Black figures like huge panicky ants dashed in and out of the glow. Men were dragging a hose from the fire engine to the pond. The wind had increased. It blew showers of snow from the trees. Someone shouted:

"Soak those pines! If the woods start to burn—"

That was the reason for the frightful tension. Even with snow on the ground the whole forest might go up like tinder.

Runabouts, gigs, automobiles of all descriptions crowded the spaces under the trees. Even in the uncertain light the two units of the fire department made glaring spots of color. Men worked, ran, hauled. No mistaking Calloway's massive figure. Reckless of self and safety he fought the blaze. There was David steadying a groaning man. He was safe, thank God!

Clang! Clang! Clang! The emergency gong of an ambulance! It must have come from the hospital in the next town.

Tree by tree Prudence crept forward. The heat was scorching. Not hotter for her than for those men working near that red inferno. She put her arm across her face to protect it from sparks and hot cinders. Could she help? There must be something she could do instead of standing here in trance-like horror. A man with eyebrows and hair scorched off dropped at her feet. His sleeves were blazing. She ripped off her dark wool jacket and crushed out the fire. She pulled off his tattered sleeves, set her teeth as his blistered arms were exposed. For an instant the trees went end over end. Then they steadied. She bent over the man who looked up at her with glazed, tortured eyes.

"I pulled out my—my duffle-bag. Everything I own—"

"Don't talk. I'll be back in a minute with something to ease the pain."

She ran and dodged her way to the ambulance surgeon, who, in his white coat polka-dotted with scorch, was applying a temporary steel splint to a broken arm. She tried to close her ears against a piercing shriek of agony. She demanded breathlessly:

"Give me oil and guaze, quick! Don't stare! I've had some training. I'll help." She obeyed his curt nod and dashed to the ambulance.

With hands full of supplies, she dropped on her knees beside the man by the tree. He opened scorched lids and tried to stretch his burned mouth in a smile.

"Say, Miss, you look—like an oriole in that orange shirt—oh, my God—how it burns!"

She did what she could to ease his pain, applied oil and gauze to three other blistered arms. Two men stumbled out of the red smoke and set a stretcher down beside her; its rubber tires were spongy from heat. One bearer slapped out little spurts of flame on his flannel shirt sleeve as he panted:

"We all went—dotty—tryin' to save a couple of fellas too drunk to find the way out. Had to pull the Big Boss out first—he dashed in ahead of everyone. Doc told us—you had supplies, Miss. Take—a look at this guy and see if you—can help him. Better pull—a fast one—he's all in."

Rodney in that inferno. Prudence shut her eyes tight to get her grip. Then she looked. The cry of

horror she swallowed nauseated her. "Don't dare go
back on me!" she threatened her dizzy brain. Teeth
clamped, she applied oil and gauze.

"That's all I can do. Take him to the ambulance,
quick!"

She straightened, threw back her strained shoulders. Rodney was safe—safe. Hadn't the men said
they pulled him out? A great stream of water was
drenching the trees beyond the blazing shell which
was once a cattle barn. She drew a deep breath. That
was a flop. She had filled her lungs with smoke and
cinders. Why didn't that huge stream stop the fire?
The wind was blowing it back, that was why. The ap-
paratus and the firemen were encased in ice. Where
could she help most? Rodney Gerard and Armstrong
were safe. They were standing together. Should she
ask them where she could be of most use?

Milly Gooch here! How had she come? Milly, her
short black hair blowing in the breeze which was
fanning the fire, was clinging to Rodney's sleeve. He
was trying to shake her off. He had succeeded. Why,
why did he go toward that burning shell again? Jim
was pulling him back. He couldn't stop the fire. He—

Roars of warning. A crash! The roof! A red-hot
girder shot into the air. A woman screamed. It spi-
raled down! Down where Rodney and Jim were
standing!

Terror paralyzed Prudence. Rodney hurt? She
couldn't bear it! Hurt before she could tell him she
was sorry. Men were crowding around something.
What? Why was she standing here when—

She ran forward and caromed into someone running with a force which swept her from her feet. An
arm caught her.

"Prue! Prue! You shouldn't be here!"

She brushed her hand across dazed eyes. Was this
really Jim Armstrong? He was safe! Was Rodney lying
there hurt—perhaps?

"Is it really—you? I saw you and Rodney—I
thought the girder hit—" She seized the lapels of his

coat to steady herself. "Is—is—he—" Had the blood gone from her head? It felt light as a balloon.

Armstrong gently but firmly loosened her tense fingers. His lips were white as he assured with exaggerated cheeriness:

"Rod is safe, Prue. Listen! Don't stare like that! He's all right. It's Calloway who is hurt. He rushed in and took the girder which would have wiped Rod out."

She could feel his shudder. "Calloway! Calloway!" What was the matter with her voice? It came from miles away. "Yes. He said he had made trouble for Rodney—and then he found out that it wasn't he—he's such a just man!"

She felt herself going, flung an arm around Jim's neck. She must hold tight to something. Was that Rodney looking at her from behind Jim? His eyes were terrible. Curious, the world was so black, the sky was—so red—

When she came out of the smothering gloom, she was sitting on a coat against a tree. Who was shrieking and sobbing? It couldn't be herself having hysterics, could it? She would die of shame if it were. David was rubbing her hands. A man in a white jacket was holding something to her mouth. Jim Armstrong was looking down at her. How queer his eyes were! Where was Rodney Gerard?

She said unsteadily:

"Don't tell me I—fainted when I might have been—of use."

The ambulance surgeon's grin slashed his sooty face. "Use! Say, there are five men who think you're an angel straight from heaven. You did your good deed for the day, all right. For the love of Mike, why doesn't someone stop that circus rider's yelling! I guess if anyone was entitled to pass out cold you were. Drink this like a good girl."

XXII

Bent over her work bench, the sleeves of her green linen smock rolled above her elbows, Prudence was intent on soldering. Her cheeks burned, her eyes felt twice their normal size, as cautiously she blew the flame from a small alcohol lamp on a tiny silver ring on a charcoal block. Silly of her to be so tense over a thing she had done a thousand times—all the other joints were protected with tripoli paste—but this was different, she excused herself, this was the last link in the collar for Jean's kitten.

She dropped the blow pipe and with pincers lifted the silver collar. She examined it link by link. Not a defect in the soldering. After it had been burnished, she would set the cat's-eyes and attach the amber pendant. That would be that. Finished. And a piece of work which made her artistic self purr when she looked at it.

She dropped the collar into a crucible of sulphuric acid and lighted the spirit lamp under it. This was the last piece of Christmas work. She had left it until her orders from a distance had been mailed; then she had finished the tourmaline necklace for Jean; and now this. Time it was ready. Tomorrow would be Christmas. She glanced at the huge spray of pine and juniper she had tied to the newel post in the hall by a broad red satin ribbon, beyond to the living room mantel banked with green, to the wreaths bright with holly in her work-room. She sniffed. She loved the Christmas smell, there was no other scent quite like it.

Christmas! Two weeks since the fire! She had not seen Rodney Gerard. Every moment she could spare from work outside had been spent at her bench, and he had not come to the red brick house. David rarely mentioned him. Why should he come? What modern man would be interested in a girl who "passed out cold" in an emergency?

Her face burned. Why, why had she collapsed—for the second time in her life—like a mid-Victorian heroine in a crisis, when she might have gone on helping! Even the fact that she had forgotten to eat before she started on her man hunt, that her heart had stopped when the girder fell, as she supposed on Rodney, was no excuse.

The collar had been boiled long enough. She extinguished the lamp under the crucible and glanced at the bay window. The sun was beginning to slant, she could tell from the pattern its light made on the rug where it filtered through the plants. It shone like a Christmas ornament spiked on the tip of a pine. Time enough to set the stones before she dressed for the party.

The party! She opened a white packet and poked the cat's-eyes on the tissue paper into the order in which she would use them. How they glowed! They were like eyes. Inscrutable eyes. Like Rodney's the night they had met hers over Jim Armstrong's shoulder. What had he thought when he saw her clinging to his friend? Only one thing he could think after she had told him that she was engaged to Jim. She had lied to set an insurmountable wall between them, and then she had found that no barrier was needed because, rich or poor, she knew that she loved him, that he would be true and fine all his life. She hadn't been sure of it, though, until Milly Gooch had flung the truth at Calloway that night in the smithy. She had wanted love without risk of heartbreak; it looked as if she would get heartbreak without love.

Prudence lifted the collar from the liquid and carefully dried it. She covered it with powdered pumice before she laid it against the emery wheel, and, foot on the treadle of the old sewing machine, polished the silver.

Had Rodney forgotten that he had ordered it? The morning after the cattle barn had burned to the

ground, every able-bodied man in the village had
dropped his own work to help rebuild. Each man of
the scorched, chastened crew, who had been able to
use his hands, had tried to do the work of three in the
woods. They had been billeted in barns. They ought
to work their arms off—hadn't their rioting caused the
damage? That wasn't quite fair; the truck which Len
Calloway and Walter Gerard had dumped at their
door had been the real cause.

The new building had gone up as quickly as if a
Radio City engineer had waved a magic wand. In
appreciation of the neighborly spirit, Rodney Gerard
was giving a Christmas Eve party to the townspeople. High Ledges was to be *en fête,* with Christmas
greens and innumerable candles, a caterer and musi-
cians from New York. Milly Gooch would not be
among those present. She had left the Puffers' the day
after the fire.

Jean had imparted the information about the proposed celebration. Although David spent most of
each day where the crew was working, he never
mentioned Rodney Gerard. They were shutting her
out. She would have loved to help in the prepara-
tions—she adored getting ready for parties—but:

"I couldn't crash in and offer my invaluable assis-
tance, could I?" she interrogated the emery wheel,
but the wheel merely threw off a spiteful little shower
of pumice in answer.

"Miss Prue! Miss Prue!"

Prudence dropped the silver collar into the pocket
of her smock, covered the cat's eyes. She was sorting
the tools on the bench when Jean dashed into the
room. Her puckish eyes brimmed with tears.

"What do you think's happened now? Mother's
here!"

"Here!" Prudence started for the door.

"Not in this house. She is at High Ledges. She's
come to spend Christmas with—with me. I don't see
why, when Father has beat it."

With a valiant attempt to repress her own dis-
mayed reaction to the news, Prudence comforted:

"But, dear, of course she wants to be with you at Christmas. She—"

"Don't talk like a schoolteacher. Uncle Rod looked as if he would bite her head off when he saw her. He and Mr. Jim were bad enough before she came; after they've been out in the woods all day, they just sit and stare at the fire and smoke like chimneys. Now everything's going to be more haywire than ever, and it's Christmas."

Prudence gave her a quick hug.

"Because it's Christmas is the reason you should forget yourself, what you want to do—and try to make someone else happy."

"I know all that bunk," Jean blinked and swallowed, "but you don't have to live with Mother. Uncle Rod said I was to receive guests with him, and I have that peachy pink dress—and now Mother will think she ought to take my place—"

Prudence stroked the short, rough hair snuggled against her shoulder.

"Uncle Rod won't let anyone take your place. Come now,

" 'Pack up your troubles in your old kit bag and
   Smile! Smile! Smile!' "

Jean beat time on the bench as her voice joined with Prue's. She administered an ecstatic hug.

"Gee, you're a peach! I don't wonder everybody's crazy about you. Mr. Jim says—"

"Jean, I have an idea." Prudence expertly shifted conversational gears. From the bookcase she took a small red package tied with gold gauze ribbon. "I had intended to have this dropped into your stocking, but perhaps you would rather wear it tonight with that pink frock."

Jean turned the box over and over in her hands. "Something you made for me?"

What a sensitive little thing she was! If only her mother were different, Prudence thought, even as she advised:

"Don't open it until you are ready to go down to receive. And, dear, forget what you want, and try to make your mother and Uncle Rod happy. You know how much he depends upon you to—" Prudence artfully left the sentence unfinished.

"I will try. I will, Miss Prue. You're a duck to give me this. I'll go home this minute and begin." On the threshold she paused with the box clasped tightly against her breast.

"I wish—I wish I could give you something. I wish I could find the emerald and diamonds that were stolen. I've tried and tried—I've picked a lot of cagey locks, but—nothing doing."

"Forget it. David told me to, said he would get them back. If he doesn't—what's the difference—run along and help Uncle Rod all you can."

"'Dearie, I'll do that little thing.' Your Christmas greens are a knock-out, Miss Prue, but just wait till you see our tree! Boxes of candy or perfume for the ladies. Pipes and smokes for the men. Bye-bye! See you tonight. Come early."

Prudence was smiling at Jean's perfect imitation of Mrs. Si, as she pulled the silver collar from her pocket and started the emery wheel. She looked at the window. Only a copper rim of sun was visible above the tree tops. The golden afternoon was slipping into a hushed rose-color dusk which was turning violet at the edges. She wouldn't get to the party at all if she didn't keep at work.

Her thoughts kept pace with her foot on the treadle. Would Rodney Gerard come for the collar? Perhaps he had forgotten it. What would she do with it? She would hate like the dickens to remind him. It had proved expensive. If they were friends as they had been that day he had ordered it—

Wheel and hands stopped moving. He had sat on the corner of the bench—she had felt his eyes on her—she had looked up—

"Never realized before how much red there is in your hair—Gorgeous," his voice had said, but his eyes—

Why live over that? It only made her heart ache as if something were squeezing it unbearably. Why had she been so obsessed with the idea that a man of wealth couldn't remain true to the marriage covenant? From her reasoning one might think that every man who wasn't rich was a paragon of truth and honor. The fact that her brother's wife and her sister's husband had been philanderers was no excuse for misjudging Rodney.

Perhaps she needed the lesson, she told herself, as on the high stool she carefully set a cat's eye in a silver rim. David had said: "Real love, no matter how unworthy the object, is a glorious adventure; it bursts the shackles of selfishness; one's world is bigger, broader, one's sympathies amazingly more tender. No matter what the result, if you haven't really loved, Prue, you haven't really lived."

She knew what he meant now. Love hadn't made her tender. She had been getting bitter, and getting bitter meant getting sharp-tongued.

"A sharp-tongued woman is the meanest work of God," she concluded aloud.

"You shouldn't be working without a light, Miss Prue."

Prudence looked up with a start. "When did you steal in, Macky?"

"I didn't steal in. I don't like that word steal, Miss Prue." The shade of the lamp rattled as Jane Mack removed it.

"My mistake. Bring the light to the bench, will you?" She held up the collar.

"This is the best thing I've done yet. It's a triumph. I'm not pleased with myself, am I? It is a collar for Jean's kitten. See the little Mickey Mouses?"

Jane Mack sniffed. "You do so much for other people, Miss Prue, it's a shame you should have—have lost that emerald and the diamonds."

"Forget it. This is Christmas. I have a feeling that those stones will come back some day. I suspect—"

"Who, Miss Prue?"

"Macky! Has the mere memory of that hold-up man

turned you white? Hurry up and make us both a cup
of tea. That will steady your nerves and make my
work hum. Everything ready for dinner tomorrow?"

"Yes, Miss Prue. Mrs. Puffer brought up the mince
pies she promised. I've had my tea. Saw a procession
in the cup. Can't tell whether it's going to be a
wedding or a party or a funeral."

Hours later, Prudence, squeezed into the back seat
beside Mrs. Si in the Puffer car; looked up at High
Ledges.

"This is the party in your cup, Macky," she said
gaily.

The windows were alight with candles. Evergreens
gay with colored bulbs bordered the drive. An all-
white Christmas tree, dripping with silver tinsel, glittering with artificial snow, glimmering with white
bulbs, loomed on the lawn in a flood of light. Cars of
every description deposited their occupants at the
front steps. Each time the door opened it let out a
glow, the scent of balsam, and a drift of music. The
atmosphere throbbed with gayety and good cheer
and Christmas spirit.

Even bulky Mrs. Si seemed wafted into the house
by the rushing impetuosity of mellow horns and
singing strings. The arrangement of pine and juniper
and balsam in the great hall was stunning. The beauty of the laden tree almost surpassed that of the one
on the lawn. Jean had not exaggerated. The decora-
tions were bounteous. Not one of the gaunt brood of
fears and anxieties old General Depression had left
behind him could live in that atmosphere. Too much
life and hope and gayety; the music set one's spirit on
its toes.

Prudence regarded herself in the long mirror in the
dressing room. For the first time since she had left the
city and festivities behind her, she was wearing an
evening gown. How white her arms and shoulders
were in contrast to its glittering ice-green! The color
was Christmasy. Should she have worn a frock so
backless to a party like this? Why not? It was her
best, and the best was none too good for this festivity.

She nodded to the looking-glass girl. "No matter what your frock is, my dear, Julie's pearls are marvelous."

Her brother joined her in the hall. "I've been looking for you, Prue. Sorry not to wait and come with you, but Gerard wanted me here early."

"He's always wanting you, David. I don't know where we would have tucked you into the Puffer car had you waited. Isn't that music heavenly! I've never seen a more gorgeous Christmas tree! Looking pretty snappy, aren't you?" she approved gaily, to camouflage the surge of thanksgiving which shook her as she looked at him, apparently so strong, so well. "I love you in a dinner jacket, and that gardenia is the last ultra touch."

"That is Rod's 'touch.' I'll say the Schuyler farmers will do credit to the party—yes? Mrs. Si said 'the folks' hoped Rod and Jim and I would dress as we would for a party at home. White ties and tails seemed out of place, so we compromised. You are not terribly hard to look at yourself. Miss Mack is doing her bit for the honor of the family. She is stiff with black glitter, and she is smiling. Shall we go down?"

From the stairs Prudence saw Jean and Rodney Gerard greeting the arriving guests. The child was really beautiful in her rose-color frock with the pink and green and silver necklace gleaming softly about her young white throat. Behind them in the living room, complacent and whispering, matrons sat in a row against the walls hung with huge holly wreaths.

Rodney Gerard looked up. The color mounted to his forehead as his eyes met Prue's. Her heart grew wings. He must have forgiven her, he must want to be friends again, or he wouldn't look at her like that. He crossed the hall and met her as she reached the lowest step.

"K.K. and I began to think you had passed up our party." He dropped the hand he had seized. "Help make people feel at home, will you?" he asked stiffly. "You'll find Jim in the next room," he flung over his shoulder as he turned away.

His voice had the effect of a shower of ice water. Anger burned away the chill. Was he afraid that she might expect him to devote himself to her if he showed even decent civility? He needn't worry. With chin up she entered the room in which dancers were swinging and humming to the rhythm of the music.

"I consider myself fairly tall, but you are looking right over me," complained Jim Armstrong. "Dance?" He put his arm about her. She saw Rodney Gerard watching them.

"You!" she crooned, with a warmth and *empressement* which narrowed Armstrong's eyes. As they glided off in perfect unison, she approved: "I have suspected that you were a superb dancer; now I know." She looked back. Rodney had vanished.

"Come out to the sun porch, Prue. I want to talk to you."

The grimness of Armstrong's voice generated prickles in her veins. Had he found out what she had told Rodney? Was he furiously angry? Perhaps he would sue her for saying that she was engaged to him. That was a cheerful thought for this merry Christmastide.

"Now what have I done?" she demanded in mock terror, as they entered the enclosed porch gay with wicker and cretonnes and plants and colored lights. She sat on the edge of a swinging seat in the secluded corner to which Armstrong led her. He drew forward a chair and seated himself so that his broad back screened her from the door.

"This is what you've done, Prue—we'll get down to facts at once. You are the finest, the best sport of any girl I know—"

"Thanks for them kind words, but don't try to soften the blow. What have I done that makes you sit there looking as grim as an executioner and—and twice as handsome?"

He refused to be diverted by her gayety. "All right, laugh, but do you realize that you have made me appear to double-cross my best friend?"

"What do you mean?"

"I feel like a brute holding you up like this when

God knows I wish—" He cleared his throat. "Why did you tell Rod that you were engaged to me?"

"Did he tell you that?"

"Hold on now, sit back in the seat and listen. Something went wrong between him and me the afternoon you and your brother dropped in on us at High Ledges. I felt it but I couldn't get hold of anything. Then things got in such a mess that I put Rod's crabbedness down to worry over the lumbering. Remember when you collapsed the night of the fire?"

"Remember! Of course I remember. I never fainted but once in my life, and when I think that I crashed when I might have helped more, mortification sends my blood pressure down, down, down."

"Don't worry about that. The ambulance surgeon says you may have a job with him any time you are ready for it. When you went to pieces that night, Rod nearly blew my head off because I left you. Your brother and the doctor were with you; I was needed somewhere else. I stayed though."

"Martyr," Prudence jeered softly. Not that she felt like being flippant, but to assure herself that her stiff lips would move.

"That night—or morning rather—when we got back from the fire the whole thing came out. You had told Rod that you were engaged to me, and he accused me of underhand methods, because the day I arrived at High Ledges he warned me that he intended to marry you."

"He did!"

"He did. Your eyes look as if they saw the coming of the Lord! Why did you tell him we were engaged? Don't answer. Tell Rod." He cleared his voice. "Promise you will explain to Rodney; you owe that to me."

"Sorry to interrupt this twosome, Jim, but Prue's brother is looking for her," announced Rodney Gerard behind him.

Armstrong rose. "Great Scott, I had forgotten! This is my dance with the village beauty. Take Prue in, will you, Rod?"

Prudence made a vain effort to clutch his coat. At

the door of the living room Gerard put his arm about her.

"Easier to dance through this bunch. Do you mind?"

She shook her head. His touch set little pulses in her throat hammering, the blood in her veins leaping, her body tingling with a fiery quality of life she never before had felt. He had told Jim that he intended to marry her! She looked up.

"I told you that I was engaged to Jim Armstrong. I wasn't. I don't love him a bit." Was that her voice, so pure, warm, and throbby, or was another girl speaking?

For an instant his eyes flamed with amazement; then he crushed her to him savagely.

"Is that true? What a place to tell me! I can't—" He bent his head.

"Rod! Rod! Not here! Not—"

Color rushed back to his face. "Think I was going to kiss you? Didn't I promise I wouldn't until—"

A hand fell on his arm. A prosperous young farmer asked diffidently:

"Dance with me, Miss Schuyler?"

With a look which set Prue's heart clamoring, Gerard relinquished her.

With the breathless sense that she was walking over a not too slumbering volcano, Prudence laughed and chatted with her partner when the music stopped. She went from group to group stopping to chat with the men and women of the village, wishing them a gay "Merry Christmas!" Mrs. Walter Gerard, in the latest in platinum metallic hairdressing and a smart black frock, bore down upon her.

"Dear Miss Schuyler, you are ravishing in that frosted green. It brings out your high color marvelously. How good of you to come to our simple little party. You've been so kind to my darling daughter. She has a fascinating uncle, hasn't she?"

To Prue's indignant fancy the last sentence seemed to ring through the room as if magnificently amplified. Her response, she could not have told what it was, shook with anger. Almost she sympathized with Walter Gerard. How could a man live with a winking woman? She turned on her heel almost into the arms of Armstrong.

"What dastardly deed are you contemplating?" he demanded, as gaily as if the conversation in the sun room never had taken place. "Your eyes are spitting sparks, you look mad as a hatter."

Prudence relaxed and slipped her hand within his arm.

"Make it mad as two hatters and you will be getting warm. Lucky you appeared. For a minute I went primitive. I felt an outrageous urge to scratch and bite and kick. That's the sort of perfect lady I am. Let's forget it. Everyone else seems to be having a grand time."

"This is some party. Rod is doing himself proud. He and Jean are distributing gifts. He sent me to look after you. Come on, let's eat."

The flames of red candles in high golden sticks were palely reflected dozens of times on the rare Chinese screens, gold all of them, which walled the dining room. The middle of the long refectory table was banked with red roses; the supper was as varied and delectable as a noted caterer knew how to serve it. The guests' eyes were wide with admiration, their cheeks pink with repletion. Perched on one of the wide window sills, Prudence pretended to eat.

"How is the lumbering coming, Jim?"

"It's a cinch. The two men who deserted to Calloway slunk back and asked for a job. We took one, but the crew rode Kusciko out of town."

"Why?"

"He dumped the truck of liquor."

"I suppose he was doing the dirty work of someone higher up."

"Of course—but he tried to knife Rod. That gets you, doesn't it? Here, drink this punch. Even if it is warranted to cheer and not inebriate, it will bring your color back. Don't care much for old Rod, do you?"

"Who are you to try to probe the secrets of a maiden's heart." Her eyes lost their laughter. "How is Calloway?"

"Better. He has made a public confession that he was solely responsible for dumping that load of liquor in front of the cattle barn and that he will pay the bills. He did it to get even with Rod. When he found out that he was wrong—"

"He is such a just man," Prudence interpolated crisply.

"He is doing his darndest to be one now. He diverted the girder which would have finished Rod. I had turned away and didn't see it coming."

Prudence shivered. "That's the worst of the horrors of that lurid night. Sometimes when I can't sleep I live over it. Oh, let's not think of it. I must find the Puffers. They probably want to go home."

As Prudence came down the broad stairs in her green velvet wrap with its broad mink collar, Rodney Gerard was waiting.

"Going? My party has been a knock-out, hasn't it?" The blue of his eyes was black, a hint of passion underlay the laughter in his voice.

"I don't like to talk about myself, but—" Prue flouted gaily. If only her heart would stop thumping, she wished wildly. "You have immortalized yourself. Good-night."

She could feel the throb of his finger-tips as he held the hand she offered.

"Are you sure Si is waiting? Then I will leave you and speed my other guests."

XXIII

"He didn't say good-night!" Prudence told herself over and over, as she squeezed in beside Mrs. Puffer on the back seat of the automobile.

"Foolish for your brother to drive home alone," Si protested, as he started the car. "Whatta mean is, he might have come along with us."

"Where?" his wife inquired practically. She laughed her soft, cushiony laugh. "No room on this seat. Miss Prue is almost out over the wheel now."

"Perhaps there wouldn't be room. I'm always forgettin', Mother, that you're not so slim as you were in the days when you and I went to the circus."

"The circus! That reminds me, what happened to Milly Gooch?" Prudence inquired.

Mrs. Si drew a long, troubled breath. "She went to pieces the night of the fire, dearie. She had hysterics hanging on to Roddy Gerard—guess if folks hadn't been scared to death thinking where those flames might go there would have been some whispering."

" 'Twouldn't have lasted, Mother. Len Calloway's confession brought out the whole story of how Roddy'd helped her. Walt Gerard had better not set his foot in the village or he'll be tarred and feathered. Gorry-me, that party was a great lay-out, wan't it? It must have made Mrs. Walt see red to have had the whole village at High Ledges."

"Now, Si, she was real friendly tonight, real nice and friendly."

Jane Mack sniffed. "What did she want? I know folks."

"Lors, Jane, she just asked me so polite if I wouldn't come up tomorrow and help Mrs. Patch put the place to rights that I said right off, 'Dearie, I'll do just that.' "

"You would, you old dear." Prudence patted the plump hand.

"But I like to be neighborly, Miss Prue. Folks were awful pleased you were so friendly tonight. You spoke to everyone, didn't you? You're the kind that makes a man straighten his tie and a female slick her hair when you heave in sight. I watched 'em tonight. Know what they say in the village when they see you coming? 'Here comes the sun!' If you have worries you don't shadow other folks with 'em. Here we are at

your door. I'll come up and help with the dinner
tomorrow, Jane. Merry Christmas, dearie! Good-
night!"

Prudence lingered outside the red brick house.
What a night! Snow covered stone walls and boulders; a field of white, crossed and recrossed by the
tracks of a small animal, sloped to the woods; giant
trees cast purple shadows; the bay sparkled between
patches of ice. Moonlight silvered the dormers of the
house. How low the stars seemed! They were like
gold dust spangling indigo velvet.

> " 'O little town of Bethlehem,
>   How still we see thee lie!
>   Above thy deep and dreamless sleep
>   The silent stars go by.' "

The song drifted faintly from the house. Prudence
swallowed a lump in her throat. David had turned on
the radio to hear the Christmas carols. She shouldn't
leave him alone with his memories on this night of all
others.

He was standing before the fire, an arm on the
evergreen-banked mantel, when she entered the living room. The setter on the rug opened one black-
rimmed reproachful eye. David smiled as he met her
eyes. Thank heaven, he could smile.

"Happy is trying to make us realize that that
spanking red satin bow on his collar is a crowning
indignity, Prue. He didn't meet me when I came into
the house, he has kept his head down as if ashamed
to face the world."

"Really, Dave, do you think it hurts his feelings?
We can't have anyone hurt on Christmas Eve." She
drew the ribbon from the dog's collar. Immediately
he sat up on his haunches and yawned.

"Remember that, Prue."

"Remember what?"

"That we can't have anyone hurt on Christmas Eve.
I'll call this a day. It is so long since I have stepped
out to an evening festivity that I am tired."

"Oh, I thought we would talk it over before the fire, David. That's half the fun of a party." She slipped her hand under his arm and laid her cheek against his sleeve. "Of course you are tired, dear. Go to bed. I will lock up."

"I want to be full of pep tomorrow. Gerard is having a big tree for the crew at the bunk-house, sort of a house warming. Come on, Happy. I would like you for company on the rug beside my bed." His arm tightened about her shoulders.

"Know what bit of verse flashed into my mind tonight at High Ledges when I saw you going from guest to guest?

> " 'When Spring is old and dewy winds
> Blow from the south with odors sweet,
> I see my love in shadowy groves
> Speed down dark aisles on shining feet.'

"No matter how dark and problem-logged the path, Prue, you bring life and gayety and courage in your train."

"Why, Dave! Dave!"

Prudence hid her quivering lips against his shoulder. His praise brought her heart to her throat. He laid his hand tenderly on her ruddy hair.

"Didn't expect your staid old brother to go sentimental, did you?" He laughed. "Well, that's my story and I stick to it. You're stunning in that frock, Prue."

Prudence lifted her head and blinked away tears. She parried gaily:

"Mrs. Walt said 'ravishing,' that green brought out my high color marvelously. When she said that, I knew that I should have worn white to tone down the aforementioned color."

"Good-night dear."

" 'Good-night, good-night, beloved,' " she hummed in a husky undertone as she watched him cross the room.

She started to bank the fire, threw on a log instead. She was wide awake, she couldn't sleep if she went

to bed. She curled up in the wing chair. Why hadn't
Rodney said good-night? Perhaps just as she had discovered that she adored him, he didn't like her any-
more. Why should he? She had been bitter and hateful. Now that love for him had slipped into her heart
and taken absolute possession, it had given life a new
value, given her a new insight into her own needs
and shortcomings.

She snuggled deeper into the chair. Perhaps she
was a washout in many ways, but David loved her.
Hadn't he said that she brought life and gayety and
courage in her train? He must have been deeply
moved to have said that. What was the line he had
quoted? She had it:

"Speed down dark aisles on shining feet."

On shining feet. The mere words had lift and buoy-
ancy. She would remember them when the aisles
ahead seemed dark and threatening. Mrs. Si had
reported that the village people said, "Here comes the
sun!" when she appeared. If she didn't watch out she
would begin to fancy herself as a sort of "trailing
clouds of glory" person, and become unbearable. Apparently she had made good as a sister and neighbor.
After this she would try to help more. As a debutante
she had learned something of the problems of her
city under a trained instructor. Many of the problems
of a village couldn't be different except in a degree.

A vine outside tapped icy fingers against a window.
A shutter rattled eerily. The fire purred. Her thoughts
raced on and on. The banjo clock wheezed and ponderously struck the hour.

Prudence counted. Midnight. How still the world
was!

> " ' 'Twas the night before Christmas
> And all through the house
> Not a creature was stirring
> Not even a mouse.' "

The words singsonged through her mind. Had
Dasher and Dancer, Prancer and Vixen, Comet and

Cupid, Donder and Blitzen been replaced by an airplane or an automobile? She smiled at the fire. Perhaps St. Nick used a car in Maine. Had one stopped? What would old Santa say if he caught her sitting up for him? Silly, what a kid she was! Perhaps that was the reason Rodney didn't like her any more—he— Someone was watching her! Who had come in? She glanced furtively at the long mirror. Her heart stopped. Rodney!

He didn't move. Was he real? Her fascinated eyes clung to his in the mirror. How he had changed since the day she had plunged into his arms in the barn! Determination and the will to grapple obstacles had remodeled his mouth; where it had been sensitive and mobile, it now set in a grim line. She had thought it too boyish. Now its sternness was like a knife in her heart; she didn't want life to hurt him, she couldn't bear it. Was she partly responsible? What would his mother think of the change if she knew? He moved, and the spell was broken.

"Merry Christmas, Prue of Prosperity Farm!"

She stood up and caught at the back of the wing chair. The guarded ardor of his eyes took her breath; his mouth was no longer stern, it was young again.

"Merry Christmas, Rodney."

"Don't look at the clock. This isn't late for the night before Christmas. Had to get the collar for the kitten. I've left him in a basket in the hall. Planned to put him in Jean's stocking in the morning. She has two dangling from the living room mantel. Dave okayed my coming."

Was that why her brother had been too tired to stay downstairs? The light in the eyes watching her seemed to get in the way of her breath. She proposed eagerly:

"Come into the shop. The collar is ready. I—I thought perhaps you had forgotten it."

"Oh, yes?" he responded enigmatically, and followed her with the rustling basket in his hand. Prudence picked up the collar from the bench.

"Take the kitten out and hold him tight while I put it on."

The ball of black fluff blinked green eyes and stretched a pink mouth in a prodigious yawn. Prudence clasped the silver collar.

"There! Do you like it?"

"It's great!" With the squirming kitten clutched in one arm, Rodney seized her hand and held it against his lips.

"Darling, did you think I would go through this night without a showdown with you? I kept away after that dance. I didn't dare trust myself. Why did you tell me you were engaged to Jim Armstrong? Why—"

The kitten squirmed and clawed and jumped. He sprang to the back of a chair. Contracted to a black ball. With a bound landed on the high top of the bookcase. His green eyes turned ruby red as he peered over the edge. The amber pendant on his collar shone like a cloudy yellow star. The man and girl stared back at him.

"Darn! Stop laughing, Rodney Gerard, you'll waken Dave and bring Jane Mack down on the double-quick for another burglar," Prudence warned in a hoarse whisper.

"Get that cane in the corner and poke the kitten down. The black imp! Do you suppose he knows that you want to tuck him into the stocking and has decided he won't go? Perhaps you can reach him if you stand on something."

Gerard balanced precariously on the arm of a chair and poked vigorously. At each thrust the quarry retreated. He moved his chair cautiously and attacked from the other end. From the middle of the lofty perch the kitten blinked at his tormenters. Particles of dust drooped from his long whiskers, dust adhered to his ruff. At the imminent risk of breaking his neck—if not the kitten's—Gerard lunged with the cane.

"Look out!" warned Prue. Her voice shook with laughter. "I'm sorry. I just couldn't help it. Your arms looked as if they were shooting off electrical energy. Every move a picture! They—"

"What the dickens is going on here?" David Schuyler demanded from the threshold, as he knotted the cord of his brocaded dressing gown. Jane Mack, still in her glittering black frock, peered over his shoulder. Gerard jumped to the floor.

"That snooty kitten walked out on us."

"Oh, was that it? Macky and I thought you had corralled her burglar at last."

Jane Mack twisted gnarled hands. "You ought to tell about that burglar, Mr . David."

"Tell about him! What do you mean? Wasn't there a burglar?"

"I was the real burglar, Prue. I had asked Miss Mack to get the emerald and diamonds for me because—"

Jane Mack eagerly interrupted Gerard. "Mr. Rodney didn't want you to know he had them. I sneaked 'em from the safe that morning you caught us three coming out of this room. Mr. David knew about it. Every time you took out those white packages I nearly lost my mind for fear you would miss the emerald. Finally I couldn't stand the strain any longer, so I just worked up that yell and burglar story, to account for them not being there. I thought I did real good," the lean, lank woman confessed modestly.

Prudence regarded her in stunned amazement. Jane Mack had taken the jewels! She said, when she could drag her voice from her throat:

"I agree with you, you 'did real good.' You are what they call a type-actress in Hollywood. But I don't yet understand why—"

David Schuyler slipped his hand under Jane Mack's arm. "Come on, they don't need us, Macky. Gerard is the only one who can explain." He looked back and smiled as he crossed the threshold. Prudence waited till the voices on the stairs were still, before she asked:

"Why did you want those stones?"

Rodney Gerard held out his hand. On the palm glittered a ring.

"Grandmother's emerald! Set in my design! What marvelous baguettes! Why did you do it?"

"Is it splashy enough? You said you wanted the stone set, didn't you—Gorgeous? I would like all my life to give you what you want. You know I love you, don't you? You know that I've been mad about you from the moment I held you in my arms in the barn. Why did you tell me you were engaged to Jim?"

He dropped the ring to the bench and caught her shoulders. "Don't turn away. We'll fight it out if I stay here all night. Answer my question."

"I didn't want to love you."

"Why—because of Milly Gooch? Calloway told me that he had poisoned your mind against me. There was not a shred of truth—"

"Please—please don't tell me that. I know it. In my heart I have always known it."

The whiteness of his face frightened her. His ardent eyes confused her. She touched the ring.

"Now that the emerald is set, what are you going to do with it?"

Color rushed back into his face, youth and gayety and laughter to his lips.

"Watch me, Gorgeous, just watch me while I make my wish come true!"

He caught her left hand and slipped the ring on the third finger.

"All right with you? This means marriage, you know—for always."

"For always," she whispered.

He looked at her without speaking. His eyes seemed to draw her heart from her breast. She pressed her cheek against the gardenia on his coat, and challenged with unsteady gayety:

"Something tells me that you are letting that silly promise—"

He crushed her so close in his arms that she had barely breath left to add:

"Don't you usually kiss a lady when you ask her to